MW01137207

The Island

Lisa Henry

Hope you enjoy!

Lisa Henry ♡

The Island

Second edition.
Copyright © February 2016 by Lisa Henry

ISBN-13: 978-1530261451
ISBN-10: 1530261457

Cover Artist: Natasha Snow
Published in the United States of America

www.lisahenryonline.com

Dedication

To my friends in the m/m community.
You know who you are.
And you're awesome.

CONTENTS

ACKNOWLEDGMENTS

Thanks to editors, proof readers, and everyone at the Loose Id team, where this book was originally published. And thanks to Natasha Snow, for designing such a wonderful cover for this edition.

CHAPTER ONE

Shaw looked out the window as the chopper came in to land.

It was a typical small South Pacific atoll: a band of gleaming white sand encircled the lush rainforest and was surrounded in turn by a brilliant blue ocean. It was shaped like a teardrop. A hill straddled the widest part. The forest swept downward from the hill toward the beach. Shaw remembered his primary school geography. This was not the sort of island that had grown patiently over the eons from the detritus of the reef, the shift of the tides, and the patronage of the sea birds. This island had been created suddenly and violently, thrown up from under the sea by the force of a volcanic eruption a million years ago.

The uniform lushness of the rainforest opened up into a patchwork of different shapes, colors, and textures as the chopper descended. Like turning the dial on a microscope, Shaw thought, and seeing a whole new level underneath. He could make out the top canopy of the trees now: waxy leaves, creepers, rubber trees, palms, and an infinite variety of flora that, just a minute ago, had appeared so unvaryingly green.

In the center of the island, at the base of the hill, Shaw saw the main house. The modern glass-and-steel structure gleamed in the sunlight. It seemed incongruous to Shaw, the wrong sort of house for both the climate and the landscape. It had not been built to complement the rainforest. It had been built to tame it.

Shaw smiled in amusement. Typical of Vornis. He was the sort of man who liked to build monuments to his own power and wealth, and that was exactly what the house was. Shaw imagined a day when the rainforest would retake the house, slowly grinding it down again until nothing remained. Like Ozymandias, Shaw thought suddenly, and wondered where the hell his brain had dredged that reference from. Was it Year Nine English? That was a lot of years and a whole other life ago.

Shaw took a breath and let it out slowly.

Focus.

A large yacht gleamed in the crescent-shaped bay on the far side of the island. It was anchored between a curve of white beach and a line of breakers that marked the reef and surrounded by a patch of deeper blue. From the chopper, Shaw thought that he could make out the safe channels between the reefs where the water was deepest. He had toured the yacht once before, several months ago now, at Mykonos. Vornis liked to show off his wealth. He liked to see other men's eyes light up with envy. And Jesus, a part of Shaw had been envious. A part of him still burned with it. King-size beds, a theatre room, an elevator between decks . . . but another part of Shaw was secretly amused. What was the point of having a yacht at all, if you stayed hermetically sealed under deck?

The island, Shaw knew, would be the same to Vornis, nothing more than a backdrop. Nothing more than a tick in a box: yacht, jet, helicopter, island. Vornis had all the trappings of wealth imaginable, but did he enjoy their use or only the jealousy they inspired in others? Shaw knew enough about Vornis to know that he found his pleasure in strange ways.

The sunlight burned on the glass panes of the

house, and Shaw squinted as the chopper came in to land. *Look on my works, ye Mighty, and despair!*

A gap in the trees — the helipad.

Game on.

The chopper hovered, and Shaw settled back into his seat. The rotors seemed louder than they had before, the exercise somehow more fraught. When they'd been moving forward, Shaw hardly felt it. Now he was conscious of the pull of gravity as they hovered slowly above the helipad, and of the churning of the engines.

Shaw's lips quirked in another smile. He wasn't a nervous flyer, but the thought never failed make itself known to him at some point: How does this even *work*?

The skids bumped against the ground, lifted again for a fraction of a second, and they were down. The engines whined as the pilot cut the power, and the rotors slowed.

Shaw unbuckled his seat belt and reached for his suitcase and laptop bag. When the pilot came around and opened the door for him, Shaw stepped down onto the helipad. He took a deep breath, hoping for sea air, but smelled only fuel.

"Mr. Shaw." A large man in dark fatigues came forward to meet him. "Welcome to the island."

He didn't smile. He didn't offer to take Shaw's luggage. It wasn't that sort of welcome. Shaw held his arms out as the man frisked him.

"My name is Hanson," the man said, straightening up. "Head of security. I'll show you to your bungalow."

"Thank you," Shaw said. He followed the man away from the helipad onto a wide sand path flanked by golden cane palms.

Hanson was at least a head taller than Shaw, and Shaw wasn't short. Hanson had the sort of width across the shoulders that you'd measure in ax handles, Shaw thought, and, despite a thickness around his middle that had more to do with age than his fitness level, he looked like he could snap a man's neck between his thumb and forefinger. Hanson had to be pushing fifty, but Shaw had no doubt he could easily take down men half his age. Not that it would ever come down to physical strength. Hanson wore a GLOCK on his hip. Fourth generation, with the dual recoil spring assembly.

Shaw forced his gaze away from the sidearm, and tried very hard not to imagine the brilliant white sand soaking up his blood like litmus paper. He looked at the fluttering palm fronds instead.

Focus.

The sand crunched under Shaw's shoes, and he wondered what it would feel like under his bare feet. His imagination took him all the way across a beach he hadn't even seen yet and into the cool embrace of the Pacific before he reeled it back.

Not that sort of trip, Shaw. Not that sort of island.

Fucking jetlag.

"How was your trip, Mr. Shaw?" Hanson asked him.

Shaw tried to pick his accent. American, maybe, but not for a long time. All the edges were knocked off. Hanson had spent a lot of years in a lot of different places. He was probably an ex-mercenary who had learned his trade in Kosovo, Pakistan, Liberia, and every dirty little theater of war in between. Shaw knew from previous dealings that Vornis was never without at least a dozen armed guards. He suspected there would be more on the island this week. This place was Vornis's sanctuary. He wouldn't leave it vulnerable.

"Good, thanks," Shaw told him.

It was a lie but not the sort that would condemn

him. He'd spent fourteen hours in economy class from LA to Nadi, transferred to Suva on what had to be the local mail run, and waited another two hours there for the chopper. An hour and a half later, and here he was—jet-lagged, unshaven, and wanting nothing more than to recharge his batteries with a hot shower, a decent meal, and a long sleep. Then he could dream about that Cézanne burning a hole in the false bottom of his luggage, and the nice fat chunk of Vornis's cash he was about to earn. And, with any luck, wake up with his head in the right place. He couldn't afford a misstep here.

Hanson turned his head and grinned, and Shaw was surprised at the genuine amusement in the big man's eyes. "Sure it was!"

Shaw smiled.

God, but it was nice to be on solid ground again, feeling the sun and the breeze. Shaw smelled salt on the air now. He heard the slow roll of the ocean against the beach.

They rounded a bend, and the beach appeared.

It was beautiful—an open, unspoiled beach and an ocean that went on forever. Shaw filled his lungs with the salt air and let his gaze settle on the horizon.

Beautiful, but don't let it fool you.

He sucked in a deep breath, rolled his shoulders, and put his prickling unease down to jetlag. Nerves? Hardly. Shaw didn't get nervous. He was at the top of his game. He kept his gaze on the horizon and let his smile win. No harm in that. *Beautiful, so enjoy it while you can.*

Enjoy the tropical paradise completely surrounded by sea.

And there was that flicker of unease again, dancing up his spine. He'd felt it in the pull of gravity as the chopper came in to land. The feeling was strange, contradictory. Shaw wouldn't walk away from this opportunity in a million years, but the illusion of free choice was always nice. Standing on the glowing ribbon of beach, Shaw shaded his eyes to watch as the chopper headed for the distant horizon, back toward Suva.

Don't let the palm trees and the sand fool you. You're stuck here now, and this place might as well be a fortress.

"You're just along here, Mr. Shaw," Hanson told him.

A bungalow sat a little way along the beach, with wooden floors, bamboo walls, and a thatched roof. Swaying palms surrounded it on three sides. The front steps led directly onto the beach. It looked like something off a postcard.

"There are six bungalows on the island," Hanson said as they continued along the beach. "They were building a resort here, but it went bankrupt. Yours is the one with the turtles, if you get turned around."

Shaw had never got turned around in his life, but Hanson didn't need to know that. Shaw was always exactly where he needed to be. "The turtles?"

He followed Hanson up onto the shaded veranda of the bungalow and saw them: three carved turtles decorated the post beside the door.

The veranda, wide and shaded, had a hammock at one end, a spa at the other, and a small table and two chairs by the door. Hanson slid the bamboo door open and stood back for Shaw to enter. Shaw walked inside and dumped his luggage on the bed.

The bungalow was open plan. It was like a five-star resort, with a massive bed, a large plasma screen, a dining table, and a self-contained kitchen. Shaw crossed the rattan matting and looked down a set of shallow steps into the bathroom. It had no floor, just crushed coral. There were walls, for the sake of privacy, but no roof above the shower cubicle. It would be like showering on the beach, and

Shaw liked the idea of that. He rolled his shoulders and let his gaze travel around the bungalow again.

The bungalow was open to the sea breezes. It was large, airy, and full of light. Luxurious, Shaw thought, but strangely simple for a man with Vornis's notoriously vulgar tastes. Shaw supposed he had the original owners of the island to thank for the bungalow. Definitely not the same crew who had designed the main house.

Hanson stood by the bed and nodded at Shaw's luggage. He didn't have to ask the question.

"Go ahead," Shaw said. It wasn't like he had any choice in the matter.

Shaw watched Hanson check through his bags. The man was an expert. He didn't miss the hidden bottom in Shaw's luggage like they had at LA and every security check since, and Shaw hadn't expected him to. Hanson also wasn't looking for a painting.

"Thank you," Hanson said when he'd finished. "Mr. Vornis will be down to see you shortly."

Shaw nodded and slid the thin door closed behind Hanson as he left. He needed a shower, but first he needed to let Callie know he'd arrived. He lay down on the bed to check his e-mail and fell asleep halfway through.

* * * *

Shaw awoke to the sound of gentle rain. He stared up at the underside of the high thatched roof for a while before he his mind caught up: Fiji. He was in Fiji to sell Vornis a stolen Cézanne.

Shit. How long had he been asleep? Shaw didn't bother check his watch. It was still set to LA time anyway. It was still daytime; that had to be a good sign. And he couldn't have slept through the whole night, because he wasn't starving.

7

Every muscle in Shaw's body ached as he hauled himself up from the bed. He closed his laptop, grimacing at that particular breach of his own security. He would have woken up if anyone had tried to take it though, right? Not that it mattered in the grand scheme of things. His laptop was secure.

Shaw grabbed his shaving kit and staggered down the steps into the bathroom. His shoes crunched on the crushed coral floor. He splashed water on his face, stared into the mirror, and marveled at the dark shadows under his eyes. He looked like crap.

He shaved and then splashed water on his face again. *Wake up. Wake up. Wake up!* Jesus, he hated jetlag. He wished he knew the time so he could figure out how many more hours he had to fight off sleep. Because the sound of the ocean washing back and forth on the beach and the gentle patter of the rain wouldn't help any. *Sleep, sleep, sleep,* the ocean murmured, and Shaw wanted to listen.

Shaw scrubbed his face dry and headed back up the stairs. He sat on the bed and pulled his shoes and socks off. He wriggled his toes on the rattan floor covering. Bare feet, that was more like it.

Shaw unbuttoned his shirt and shrugged it off, reaching back into his suitcase for a fresh one. He was about to change his trousers and underwear when he heard the squeak of the boards on the veranda, followed a moment later by a knock on the doorpost.

"Shaw? You in there?"

Vornis. *Game on.*

Shaw rose. An easy smile spread across his face as he walked to the door and slid it open.

"Shaw," Vornis said, extending his hand. "It is good to see you, my friend."

Shaw shook his hand. "It's good to be here,

Vornis."

Vornis wasn't a large man, but he still managed to seem physically intimidating. He stood at just under six feet, with a paunch around his middle. His dark hair was gray at the temples and thin on top. His dark eyes were set into a pale, fleshy face. He wasn't an attractive man, but he exuded an air of power that only the very naive or the very stupid didn't see.

Shaw wasn't stupid, and it had been a long time since he'd been anything like naive.

"How do you like my island?" Vornis asked, walking into the bungalow.

"It's beautiful," Shaw said. No need to moderate himself there. God's honest truth. "I can't wait to have a walk around."

He knew Vornis had bought his Fijian island outright twelve years ago. It was remote, an hour and a half by chopper from the main island, but Vornis never arrived by chopper. The yacht, anchored in the secluded bay on the other side of the island, was his preferred method of travel. It would be Shaw's as well, if he ever had that sort of cash. It was the sort of luxury Shaw could only dream about, and often did.

Vornis opened the fridge and drew out two beers.

Shaw had never seen Vornis drink beer before. He wondered if it was the relaxed atmosphere of the island, or, more exactly, if drinking a beer was the sort of thing Vornis felt he ought to do on a tropical island to show that he was relaxed. With Vornis, everything was for appearances.

Shaw accepted a beer and twisted the top of it. "Cheers."

"Shall we sit outside?" Vornis asked.

They headed onto the veranda. So beautiful here, Shaw thought, so peaceful.

So remote. So dangerous.

Shaw looked out at the ocean. It had vanished under clouds now, but the rain was only soft. It was tropical rain. It smelled sweet, and Shaw knew that it wouldn't be cold. A part of him wanted to get out underneath it, to tilt his face up to the sky and taste it.

God, the smell of it hit him like homesickness. His own fault. He'd let the Pacific work its old magic already. He'd been a different person the last time he'd stood on a beach with a beer and watched the rain on the Pacific.

Focus. You're supposed to be smarter than this.

Vornis rested his beer on the rail of the veranda and watched Shaw watch the ocean. Shaw sensed his gaze — he felt it sliding over his skin like a touch — and didn't comment on it. Nothing like the narrow, heated scrutiny of a predator to sharpen the senses. He should be thanking Vornis.

Shaw ran his thumb up and down the cold beer bottle, collecting condensation. He knew he looked relaxed. He almost believed it himself, and why not? There were worse places to be than on a Fijian island. In a tropical paradise, even the rain was nice.

At last, Vornis spoke. "I'm glad you're here, Shaw. I have always enjoyed your company. I have been growing a little bored with nothing to do except play with my toy."

"Toy?" Shaw asked.

Vornis was looking out into the rain. Shaw followed his gaze. He looked up into the line of trees, and he saw, and a moment later understanding caught him.

His stomach flipped.

Fuck.

Vornis had left his toy out in the rain. The toy was young, male, and lean. When he moved, his muscles shifted under his captivity-pale skin. He was walking in the rain like he couldn't remember the last time he'd stood under a natural sky. A few steps forward and a few steps back; he was held close to the tree line by an imaginary leash. His skin gleamed under the rain. Shining droplets caught on full lips that were parted as he looked blankly at the world, his jaw hanging like a gormless child's. His bare feet sank into wet grass. His long pants, hanging low on his hips, flapped wetly around his feet.

It was the pants that gave him away. They were khaki cargoes with a camouflage pattern. They were thin with wear and stripped of any identifying labels, but Shaw could hazard a guess.

Focus. Take a breath and focus.

He leaned on the veranda rail. "Military," he asked Vornis, ignoring the sudden wild thumping of his heart, "or mercenary?"

Vornis only laughed.

Shaw shook his head wonderingly. "Christ, Vornis, you do like to walk on the wild side. Couldn't you at least get him some new clothes?"

Vornis laughed and took a swig of his beer. "But I like to remember where he comes from. One of us ought to!"

Shaw raised his eyebrows and looked out at the young man again. He was hardly more than a boy. He didn't look much older than nineteen or twenty. He couldn't have done a lot of living before he was brought here, and Shaw didn't like his chances for the future.

Shaw raised his beer bottle to his lips and forced himself to swallow.

Jesus, he did business with some frightening fucking assholes. Truth be told, Vornis wasn't even the worst of them. Sure, he was a murdering drug lord, but at least he was up-front about it. And here, on his secluded little island, Vornis was almost friendly. His friendliness had a lot to do with the fact that Shaw had a Cézanne to offer him. Like a lot of thugs, Vornis liked to pretend he was cultured. The fact that he kidnapped, raped, and murdered anyone who crossed him was beside the point. He appreciated fine art and classical music. He must have been a gentleman.

"So, which was it?" Shaw asked. "Military or mercenary?"

A pair of armed security guards stood some distance away: more of Vornis's private security team. They watched the boy intently, their hands on their utility belts. Shaw watched them as they watched the boy. They were too far away to hear what they said, but Shaw saw the way one of them smirked in his direction. There was something predatory about that smile, something proprietary. Shaw hid his misgivings under the gentle curve of his own smile.

Vornis sipped his drink. "That is the only surviving member of a covert team who made a strike on my Colombian compound eight weeks ago. The uniform is not American, but the boy is. CIA, I suspect."

"CIA?" Shaw asked. The boy looked way too young to be a specialist in any field, let alone in black ops.

Vornis only shrugged. "What does it matter?"

Shaw raised his eyebrows. "In your place, I might be worried he had friends coming after him."

Vornis laughed. "We're a long way from Colombia now."

Shaw watched the boy as he shuffled in the rain. "True."

Watched, and tried not to see.

Shaw had an idea he wouldn't like himself much if

he had to keep looking at that boy and imagining the things Vornis did with him. Shaw had made a career out of morally reprehensible dealings, but he didn't usually have his nose rubbed in them. Shaw liked to pretend he was a gentleman. It felt so much more civilized when he could pretend Vornis was a gentleman too.

Focus.

The palm fronds waved in the breeze, tipping rivulets of water into the sand. The sea was gray under the clouds, and Shaw hoped he'd at least get one postcard-perfect glimpse of the brilliant blue Pacific before he left. He had been hopeful that Vornis would extend his hospitality even before he'd seen the beauty of the island. He hadn't anticipated any problems. He'd known what he was walking into.

Palm fronds, sand, the clouds and the ocean, but somehow Shaw's gaze kept coming back to the boy. He didn't just see flesh either. He saw straight past that, straight to his own . . . *culpability?* No, that wasn't fair. He hadn't kidnapped the boy. He hadn't brutalized him and broken him. That was all Vornis, and in Vornis's world, payback wasn't only justified, it was necessary. It was the only currency men like Vornis dealt in: force. Shaw understood that.

And the boy must have known what he was getting himself into. He must have known the risks. Somewhere along the way, he'd signed on the dotted line and given his life away. He'd probably never seen this coming, though. Shaw wondered which was worse in theory, getting shot in the head or getting raped daily by Vornis? It wasn't a choice he'd want to make, but any man who entered Vornis's world had to know the risks. You knew them, you calculated them, and you decided whether or not to take the chance. Heads, you win, tails you lose, but nobody forced you to play. It was the kid's own fault he was here

The breeze tasted of salt, and Shaw swiped his

13

tongue over his lower lip. Being on the same island at the same time wasn't culpability at all. It was coincidence.

Shaw smiled again. How useful that he could always soothe his own conscience. Soothe it or smother it, same thing. It took a special sort of pathology to look at Vornis's captive American and blame him for his own misfortune.

Vornis saw where he was looking, saw his smile, and his eyes danced. "Nice, yes?"

Shaw couldn't deny that. His cock had twitched the moment he'd seen the boy, but he'd put it down to jetlag, alcohol, and a long dry spell. "You're a man of impeccable taste. I've always said so."

Vornis laughed again, and Shaw pressed his advantage.

"Particularly in art."

Vornis clapped him on the back. "It is late, my friend. We have plenty of time to discuss my latest purchase tomorrow. What is your rush?"

Shaw took another sip of his beer. "No rush."

"Good," said Vornis. "Make yourself at home. You look tired. Have a shower, and I'll have something sent over from the main house for you. Business can wait for the morning, agreed?"

"Agreed," Shaw said. "The morning."

Shaw watched as Vornis walked down the steps. He stepped onto the winding path that led back away from the beach toward the main house and whistled sharply.

"Christ," Shaw said under his breath.

He had the boy trained like a dog. One whistle and the kid almost tripped over his feet in his hurry to get to heel. Cowering and eager, just like a fucking dog. Shaw felt himself tense as Vornis ran a hand down the boy's naked back, and he turned away. The beer he'd swallowed churned in his guts. Shaw drew a quick, deep breath and held it.

Focus.

It was none of his business. None of his fucking business.

He had to remember that.

CHAPTER TWO

The shower was not as relaxing as Shaw had anticipated. His feet crunched in the coral as he washed his hair. It was the strangest sensation to be showering under the rain. The water from the showerhead was hot and the rain wonderfully cool. Even as he stood under the jets, Shaw could see the clouds slowly dissipating. The patches of blue sky were already beginning to darken into dusk. It felt good to be surrounded by nature. Too much time had passed since Shaw had been out of the city, or even spent the day barefoot. The tenderness of his feet against the coral attested to that. The shower could have been relaxing, it could have been heaven, except for Vornis's American boy.

Shaw closed his eyes, sighed, and tried not to think about him. The boy was out of sight, out of mind. Out of sight, out of mind. If he kept repeating it to himself, sooner or later it would be true. He didn't need to wonder where he was now or what was happening to him. He didn't need to speculate.

None of his business. Not his problem. Too fucking dangerous.

Focus.

Shaw turned off the shower to find the rain had stopped. He crunched across to the sheltered half of the bathroom and wrapped himself in a towel.

He headed back up the steps into the main bungalow, and for a moment, the view of the ocean took his breath away. He could smell the saltwater. God, he'd love to have a view like this every day. The beach stretched out before him, the ocean receding all the way to the horizon. It was like looking at eternity.

There were no windowpanes in the bungalow. There were storm shutters, currently locked open, but the wide windows let the sea breeze straight through. There was a ceiling fan above the bed, but Shaw doubted he'd need it.

The grass matting scratched his feet as he crossed to the bed. He lay on his back, letting the breeze dry him, and pretended he was on a deserted island. There was no main house just up the path. There was no massive yacht anchored in the other bay. There were no armed guards. There was no tortured captive.

"Mr. Shaw?"

Shaw opened his eyes to see a woman by the door. "Yes?"

She entered and set a tray down on the table. "Your dinner, sir."

The woman was thin, older, her golden hair fading to gray. Her face was unremarkable. Shaw thought her accent was possibly Eastern European, but it had been tempered with something else. She had spent a lot of time in America, he realized. Probably one of Vornis's many relations. Vornis didn't outsource except when he couldn't avoid it. He'd been a hard nut to crack for Shaw. It had taken years to exploit an opportunity to work with the man, let alone build up enough trust to be invited to his private island.

Shaw tucked the towel around his hips as he stood. "Thank you."

She nodded and left, her cheeks flushed.

Shaw was used to that reaction from women. He didn't kid himself that he was anything special, but he kept himself in good shape. He was twenty-eight, six feet two, and he had good muscle tone. He wasn't some oiled, ripped gym junkie either who looked like his skin was about to burst. He kept in shape by running.

Shaw ran a hand through his hair and sat at the table. He removed the cover from the tray.

Dinner was lobster. Of course it was lobster. Nothing but the finest for Vornis and his guests. It was probably a local catch, and it wasn't ruined with some chef's idea of an exotic sauce. Lobster and coral trout and coconut crab, accompanied by a bottle of wine. Shaw checked the label. Apparently, Vornis didn't trust the locals with that. The wine was French.

At home, Shaw usually put on the television when he ate. It always felt like a waste of time when he wasn't doing at least two things at once. Here, he realized, he just wanted to watch the sun go down and listen to the sound of the waves against the beach. It was so relaxing, and so easy to push everything else out of his mind. Except that one thing that niggled: the boy. He was there at the edges of Shaw's mind, standing in the rain. A beautiful, dumb thing, like a piece of art.

Shaw sighed as he ate. The food was perfect. The wine was perfect. The location was perfect. And the job was what it was. He was here to sell a stolen painting and make some contacts, nothing else.

He finished eating and pushed the tray away.

The woman was back almost immediately. Surveillance, Shaw wondered, or just good service? In Vornis's position he'd keep a close eye on his guests as well. *If I were a hidden camera, where would I be?* Shaw knew better than to look for it.

18

"That was lovely, thank you," he told the woman.

She nodded at him and placed a sports bag on the table. "Your welcome present from Mr. Vornis."

"Welcome present?" Shaw asked curiously.

The woman pursed her lips together briefly and nodded. "Good evening, Mr. Shaw."

She left.

Shaw leaned back in his chair for a moment before reaching for the bag. He tipped it up, and the contents spilled out onto the table. A silk scarf. A pair of cuffs with the key attached. Condoms and lube. A flogger. Nylon ropes. Plugs and clips. A *cattle prod?*

Realization dawned. Shaw rose, a hard knot forming in his gut. He stepped out on the veranda.

The boy knelt on the wooden boards, his head bowed.

Shaw looked around, but the woman had already gone. *Shit, shit, shit.*

Shaw leaned in the doorway and looked at the boy. The sunset made his skin glow. Shaw watched him breathe. He wasn't even afraid. He'd been captured eight weeks ago and undergone God only knew what. He was probably beyond fear.

Shaw had thought he was like a dog, but that was wrong. He was less than that. He wasn't even an animal anymore. He was just a thing, an insensible thing.

Shaw looked out at the ocean and then back at the boy. He didn't want the boy, not like this, but Shaw had worked too hard to win Vornis's trust. He didn't know if Vornis was testing him now, or if it was simply what the woman said it was: a welcome present. Either way, he couldn't refuse.

"Get inside," he said to the boy.

The boy rose, still looking down. That was interesting. Did it mean fear and shame, or had it just been trained into him not to look men in the face? Shaw had never seen the attraction in fucking someone who wouldn't look him in the face. Still, he didn't doubt that Vornis got off in other ways. A cattle prod, for Christ's sake. He was a sick fuck.

The boy shuffled inside.

Shaw watched him. He was attractive. He would have been more attractive if he'd actually had some spirit left in him, but he was attractive. He was young, his body all lean muscle. He hadn't filled out yet. He looked like was caught between gawky teenage years and adulthood, that phase that looked awkward on most guys and fucking gorgeous on just a few. There were lines at the corners of his eyes, though. He wasn't as young as he appears. Probably one of those guys who'd look baby-faced until his hair turned gray. Not that he'd live that long.

Shaw exhaled slowly. Any other time, any other place…

The boy's head was bowed. Dark lashes caressed his cheeks as he closed his eyes. Shaw mapped the boy's face with his gaze. He would have preferred do it by touch.

The boy's mouth quirked. Not a grimace or a smile or any expression at all. Just a twitch. His top lip made a perfect cupid's bow. His bottom lip was full and marred with teeth marks. The boy chewed his lip, his eyes still closed, and Shaw wondered where his mind had taken him. A long way away, if he was lucky. What tiny corner of the world was home for him? Who missed him?

Careful. Focus.

Shaw took a step back.

When Shaw had first seen him in the rain, he'd thought the boy's skin was unblemished. Now he saw it wasn't. His skin was marked with narrow welts across his back, bruises from rough handling, and tiny red scorch marks from the cattle prod. Black shadows rimmed his eyes. His arms hung slackly at his sides, and Shaw saw the track marks. He'd been drugged into oblivion. Probably the only way Vornis could get him to make any sounds at all was through torture.

"How old are you?" Shaw asked him quietly.

The boy looked up briefly. The light caught in his brilliant green eyes. They were unfocused. His head dropped again.

Christ, it was almost easy to look him in the eye and see nothing human looking back. Shaw knew that trick. He knew it, and he used it, because it was smarter to dispassionately evaluate the boy than it was to acknowledge just how fucking wrong this was. *Stay buried, Green-eyes. You wouldn't like it out here.*

Shaw resisted the urge to raise his hand and trace the boy's bruised jawline.

He couldn't have been more than twenty-four at the outside, Shaw thought, and that was a generous estimation. There was no way in hell he was CIA. He didn't have enough muscle, and he didn't have enough years. This kid should have been serving his country by getting blown to pieces in the Middle East, not launching an attack on Vornis's Colombian compound. Something wasn't right here.

Shaw allowed himself a cynical smirk. *Nothing* was fucking right here.

"Get in the shower," he told the boy, nodding toward the bathroom.

The boy shuffled down the steps, and Shaw followed him down.

Shaw watched as the boy fumbled with the button on his fly. Even now he wasn't breathing heavily. He finally popped the button. Shaw heard the rasp of a zip, and the boy's cargoes pooled at his feet.

He was lovely, all angles and planes. Shaw felt his breath catch in his throat as his eyes trailed down the boy's chest and abdomen, following the narrow path of hair from his navel all the way down to his cock. It was lean like the rest of him, a good length, and Shaw wondered what it would look like thick and engorged with blood. His own cock twitched when he imagined getting on his knees and tasting the boy.

Any other time, any other place…

Even any other fucking bathroom would do. Shaw's apartment in Sydney or the one in LA. The bathroom with the full-length mirror or the one with the spa? Or, Jesus, even the bathroom at Shaw's favorite pub in King's Cross, with the suspiciously sticky floor, the stalls that didn't lock properly, and the condom machine that only worked when you punched it just right. Shit, yeah, the fun he could have with this boy in a filthy stall, a back alley, or up against a parked car. Dirty, cheap, and as hot as hell. Shaw could paint that vivid fantasy anywhere but here, because the boy had no choice here. Shaw was a lot of things, but not that.

There's a line.

Shaw ripped his gaze away from the boy's cock. If he'd seen any indication at all that the boy was turned on, he wouldn't have hesitated, coral floor or not. But Shaw wasn't a monster.

His stomach churned, and he tasted bile. Not a fucking monster.

Shaw dropped his towel and stepped past the boy into the shower. He turned the tap and felt the warm water against his skin. It wasn't as relaxing this time, not with the naked boy standing right there. Shaw reached out for him and pulled him under the water.

He held the boy by the shoulders and looked into his face.

The boy blinked water out of his eyes. Something like confusion passed over his face, and then a flicker of what might have been panic, and then he was blank again.

"What's your name?" Shaw asked him under the noise of the shower.

The boy sighed and turned his face up to darkening sky. The first stars were appearing.

Shaw gripped his jaw and angled his face back down again. "Listen, Green-eyes. What's your name?" He wondered if there were cameras in the bathroom as well. He pulled the boy closer, loving the feel of the boy's skin against his and hating that he loved it—*not a monster!*—and put his mouth on his ear. "Name, rank, number."

Shaw felt the boy's body stiffen suddenly and knew he'd gotten through past the drug for just a second. That was what the military trained into them, wasn't it? Name, rank, and number. He hoped it was second nature to the boy.

Shaw drew away and saw the sudden, awful fear in those brilliant green eyes. He didn't know if it was because Green-eyes realized exactly where he was and what was happening, or if he was just terrified he'd be punished for not being able to answer.

"Tell me your name," Shaw said.

The kid's jaw worked silently for a moment, but nothing came out.

"It's okay," Shaw said. "Doesn't matter."

And it didn't. Shaw needed to back off. Jesus, Vornis would kill him if he found out he'd been prying. He'd killed men for less. Shaw was just here to sell a stolen Cézanne and make a few valuable contacts.

Fucking jetlag. That was all. Jetlag messing with his head. Jetlag and the wine he'd had with dinner.

Shaw turned off the water and reached for his
towel. He wiped himself down quickly, did the same for
the boy, and dropped the towel on the coral floor. He put a
hand on the boy's shoulder and pushed him back upstairs.

It was night, but the moonlight was brilliant. It
softly illuminated the entire bungalow. Shaw could hear
the sound of the waves rolling endlessly on the beach and
the wind rustling in the palms. There was no one waiting
at the door, so Shaw supposed Big Brother had decided he
wasn't done with the boy yet.

Shaw didn't allow himself time to hesitate.

He collected a condom and the lube from the table,
even though he had no intention of needing them. He
pushed the boy onto the bed and drew the mosquito
netting down. It reminded him suddenly, ludicrously, of a
bridal veil.

The boy lay on the bed, his eyes half-closed.

Shaw crawled in on top of him and pulled the sheet
up. He kept his face impassive as he looked at the boy
lying underneath him. Jesus, he was beautiful, but Shaw
was no fucking rapist. He'd done a lot of things in his life
he regretted, but he wasn't going to do that. The boy with
the brilliant green eyes had enough bruises.

Showtime.

Shaw unwrapped the condom, squirted lube into it
and tied the end off. The oldest trick in the book, if nobody
looked too closely. And really, who would?

Shaw hoped the sheet and the mosquito net would
provide enough camouflage for what he was doing. Or not
doing. He knelt between the boy's thighs and positioned
himself. Then, before he could remind himself that this
wasn't his smartest idea, Shaw grasped his hard cock in his
hand and hunkered over. The boy raised his knees and
spread them. Shaw moaned, bit his lip, and began to

stroke himself.

Shouldn't, he told himself. Shouldn't, but the boy was beautiful, he was right there, and it had been a long fucking day. No harm, no foul. The boy wouldn't even remember it.

It was awkward, uncomfortable, and, feeling the heat rise off the boy's body, Shaw wanted nothing more than to fuck him. He raked his eyes over the boy's body, ignoring the bruises, and his cock leapt in his fist.

Shaw groaned again, and the boy's eyes flashed open. He looked far too fucking comfortable for someone who was supposedly getting raped. Shaw jabbed him in the abdomen with his forefinger, and the boy gasped and arched. That was more like it.

Fuck, he wished it was real. Shaw wanted to taste the boy, to pinch him and tease him, to shove his cock inside him and watch him squirm. He wanted to see his face when he came.

He jabbed the boy in the abdomen again, and the boy's eyes widened with sudden understanding. Shaw remembered the pull of gravity as the chopper came in to land. He remembered the rainforest: green, green, green, before it opened up into a hundred different nuances. It had seemed dull and uniform before it had revealed itself to his gaze. And what was underneath was beautiful and dangerous.

Shaw jabbed him again.

The boy arched again, and this time he cried out. *"No! Please, no!"*

Shaw met the boy's gaze. Clever, despite the drugs. He still had a brain after all. And that was a crying shame. Shaw tore his gaze away from those green eyes and back to the boy's body: smooth pecs, the dip of his sternum, the ridges of his abdomen. The boy's body deserved worship, not torture. Shaw stroked himself more quickly, worshipping the boy's flesh the best way he knew how.

No harm, no foul.

The boy whimpered and began to twist back and forth.

Well, give Green-eyes a fucking Oscar. Shaw felt his balls tighten and contract, and he jerked his hips forward as he came, his semen splashing across the boy's abdomen. His thighs ached from holding himself away from the boy, and it wasn't acting when he fell forward on top of him.

The boy grunted as he took Shaw's weight.

Underneath the sheet Shaw felt the boy's fingers entwine with his. The boy squeezed his hand tightly and then released it. He sniffled, and Shaw wondered if he'd hurt him. It took him a moment to realize what the sounds meant: gratitude and relief.

Shaw rolled off the boy, patting him on the shoulder. He listened to the boy as he cried quietly in the moonlight and wished he could show him some real affection.

"Shut your mouth," he said instead, his tone harsh.

The boy stiffened immediately, choking back the sobs.

Shaw sought out his hand under the sheet, and held it. He rubbed his thumb back and forth over the boy's palm, back and forth, back and forth until the boy slipped into sleep.

Dangerous. Remember this is dangerous.

You need to focus.

Shaw wondered what the fuck he was doing.

* * * * *

Shaw sat at the table and flipped open his laptop. What time was it in Sydney? It didn't matter, he supposed. It was never too early or too late to contact Callie. The woman was a godsend.

He looked across at the bed. The boy was sleeping there. His body looked otherworldly in the moonlight. The planes of his back glowed, and Shaw wanted nothing more than to lie beside him and trace the path of the moonlight across the boy's skin with his hand.

Shit, shit, shit. Shaw stared at the boy until he saw past the lure of his glowing flesh. He was too pale, Shaw thought, and too thin. Vornis needed to let him into the sun more often and maybe feed him once in a while. That was a victim lying in Shaw's bed, not a temptation. He had to remember that.

There was a new message from Callie regarding his flight from Nadi to Sydney. The ticket had been prepaid, but the date had not yet been confirmed. It had been too long since he'd been home, and the thought of a few weeks in Australia sounded good. Shaw was sick of Los Angeles, and Callie had known it, clever thing.

She'd sent a picture of Molly as well, and Shaw smiled when he saw it. He'd missed Molly, even if the last time he'd seen her she had chewed the handle off his briefcase and managed to pee everywhere except the newspaper he'd put down. She'd grown. She wasn't a puppy anymore.

When he was back home, he'd pick up Molly from Callie's place and head north. A few weeks in Ayr playing on the beach with Molly would clear his head.

He replied to Callie's e-mail. He and the merchandise had arrived safely. Things were going well. He looked forward to catching up.

Shaw looked across to the bed again, at the sleeping boy, and then back to his laptop. He stretched, rolling his shoulders, then hunkered forward to protect the screen from prying eyes: *8 weeks ago a US (?) unit attacked V's Colombian compound. Find out who. One survivor is here. Shaw.*

It was risky, but he had to know. He sent it before he could regret it.

CHAPTER THREE

What's the first thing you remember?

He always asked himself the question. He didn't know why, but he knew it was important. It was something beyond the bruises and the blood and this body that was racked with pain. It was something *before*. That was it. That was what he had to remember. There was something before.

He moved his fingers down his body and discovered a round mark on his hip. He pressed it, and it flared with pain. A burn. It was a burn.

He remembered the cigarette now. He remembered the ember coming closer and closer, and how he'd tried to twist away even though it didn't matter. It never mattered. Never made a difference. They always hurt him.

But there was something before. There was someone he had been, in a different place from here.

A moth fluttered up toward the lights inside, brushing against his face. He felt its fragile wings snag in his eyelashes. He raised a hand to sweep it away, but it was already gone. There were lots of insects here because it was so hot. Even the nights here were warm.

He frowned. If he knew the nights were warm here, had he once known different nights? He searched for them in his memory, but there was nothing.

What's the first thing you remember?

He remembered the sound of the ocean. No, he wasn't remembering that. He was hearing it now, the tiny waves chasing one another up the beach and the low, rhythmic pull of the water as it drew them back. The ocean was very loud. The only time he didn't hear it was in the room in the house where they took him.

He shivered. The only thing he heard inside that room was the men laughing, and the sounds that were wrenched out of him when he did the things that made them laugh so hard.

The ocean was good. If he could hear the ocean, he wasn't in that room. So where was he?

He was kneeling on wooden boards. He twisted his head. There was light coming from a doorway, the same light that had drawn the moth from out of the darkness. There was a carving on the doorpost. Turtles. Three turtles.

He ran his tongue over his dry lips.

He heard voices farther out in the darkness. It was the men who had brought him here. He didn't like them. He was afraid of them.

Once, before, he'd been something else. Why couldn't he remember? It was important to remember.

He closed his eyes. Sometimes it hurt to remember, but it was a different sort of hurt than he was feeling now. He remembered that. Nothing else, though. He couldn't catch his own thoughts. They were there, fluttering just out of reach, like moths looking for the light. He reached for them, dumb, clumsy, and missed them every time.

He opened his eyes again and scratched the inside of his elbow. There were scabs on his skin. He couldn't see them in the darkness, but he felt them flake off as he snagged them with his fingernails.

He was on drugs. That was the problem. That was why he couldn't catch his own thoughts. The slow realization brought a frown. Why was he on drugs? That wasn't right. How had that happened?

What's the first thing you remember?

He remembered the rain. It had rained. It had happened earlier, but he didn't know how much time had passed. The rain had felt good on his skin. Clean. It had tasted good as well.

He squeezed his eyes shut.

Concentrate. What's the first thing you remember?

Snow. He remembered snow. Snow that melted on his tongue. He remembered the smell of pine needles. He remembered being home for Christmas.

His breath caught in his throat. *Home.*

Snow. Pine needles. Christmas.

Hold it. Hold it. Don't let it go.

Too late. There were insects buzzing in the air, like static. He turned his face to the sound and opened his eyes. A small brown frog made its way across the boards of the veranda. It didn't jump. It crawled instead, extending its long, thin back legs as it propelled its way tentatively along. He watched it for a moment and forgot that he'd ever been anywhere else.

The night was warm. The gentle roar of the ocean made him tired, like it was whispering a lullaby to him. He wanted to sleep—he *always* wanted to sleep—but he couldn't. They'd put him here on his knees, and even if he didn't know his own name, he knew what that meant. They weren't finished with him yet. He swayed on his knees.

The frog reached the edge of the veranda and leaped into the darkness.

It was dark, and he was tired, and he hurt.

He heard the woman's voice from inside: "Good night, Mr. Shaw."

Irina. That was her name. She was nice to him. It

hurt when she put iodine on his broken skin, but she blew on it afterward to take away the sting. She called him *ukochany*. He didn't know what it meant, but he liked the sound of her voice when she said it.

Her shoes creaked on the boards of the veranda.

He watched as a mosquito floated drowsily around his forearm. He turned his arm and tried to make a fist to crush it in but missed. He always missed. He sighed and closed his eyes again.

The veranda boards creaked again.

He opened his eyes and saw bare feet and legs. He didn't look any higher. He was too tired for that.

"Get inside."

His aching muscles obeyed the tone of command in the voice before it had even registered in his mind. He rose and moved into the light, blinking. He saw a carved post by the door: three turtles. They seemed familiar, but he couldn't remember having seen them ever before. Rattan matting scratched his feet. There were steps.

His body knew what to do when the man told him to get into the shower. He fumbled with the button on his fly. It took his fingers a long time to manage it. The floor was coral. Like a beach.

What's the first thing you remember?

The rain.

No, this wasn't rain. He looked up and saw stars. He was standing under the sky. The man was talking to him, touching him, but he only saw the stars.

"Name, rank, number."

A shudder ran through him, and he didn't know why. *Before.* There was something before. Oh God. Pine trees and snow and Christmas, and something else. Something important. A helicopter. Mountains. A dark green landscape he had never seen before. *Get down! Get down!* But it was already too late.

It was important to remember. But why was it important? It would hurt. God, he knew it would hurt.

He was naked. He was standing under a shower under the stars, and then he wasn't. The man put his hand on the small of his back and propelled him up the steps. Moths pinged against the lights. He looked up, and coronas appeared. He blinked.

What's the first thing you remember?

Don't want to. Don't want to.

The mattress was firm, but it was the softest thing he had felt since...since...

Doesn't matter.

The man moved above him, but he didn't feel anything. That was strange. It should have hurt. It usually hurt. They always made sure of that. Something was different this time, and he wasn't sure what to do with different.

It didn't hurt, and the man didn't look pleased.

He had a handsome face. His hair was dark blond, sun-bleached. He had a strong jawline and nice lips and hazel eyes. He wasn't old, and he wasn't ugly, and it didn't hurt.

Then, suddenly, it did, but not in the way he'd expected.

The man jabbed him in the abdomen, and he twisted away. He met the man's eyes. *That's it,* he thought he saw there; *that's it.* The man jabbed him again.

"No! Please, no!" The words came so easily. They were always waiting in his throat, fully formed, until he could just get enough breath behind them to push them out. They had become the most natural words in the world.

The man smiled slightly. It was a pleased smile, but

it was also a tight smile. A moment later, he felt the man's hot cum splash against his stomach, and the man fell forward.

Tears constricted his throat. The man hadn't hurt him, not really. He couldn't remember the last time a man had made the choice not to hurt him, and it overwhelmed him now. He was lying in a bed, and the man was holding his hand and stroking his thumb across his palm, and he hadn't hurt him.

What's the first thing you remember?
This.

* * * * *

Afterward, Irina came and fetched him back to the house. She took him to his room there—a tiny, dark place very close to the room he hated—and sat him down on the thin, stained mattress. She murmured soothing words that he didn't understand as she wiped a warm sponge over his shivering flesh.

He liked Irina. He loved her, he thought. She was the only person he could remember who had ever shown him any kindness.

He thought back to the man with the hazel eyes. Except until tonight.

Irina left him and locked the door.

This isn't a sanctuary, he told himself without understanding what it meant. This is a prison.

But nobody ever hurt him in his dark little room.

He sat on the mattress and leaned his head against the wall. Irina had left him a cup of water, but his hands were shaking too much to risk reaching for it.

He thought of the man in the bungalow with the

turtles. What had happened there, he knew, had to stay a secret. The others wouldn't like it if they knew the man hadn't hurt him.

He sighed and closed his eyes. It had been so long since he'd had a secret he wasn't sure what to do with it. He wasn't sure if he would even remember it, or if it would just fade away like everything else, lost in the static in his head. A wave of fierce desperation rose up in him, and he was shocked at its intensity. *What's the first thing you remember? This is important!*

He remembered the jungle. He remembered the color of the mud on his boots. He remembered someone shouting: *"Get down! Get down!"* He remembered thinking he was going to die. But he hadn't.

His eyes flashed open, and his heart raced. He should have been dead, but he wasn't. He should have been dead. He'd *wanted* to be dead.

The thought unsettled him because he didn't understand it. It hinted at complexities he didn't know he had, hidden so deep inside him that he couldn't find them. He existed only in this moment, didn't he? But there must have been something before.

He remembered this room. It was four steps deep and six steps wide; too small to stretch out in, and too low to stand up in. In the gloom, he could make out the marks on the wall where the shelves had been removed. It wasn't really a room. It was a closet. He shouldn't have liked sleeping in here. He shouldn't have become the sort of person who was glad to be locked in a closet.

He would have railed against it, once. Before, when he'd been a different person. He would have fought.

He closed his eyes again. He *had* fought. He'd fought every way he knew how, but it didn't matter. It hadn't made a difference.

"Come on. If you give up now, we'll never make it."

Tears pricked his eyelids, and his throat ached.

"My feet hurt, Dad. I want to go back."

Whose stupid idea was it to go camping at the lake anyway? The lake was miles away from the road. There were plenty of good camping spots that were easier to get to. It was going to take hours just to get there, and they'd only have to hike out again in the morning. It was pointless, and it was dumb, and he'd rather be at home playing video games.

"Come on! Keep going!"

He opened his eyes, and wished he could remember his father's face. It hurt to remember his voice, but it was so important not to forget. He wanted more. He wanted all his memories back. He wanted them to fill his mind and push away all the confusion there. He wanted to know who he was *before*.

"Come on," he whispered in the darkness. "Keep going."

One foot in front of the other, all the way to the end.

He ran his fingers across his chest. There was a small scar in the dip of his sternum. One of the earliest.

That one stood for Colombia.

Shit. He swallowed down the wave of panic that threatened to drown him, and looked his memories in the face.

In the beginning, he'd wanted to leave himself notes so that he didn't have to go through this every time they drugged him, but they didn't give him anything to write with. But that scar, he remembered, that one stood for Colombia. The helicopter, the jungle, the mud, and the men who had died there.

He skirted the scar with his fingers, forcing himself

to breathe through the sudden nausea. He slipped his fingers up to the whorl on his shoulder. He'd given every scar on his body a story. He'd made them signify. That one was for Vornis, made by the man himself with a fat Cuban cigar.

"Come on. Keep going." He closed his eyes again and read the scars on his body like Braille.

Colombia, and his team. Vornis, Hanson, and the guards. And, hidden in the curve of his ribs, himself. His mom, his dad, last Christmas at the house he'd grown up in, snow and pine needles.

"*Come on,*" his dad had said on the hike to the lake all those years ago. "*If you give up now we'll never make it.*"

He remembered his name. He remembered his family. He remembered everything that had happened to him in Colombia and on this island.

He drew a shaking breath.

There was no scar for the man in the turtle bungalow. Mr. Shaw, Irina had called him. He'd left no scar and no broken skin or throbbing wound that would transform into one and allow him to retain a memory of what had happened in the bungalow once they drugged him again.

He moved his fingers down his body and pressed them against his abdomen where the man had jabbed him. He felt a faint tenderness that probably wouldn't even translate into a bruise by morning.

Remember him.

The man in the turtle bungalow was the only man since Colombia who had never hurt him. And maybe that was important as well.

Remember him, even if he didn't leave a scar. Remember him because *he didn't leave a scar. This is important.*

CHAPTER FOUR

Shaw woke. The boy was gone, leaving nothing behind but twisted sheets and Shaw's lingering sense of worry.

Out of sight, out of mind. You don't need the fucking distraction.

Shaw scowled at the underside of the thatched roof for a moment and thought hard about not thinking about Green-eyes.

Fuck it.

Shaw rose and checked his e-mail. Callie had been quick to reply: *I will make enquiries. C.* The answer was short, sweet, and to the point, just like Callie. Shaw was the face of the operation, but Callie put everything together behind the scenes. She was his Girl Friday. He'd made the mistake of telling her that once as well, and the only reason she hadn't ripped his head off for being a chauvinistic prick was because they'd been on different continents at the time.

Shaw closed his laptop and looked out the wide window to the ocean. It was blue today, that brilliant, luminous Pacific blue he'd hoped for the day before. There wasn't a cloud in the sky. Surf broke over distant reefs, crowning them in white foam. He let his gaze drift out to the horizon. Shards of sunlight pierced his vision, and Shaw reached for his sunglasses.

Beautiful, Shaw thought as he gazed at the view, and dangerous, and suddenly he was thinking of Green-eyes again. He pulled his thoughts back to the view with difficulty.

It was earlier than he was used to waking. His watch told him it wasn't even six a.m. Shaw was at nature's mercy here. He would wake with the sun and sleep with the night. His body clock would set the pace here, not his Tag Heuer. He might have found the thought strangely relaxing if his host wasn't a monster.

He showered, shaved, and dressed.

Breakfast awaited him on the table on the bungalow's veranda. Fruit, toast, and cereal, and a fresh pot of coffee. The service here was better than at any resort. There was even a newspaper beside the tray, the *New York Times.* It was only a day old.

Shaw flicked through it without really reading it. It spoke again of Vornis's sense of luxury. Vornis didn't care about the cost of getting the *New York Times* to an isolated Fijian island every day. It didn't matter that Shaw had a smartphone and a laptop and news at the touch of a button. It was all about appearances for men like Vornis. The newspaper was a symbol of wealth and power for his guests, and Shaw respected that.

There was a card on the table as well. *Come up to the main house when you're ready to talk business.*

Shaw swallowed down the last of the coffee. Showtime.

He returned inside and checked his outfit. Chinos, a linen shirt, and canvas shoes. Island chic. He'd rather be in board shorts and bare feet, but this was Vornis's tropical paradise, not Shaw's. Shaw thought of the *New York Times.* Appearances were everything.

He checked the lock on his laptop case, knowing it was secure. Even if someone broke into the bag, and he didn't doubt they would, the laptop was protected with so many levels of encryption that it would take months to get anything off it. Callie had set that up for him as well.

Shaw moved on to his suitcase, turning it upside down and opening it to access the false panel. It wasn't exactly creative, but it had served his purpose. Customs agents were looking for drugs and explosives, not paintings. A piece of rolled-up canvas didn't attract their attention at all. The sniffer dogs went right past it.

Shaw drew the painting out and tucked it under his arm. He locked his suitcase again and headed outside.

A pair of security guards stood on the beach. Muscles, dark uniforms, sunglasses, and sidearms. Shaw forced himself to see security guards, not mercenaries. Men, not atrocities. They looked at Shaw as he left the bungalow, and he nodded a greeting at them.

"Beautiful day." He smiled, and they nodded and smiled back at him.

Out of sight, out of mind. Don't think about what they've done to Green-eyes.

Don't think about what they're going to do to him.

Jesus, don't give him a fucking name either.

Focus. Just focus.

The main house was only a few minutes away, and it was a pleasant walk along a meandering path shaded by palms and bordered by lush ferns. The sand crunched under his shoes as he walked. So beautiful here, Shaw thought, so peaceful.

Out of sight, out of mind.

Shaw recognized duality. He worked with it every day. He could still differentiate between hypocrisy and necessity, couldn't he?

Game on.

Intersecting sharp angles of steel and glass came together under a brilliant sky to make up the main house. The structure glittered in the sun, and Shaw was glad he'd remembered his sunglasses. This was what he'd expected from Vornis all along, a show of decadence and wealth.

Shaw was admitted by the same woman who'd brought him dinner the night before.

"Mr. Vornis is in his study," she said, nodding up the stairs. "Please go ahead."

"Thank you," said Shaw, looking at her questioningly.

She pursed her lips, but a slight flush darkened her cheeks. "Irina."

"Thank you, Irina," Shaw said with a smile, heading up the stairs. Charm the women, befriend the men, and debase the toys. Shaw knew exactly how to do business with men like Vornis.

Vornis was waiting for him, and Shaw didn't waste any time. He crossed to the desk and placed the painting down. Vornis came to stand beside him.

"*Jeune garçon au gilet rouge.*" Shaw unrolled the canvas. "*The Boy in the Red Vest*, by Paul Cézanne. Painted in 1895."

Vornis rubbed his chin with his fingertips. "And stolen in 2008."

Shaw shrugged.

Shaw didn't know a lot about the painting's provenance. He didn't have to. What did it matter to him if the painting had gone through a lot of different hands in the years between 1939 and 1945? Something about *Jeune garçon au gilet rouge* would always stink of the death camps to Shaw. He was just the last in a very long line of profiteers.

The painting wasn't to Shaw's taste. A boy in a red vest sat at a table with his face cupped in his hand. His white shirt wasn't white at all. It was green and brown and purple and yellow, but all of those colors together gave the idea of light and shadow caught on a white shirt. The boy's face was the same. A palate of different colors made up the planes of his face. It was almost messy, almost splotchy, Shaw thought, until he took a step back and brought it into perspective again. Like one of those Magic Eye pictures that suddenly coalesced into something recognizable.

It wasn't the nicest painting Shaw had ever seen, but that didn't matter to him. It didn't even matter to Vornis, he suspected, who was only interested in buying a name. The painting was a symbol of wealth and power to Vornis. He wouldn't appreciate it purely as a thing of beauty. In a museum, he wouldn't even glance at it. Vornis needed to *own* things. *The Boy in the Red Vest*, mute and pretty, was not that different from Vornis's other nameless boy.

"At the time of its theft, it was valued at ninety-one million." Shaw let his hands linger on the edges of the canvas. Funny that a little bit of paint could be worth that much. "I wonder if it's worth even more now."

Vornis laughed at that and moved to stand beside the desk. He drew his bushy brows together as he studied the painting, and Shaw wondered for a fleeting moment if he'd misjudged Vornis. Maybe he saw the painting after all, not just the price tag.

"You liked my little present last night?" Vornis inquired as he gazed at the painting.

Shaw stepped back to give him space and light. "Very generous, thank you. Nothing like a good fuck to get over jetlag."

"I have always found it so," Vornis said.

Shaw wondered what Vornis thought of him now. It shouldn't have rankled if Vornis thought they were the same. That had been the point of the charade, after all. But Shaw had always tried to believe he was better than his clients. He needed to.

Shaw looked out the window. From here he could see the rooftop of his guest bungalow down on the beach. He could see palm trees and shaded paths, sand so white that it almost blinded him—none of Cézanne's ambiguity there—and the endless brilliance of the Pacific. It was beautiful here. Spoils to the victor, he supposed. You don't get a private island in the Pacific by playing fair.

Vornis saw him looking.

"This view," Shaw said, shaking his head. "It's better than a Cézanne any day."

"You're not an art lover, then, Shaw?"

"I like a good painting as much as the next man," Shaw said, seeing an opportunity and taking it with a teasing smile. "I just don't see how a bit of paint on canvas is worth ninety-*five* million."

"Inflation these days." Vornis shrugged. "Blink and it's gone through the roof! A drink, Shaw?"

They sat in leather armchairs totally unsuited to the climate. The main house, modern and hermetically sealed, hummed as cool air whispered through the vents. The leather armchairs were cool to the touch, almost chill, but Shaw preferred the bungalow. He could see the ocean from here, but he couldn't hear it. Couldn't smell it.

Shaw wondered if Vornis ever swam in the ocean or if the Pacific was like another expensive painting to him: something to look at to make himself feel rich and powerful. What a waste. Shaw couldn't wait to get into the ocean. There were no stingers here, and the reef sharks were small and generally shy. The only real predator on the island was Vornis.

"Thank you." Shaw took the drink Vornis handed him.

Vornis eased himself down in the opposite chair. He seemed almost relaxed today, more relaxed than Shaw had ever known him, but Shaw knew his generous mood could change in a heartbeat. He'd seen it happen before. And every time he'd seen it, Shaw had wondered if one day he'd be on the receiving end. He wasn't afraid of Vornis, not exactly, but he was always wary.

"Extraordinary," Vornis murmured, his gaze settling on the painting.

Drugs were only the thin edge of the wedge with Vornis, Shaw knew. Vornis had married into the trade. The plantation in Colombia had been his father-in-law's. Vornis himself favored money laundering and organized crime, trafficking over production, or at least he had until he'd stepped on too many toes in America. He'd disappeared from the radar for a while, appearing several years later with some new associates. There was big money in terrorism. It had more links with the corporate world than it did with the scrawny, impoverished kids who were convinced to strap bombs onto their bodies. Men like Vornis were in it for the money, not the ideology. And there was a lot of money to go around.

Shaw wasn't really here for the Cézanne. He was here to make valuable new contacts, and Vornis was the best way. This was the opportunity of his career.

"I will pay you ninety-five," Vornis said, "if I can bring in an expert to verify the Cézanne is genuine."

"Deal," said Shaw.

Vornis smiled at him, but there was nothing friendly in the way he twisted his lips and showed his teeth. It was the approximation of a smile. There was no real warmth behind it. There was nothing there at all. "And you are welcome to remain my guest in the meantime." Vornis's gaze lingered on his face, and Shaw felt his nerves tighten. That quick thrill of sick anticipation. There was nothing like it. He fucking loved it, and that wasn't right. There was a pathology at work that Shaw didn't question. It made him good at his work.

Very good.

Shaw ran a hand through his hair, tugging it slightly, tightening his fingers just enough so that a man of Vornis's tastes would freely make the association. Not an invitation, no way in hell, but if Vornis was suddenly imagining his own fist in Shaw's hair it was no accident.

Vornis's black eyes flickered.

Shaw had always known that Vornis found him attractive. Not because Shaw was particularly stunning, but because he was young, masculine, and self-confident, and Vornis liked strong things that he could break. He was a sadist, pure and simple. Green-eyes was proof of that.

It would never happen. No way in hell would Shaw let Vornis cross that line with him, but if Vornis wanted fuel for his nasty little fantasies, then Shaw was happy to provide it. Shaw took any advantage he could get, always.

And now Vornis was trying to sweeten the deal. "I have some associates visiting later in the week. You might like to meet them, Shaw."

"Associates?" Shaw asked, swirling his glass to hear the clink of the ice cubes. He didn't want to sound too eager. There was no telling what Vornis would ask for if he knew how much Shaw wanted this. He'd chased this rumor for months because this, finally, would put him in the big league.

"Men who are always glad to meet a trusted facilitator such as yourself," Vornis said.

Shaw leaned back in his seat. "You're not my only client, Vornis. I have appointments next week."

That was a lie, but Vornis didn't need to know it.

"I suggest you clear your schedule," Vornis said. He upended his glass with his blunt fingers and swallowed the rest of his drink down. "You will not want to miss this opportunity."

Shaw nodded like he was really thinking it over.

Vornis's dark eyes settled on his face. They reminded him of a shark's, flat and cold. "It will be worth your while."

Shaw swirled his glass again. The condensation on the side made his fingers damp. "Okay."

Vornis leaned back.

Shaw shook his head and laughed as though it had just occurred to him. "Jesus, I didn't even bring a book. What am I supposed to do to kill time on a fucking island?"

Vornis had always liked Shaw's self-deprecating sense of humor as well. He leaned forward again and raised his eyebrows. "How about what you did last night?"

There was no mistaking the flash of interest in the man's eyes. A sadist and apparently a voyeur. But Jesus, the last thing Shaw needed was to spend more time with Green-eyes. The last thing he needed was to get distracted and start feeling sorry for the kid. No, he reminded himself, it was okay to feel sorry for him, but it would be unacceptable to try to do anything about it. Shaw knew where the line was.

Shaw moistened his lower lip with his tongue, all for Vornis's sake, and felt a chill as Vornis's eyes followed the path of his tongue. This was a dangerous game.

But he needed this.

"Yes," Shaw said, ignoring his misgivings. "All right. I'll stay."

* * * * *

Shaw took his laptop down onto the beach and sat in the shade of a palm. He was wearing board shorts and a singlet. The sand burned his toes pleasantly. He sent a quick e-mail off to Callie, to advise her of the change in plans. Well, the change in Vornis's plans; it had been Shaw's intention from the start to stay on as long as he could and meet some of Vornis's other associates.

The beach was almost deserted. A pair of armed guards trudged through the sand a few hundred meters away. They were dressed in black fatigues, and Shaw smirked at that. No wonder all of Vornis's security detail looked so mean. They were melting underneath their uniforms in this heat.

Shaw wondered whom he could expect to arrive at the island at the end of the week. An art expert, obviously, but who else? Would it be hoping for too much that Guterman was one of Vornis's guests? Guterman was the head of a private bank that apparently laundered funds for a major terrorist organization. He would be a very valuable man to know. Shaw had wanted to meet him for years, but Guterman guarded his privacy. So would Shaw, if every intelligence agency on the planet had him in their sights.

Maybe Bashir would be here as well, or Atmadja, or Hale, or Ruiz. His heart beat faster at the thought of them. Shaw closed his eyes and smiled. Fuck, he was as good as having a wet dream about terrorists. But these weren't the guys who spouted hate on the news. These guys were above all that. These were the guys with the money who gambled against world governments. Serious fucking money.

Shaw felt a shadow fall across his legs and opened his eyes. He sighed when he saw the boy standing there, dazed and gorgeous. Ready for the taking, except Shaw still had some morals. Not many, but some.

Shaw closed his laptop and slipped it back into his bag

"Sit down, Green-eyes," he told the boy and wondered why the kid didn't run screaming for the ocean instead. Or at the guards, forcing them to shoot. Shaw would have. Because the kid had to know, didn't he, that there was no other way off the island?

Whatever they were injecting into his veins, it did the trick.

There was nothing in the boy's blank face to show that he remembered Shaw from the night before. That was probably for the best, Shaw reasoned. The last thing he needed was the boy thinking he was some sort of soft touch.

The boy settled into the sand. His gaze flicked to the ocean and stayed there, hypnotized by the waves that rolled back and forth on the sand. The sunlight shone in his green eyes.

Shaw leaned back against the palm and studied the boy's back. He saw a web of faint welts, old scars, and thin, new bruises. Vornis had certainly taken his revenge for what had happened in Colombia. Passing him on to someone new was probably only a variation on his old cruelty: let the boy suffer all over again from someone who wanted to take it from the beginning. Jesus, the kid was dead the moment Vornis was bored with him. And Vornis would make sure he felt it.

Shaw tried to ignore the sudden wave of pity that

washed over him like the ocean.

How easy it would be to find a boat. There had to be one on the island somewhere. There would be lifeboats on the yacht at least. How easy it would be to find a boat and launch it in the night and take Green-eyes away from this place. So easy, but Shaw couldn't do it. He'd worked too hard to get to this point. No pretty face was worth that. No scarred flesh was worth that.

Shaw reached out and ran his fingers across the boy's shoulders.

Maybe it was the tenderness of the touch, but the boy didn't jump. He leaned back slightly to allow Shaw better access and exhaled heavily. Shaw moved his hand down the boy's spine, feeling the pads of his fingers graze against the Braille map of cruelty that was the boy's body. Shaw kept his touch light. Even if the boy was beyond caring, Shaw didn't want to hurt him.

Green-eyes was a mystery, and Shaw's problem was that he loved to unravel those. He always had. Give him a puzzle to solve or a secret to ferret out, a maze to navigate, and he was happy. His mother had always said he was too clever for his own good, and Shaw supposed that was what had led him to his strange career path. It wasn't the danger he liked; it was the intrigue. Sometimes the danger brought him out in cold sweats in the middle of the night, not that he'd ever tell anyone that. He'd chosen this life. He'd made his own bed.

The boy drew in another breath, and this time it was shaky. That was probably reality knocking. He must have heard it sometimes. Underneath the drug-induced stupor, it probably screamed at him.

Green-eyes would never make it off the island alive. Shaw pitied him for that. His flesh was warm to touch, but it wouldn't last much longer. Shaw felt every intake of breath, every fragile beat of the boy's heart underneath his fingertips. It was a crying shame.

"You didn't hurt me."

Shaw started when the boy spoke but, always conscious of being watched, he kept his hand on the boy's back. What was that accent? Vornis was right. American, no question. Midwest, even? Shaw had a good ear for accents. The boy's was disguised under his low whisper but still recognizable.

"And I won't," Shaw murmured, "if you shut your mouth and play the part."

The boy dropped his chin to his chest.

"Good boy," Shaw said, hating the sound of the words. He doubted they could be overheard on the beach, but they could be seen. And you didn't speak to a fuck toy.

He wondered what was running through that pretty head. Probably nothing.

Shaw let his hand drop at last, and the boy turned his head to look at him.

Jesus, those eyes. They did it to him every time. Shaw didn't know if he wanted to spirit the kid off to safety or hold him down and fuck him senseless. Those brilliant green eyes, that jaw, those full lips, and that dark hair that eight weeks ago might have been a buzz cut but was now starting to remember how to curl. He looked like something Raphael might have painted, something rapturous and glorious and beautiful. Shaw almost laughed at the old cliché: he might not know art, but he knew what he liked. Just looking at the boy, silent and compliant, Shaw felt his cock stiffen. Then he remembered the poor fucking kid was going to die here.

Shaw felt the pity cross his face.

The boy saw it and latched on to it. Shaw hadn't hurt him. Shaw felt sorry for him. Probably that was all it took to earn his devotion, the sorry bastard.

His green eyes wide, the boy twisted around and leaned his face toward Shaw's.

Shaw got a hand on his thumping chest and pushed him away. "No."

Showing affection was the worst thing the kid could do.

Confusion washed over the boy's face.

"Not here," Shaw said in a low voice. "You don't even look at me, understand?"

The boy nodded quickly and turned away again.

Shaw castigated himself for letting it show. He didn't have to hurt Green-eyes, but, Christ, he didn't have to offer him a shoulder to cry on either. Vornis had only loaned him the kid to scratch an itch, and the nastier the itch, the better. This wasn't a fucking romance. Romance didn't come with a sports bag full of torture gear.

Shaw shook his head. He'd probably have to mark the kid at some point as well, to make it seem real. It would have been easier if Green-eyes didn't already trust him not to hurt him. It was wrong, earning that amount of trust so quickly, so unquestioningly. It wasn't the sort of trust anyone should give away. Even dogs that had been kicked half to death were wary the first time a kind hand touched them. The kid was just so desperate.

Shaw closed his eyes and thought of Molly. Molly was Callie's fault. Callie's sister was a vet, and when the yellow Lab puppy had been brought in with half an ear cut off, scorch marks on her belly, and all her ribs busted, she should have been put down. That would have been the kindest thing. How Shaw had ended up agreeing to take the bloody animal, he didn't know. He'd been taking a break at the time, and he'd been at a loose end, and he'd never been able to say no to Callie.

That first week had been torture, for both of them.

Molly had peed everywhere, and Shaw couldn't yell at her for it. She had been too afraid of him, and seeing that small animal cowering even when he tried to tempt her with treats had been heartbreaking. Now, a year later, Molly was the rambunctious, naughty dog she was supposed to be. And Shaw missed her. She stayed with Callie when he worked overseas. She was their baby. Shared custody and visitation rights, just like the real thing.

And, strangely, all the reprehensible things he had to do, all the awful things he'd seen, Molly somehow made it better. Shaw wasn't a monster. He'd rehabilitated an abused dog. He wasn't a monster. Molly loved him so much she could burst with joy when she saw him. He wasn't a monster.

Shaw shook his head. And Vornis wasn't a monster either, because he liked art. Jesus, everybody had some delusion they clung to pathetically to convince themselves they were better than the next guy.

And why was he even thinking of Molly? He should have been keeping his head in the game. It was because of Green-eyes. What did he imagine? That they could sail away, and back home Shaw could put down newspaper for the kid and make *shh-shh* noises until he could sleep without whimpering? There was too much at stake here for stupid fantasies.

True, somebody probably wanted Green-eyes back. And information was the most valuable currency in the world. Callie would find out where the boy came from, and Shaw would contact his people when his own business here was finished. Then, if Green-eyes was still alive, they could come and get him themselves. And maybe not fuck it up like they had in Colombia.

That would soothe his nagging conscience. He'd make the call once he was gone, and even if it only offered the kid the slimmest chance in the world, it was still better than nothing. It was more than the kid had any right to expect.

Shaw stretched. It was getting too hot to stay under the palm. He wanted to retreat to the cool of the bungalow. Maybe he'd have a shower, put the fan on, and lie on the bed for a few hours. He had a week to kill. He might as well catch up on some sleep while he was here.

He stood, brushing the sand from the back of his shorts.

The boy looked at him warily, expectantly, through his dark lashes.

Fuck. That went straight to his cock.

"Come on," Shaw said, leaning down to pick up his laptop bag. "You're with me."

The boy followed him.

CHAPTER FIVE

Packed off to keep busy with Green-eyes, Shaw was on edge. He'd shown Vornis the painting, he'd agreed on a price, and now he had nothing to do but kill a few days until Vornis's other guests showed up. Shaw discovered that he didn't really want to spend a lot of time with the boy. He didn't like the way the boy's proximity — his breath quickened and his green eyes widened when Shaw came close — had him veering between lust and pity. And he couldn't tell which one was more dangerous.

He needed to get some space.

"You run?" Hanson asked that afternoon when he saw Shaw sitting on the bungalow steps lacing his shoes. The big man was running as well. His face was red, and his body streamed with sweat. He lifted his arm to wipe his sweaty forehead, and Shaw noticed the way his biceps bulged. The hair under his arms was matted with sweat. Not Shaw's type, but he could see the appeal. And there were worse things he could do than make friends with the head of security.

Hanson looked just as intimidating in his sweats and joggers as he did in his black fatigues with a GLOCK. The man radiated physical strength.

"Do you mind if I tag along?" Shaw asked.

Screw the heat, he needed the sense of clarity that only running brought him. A couple of laps up and down the beach would sort him out.

Running in sand reminded Shaw of home. He liked listening to the crunch and squeak of the sand under his shoes and having his own breaths drowned out by the noise of the ocean.

The sun was slowly sinking into the sea, blazing in its death throes and turning a narrow bridge of the ocean into molten gold. The breeze was cool, chasing away the last shreds of thin clouds. Tonight, Shaw knew, would be spectacular.

It took thirty-five minutes to do a circuit of the island. Shaw guessed that Hanson could do it faster, but he'd slowed down to match himself to Shaw's pace. Shaw could do it faster as well, but screw it, it was hot, and he didn't feel like wiping himself out completely. And he wanted to take in the view. They passed the other guest bungalows on the way, the jetty, the collection of low buildings on the far side of the island — storage sheds? — and the path that led up to the helipad and the main house.

Approaching Shaw's bungalow again, Shaw invited Hanson to join him on the shade of the veranda. The big man agreed, and Shaw slipped inside to grab a bottle of water each.

He'd left Green-eyes kneeling on the floor by the bed because he had no idea what to do with him, apart from the obvious. And that was out of the question. The kid had fallen asleep while Shaw was out. He was lying curled up on his side as though he'd drifted off hugging his knees. One arm was out flung, stretched out across the grass matting. Shaw could see the bruises and the track marks on the pale inside of the kid's elbow. It was probably the most pitiful thing he'd ever seen.

One of the puncture marks was bleeding. A fresh wound. Had someone been here when Shaw was out running?

He joined Hanson on the veranda.

They sat at the table. Shaw stretched his legs out. His muscles felt tight. It had been too long since he'd been on a decent run. He used a treadmill back in LA, and it didn't give the same resistance as running on sand. Sand was a bastard.

"Have you dealt in art for long?" Hanson asked suddenly.

Was this an interrogation, Shaw wondered, or polite conversation? It had to be polite conversation. He'd worked hard to earn Vornis's trust and had a lot of dealings with Hanson's equivalent back in the States. He would never have made it this far if they were suspicious of him.

"I don't deal in art exclusively." Shaw leaned back in his chair. "I *facilitate*. I put buyers in touch with sellers, whatever the merchandise." He took a swig of water. "I've been in business for about six years."

"You must have started young," Hanson said, looking him up and down.

Shaw got that a lot. It didn't rankle. His reputation spoke for him. "I did."

Hanson's eyes gleamed suddenly. "Do you like the kid?"

Shaw smiled and tasted guilt. "Sure. What's not to like?"

"Well, he's docile now," Hanson said. "Should have seen him at the beginning. He fought like a fucking animal." A slow grin spread across his face.

Shaw didn't even want to imagine it. He looked out at the ocean. "Sounds like you did all the hard work, and I'm getting all the benefits."

Hanson laughed. "Hard work is its own reward!"

Shaw laughed as well and marveled at how natural it sounded. Jesus, he did business with some scary fuckers.

And he didn't need to know this shit. It was bad enough looking at Green-eyes and seeing what he was. Shaw didn't need to think about what he had been once and how hard he'd fought before they'd broken him. Eight weeks wasn't a long time, not really, but for Green-eyes it must have felt like eternity.

"Want to see him perform?" Hanson asked.

Crap.

"Why not?" Lie down with dogs, Shaw thought, and you'll get up with fleas.

Hanson rose from the chair and entered the bungalow. Shaw leaned in the doorway, absently tracing his fingers along the lines of the carved turtles on the post.

"Boy," Hanson said.

Green-eyes flinched awake, drawing his arms protectively against his chest. He looked around, blinking his dazed eyes to try to focus, and hauled himself up on his knees slowly. He reminded Shaw of a newborn foal struggling to find its fragile balance for the first time.

Hanson winked at Shaw. When he spoke, his voice was pitched low. "Get over here, bitch."

Don't, Shaw thought, and it shocked him how close he came to speaking the word aloud. Focus. Watch. Smile.

The boy drew himself to his feet. Still hugging his chest, he scuffed his way across the grass matting on bare feet. He stood in front of Hanson and sank back down onto his knees without even looking up.

"What do you want, boy?" Hanson asked. His tone was severe, but he was smiling.

A shiver ran down the boy's back. The thin scars on his flesh rippled. "Please, Mr. Hanson, please let me suck your cock."

Shaw's chest constricted. A perfect, coherent sentence, and it was a fucking travesty. He wondered how long it had taken them to beat that into Green-eyes. He forced a smile for Hanson's benefit.

The boy looked up. He swayed on his knees slightly. He swiped his tongue across his lips. It might have been hot, Shaw thought, except for his eyes. He was out of it.

Hanson laughed and reached down to pat the boy's head. The gesture was almost affectionate, but Shaw saw how Green-eyes tensed under Hanson's touch; obviously, not all of their interaction was as gentle.

The boy swayed again. His flesh had taken on a grayish pallor.

Too sick, Shaw thought, too broken, and too drug-fucked. How the hell was Green-eyes still breathing?

Hanson clapped him on the shoulder. "I'll leave you to it."

Shaw's expression was on the right side of lewd. "Thanks for the run."

Hanson slid the door shut behind him.

Shaw wanted to lean against the wall, maybe sink to the floor. This was too fucking much. He'd known of Vornis's proclivities for years, but at least Vornis had the decency to keep them mostly under wraps in LA. Apparently, on his own South Pacific island, he wasn't as constrained, and neither were his men.

I know he's a monster. I've always known. I just preferred it when he pretended to be a gentleman.

"Get up, boy," Shaw said at last. "Get in the fucking shower."

*****

Shaw pulled the boy under the shower. "What drug do they have you on?"

Green-eyes squeezed his eyes shut as the water hit them. He was shaking.

Shaw pushed him back against the cubicle wall. "What do they have you on?" He pressed his thumb into the inside of the boy's elbow, against the bruises and the track marks, and Green-eyes hissed. "What drug do they have you on?"

The boy shook his head. "Don't know."

"Someone came in here when I was out. Who was it?" Shaw asked him. He was half-afraid the kid would collapse and not get up. And half-afraid he wouldn't. It would be the best thing for him.

The boy's eyes flickered over Shaw's face, to his throat, and lower. They widened. His jaw worked, but no sound came out of his mouth.

Shaw tightened his grip on the boy's elbow. So he had a hard on. Of course he had a hard on. He was naked, in a shower with a hot young man who was also naked. Didn't mean he'd do anything about it. "Look at me. Focus."

The boy frowned. He dropped his chin onto his chest. Rivulets of water ran off the end of his nose.

Shaw slipped a hand under his chin and tilted it back up again. "I need to know who came in here."

What he needed to know was whether or not they'd tried to hack his laptop. Then he had to decide if Vornis was being cautious or paranoid. Both could be dangerous, but Shaw would take cautious any day, thanks. Paranoid, in Vornis's world, translated so quickly to homicidal.

Shaw slid his thumb along the kid's jaw. "Focus, Green-eyes."

Those brilliant green eyes widened, and a shudder ran through the boy's body.

"It's Lee!" he gasped. "My name is Lee!" It sounded as though he'd ripped it from a place deep inside him. It opened the floodgates. His face contorted, and he began to struggle. "Oh fuck! Oh fuck!"

Shaw was stronger. He held the boy by his shoulders and got a leg between his to anchor him. "Calm down. Just calm down, okay? I'm not going to hurt you. Just calm down."

Shaw wondered how it would feel to say Lee's name aloud.

Dangerous, Shaw, it would feel fucking dangerous.

Lee tried to push him away.

Shaw slid his hands down Lee's arms, gripping his wrists and pinning his arms up above his head. "It's all right. I won't hurt you. You remember that, right?"

Lee shook like a leaf. He nodded, but a small whimper escaped his throat.

"If I let you go," Shaw said, "you have to promise you won't fight me. Promise?"

Lee nodded again, more slowly this time.

"There are cameras in the bungalow," Shaw said. "I don't know if they have sound or not, but we're not going to risk that, are we?"

Lee nodded again, eyes wide.

"We can talk in here," Shaw told him. "This is the only place we can talk. Fuck, I hope you remember some of this tomorrow, because I don't want to go through this shit every day."

All the fight had gone out of Lee. Shaw thought if he released him, he'd just slide to the coral floor.

"I'm not going to fuck you," Shaw said. "But

Vornis has given you to me for the week. He's just a good host that way."

Lee shuddered.

Shaw leaned closer. "So this is the deal. We act the fucking part. You with me?"

Lee was breathing heavily now. "Why are you different?"

"Not everyone's a fucking rapist," Shaw told him. "Instead of asking questions, you could shut your mouth and be grateful."

Lee nodded again.

"What's your last name?" Shaw asked him.

He stumbled over that a bit. "*Um,* Anderson. Lee Anderson."

"And what are you?" Shaw asked him. He shook his head as confusion washed over Lee's face. "What government are you with? What agency? What were you doing in Colombia?"

Lee paled. "I don't remember."

"You try," Shaw said, carefully releasing his grip on Lee's wrists. He was surprised to see Lee kept his arms above his head. He'd been trained well. And what the hell was wrong with Shaw? Despite everything he'd just told the kid, he wanted to take advantage of that. Lee just looked so vulnerable like that, so sweet, that Shaw wanted him. He pulled his thoughts away with difficulty. "You try, you tell me, and when I'm off this island, I'll get a message to your people."

Shit! Where the fuck did that come from? Keep it together, Shaw! He scowled. *Information is currency, and you've just handed the kid a blank fucking check! Better cross your fingers he doesn't blurt that out to Vornis.*

Shaw was gambling on the fact that Vornis didn't like his toy to make any noise except cries of pain.

Big fucking gamble, Shaw.

Lee closed his eyes. "I don't remember. Oh God."

"But you say anything to Vornis, and I'll kill you myself," Shaw told him harshly. *Right before Vornis kills me.* "Understand?"

Lee nodded. "Thank you." He opened his eyes again. "Thank you."

Thanked for a death threat; that was new. The pathetic look in the kid's eyes made Shaw regret even trying. The kid was probably going to die here anyway. It would have been better if he'd been resigned to it. The last thing Lee Anderson needed was hope. That would just give Vornis one other thing to destroy.

"It's okay," Shaw said. He could feel his cock pressing into the boy's hip. It was high time he stepped back. Shame Lee's skin felt so good against his. Shame he liked the heat and the friction. Shame he liked the way Lee just stood there, arms above his head just waiting.

"Thank you," Lee murmured again. He tilted his chin forward and brushed his wet lips against Shaw's. The gentle contact coursed through Shaw's veins like electricity, and went straight to his balls.

Jesus!

Shaw stepped back to get some space between them. Some space and some fucking room to breathe. "You don't have to do that."

"Wanted to," Lee murmured, closing his eyes again.

"No, you didn't," Shaw said, turning his back on him and reaching for his shampoo. "It's the drugs, and it's something they beat into you. Get out, and go and wait by the bed."

He heard Lee's feet crunch in the coral.

Shaw looked up at the sky. The stars were just

beginning to appear.

Shaw lathered his scalp roughly and then stuck his head under the jets.

It had been a mistake, probably, telling the kid what he intended. But he had to offer something, something that would cut through the kid's drug-addled brain and stick there, something that would buy his silence and convince him to play along. It was a risk, but Shaw had taken plenty of those before. He just wasn't sure this time why he'd done it. He didn't owe anything to the kid.

Shaw sighed. No, he knew exactly what had happened. The kid wasn't some anonymous victim anymore. He had a name: Lee Anderson. And once a thing had a name, Shaw knew from his experience with Molly, you had to at least try to help it.

Shaw wished he'd never seen Lee Anderson. He wished Vornis hadn't trusted him enough to show off his little toy. But he had, and now it was too late. Against all his better judgment, Shaw was involved.

He stood under the jets until the water ran clear and then turned off the shower and reached for his towel. The worst part of the deal, he supposed, was the fucking peepshow. It would have been all right if he could have just ignored the boy and got him to sleep on the floor. That was safe. But no, he had to crawl between his thighs and jerk himself off inches from the boy's asshole. The week was going to be torture.

He walked up the steps to the bungalow.

Lee was waiting for him on his knees beside the bed. He was still wet from the shower. His naked body gleamed under the lights. His head was bowed. Droplets of water chased down his back.

Long runs on the beach, Shaw told himself. They were a much better way to work himself into a hot sweat. Long runs, long swims, and maybe he'd be able to keep his head.

Shaw remembered how Vornis had attracted the boy's attention. He whistled sharply, and Lee's head snapped up. Shaw gestured to the bed and watched as Lee climbed up and lay on his back. He was all long limbs and angles.

Shaw moved to the table, picking up another condom. He looked at the rest of the equipment. Not the cattle prod, Jesus, but the scarf and the cuffs? He'd put them to good use in the past. It was a shame they were instruments of torture to the boy. He couldn't use them.

A large moth tapped and pinged against one of the lights on the ceiling.

Shaw dropped his towel on the floor and crossed to the bed. He settled himself between Lee's spread thighs and looked down at him. The boy's cock was hard, and Shaw felt a jolt of surprise. It grew as he watched it, thickening, hardening, and slowly rising to push up against Lee's stomach. Shaw wished he could touch it, feel the weight of it in his hand, and trace the thick vein underneath with his thumb. Christ, maybe the kid wasn't straight after all.

He looked at Lee's face, and there was no denying the hungry look on it. It couldn't all have been misplaced gratitude. His green eyes were half-closed, and his lips hung open slightly. He wasn't passive like the night before. He was eager. Shaw felt even more sorry for him. How long had it been since the kid had equated sex with pleasure? Too bad that Shaw was in no position to give it to him.

Shaw drew the sheet up again, and saw a flash of disappointment cross Lee's face. Shaw frowned at him.

"Legs up."

Lee shivered at his harsh tone.

"Hurry the fuck up," Shaw snapped.

Lee raised his legs, folding them back against his body and holding them there. Shaw eased himself down, checking the sheet was still in place, and made a fist around his cock. He began to rock, leaning his weight on the boy's legs. The sight of Lee's body spread underneath his own was almost enough. Almost. He wanted to push his cock into the boy's tight, hot ass, but this would have to do.

Lee cried out, and it sounded so much like pain that Shaw almost stopped moving.

"Shut your fucking mouth," he said, and the resentment wasn't all feigned. This was torture.

"Sorry, sir," Lee murmured, and the *sir* made Shaw's cock leap in his fist.

Lee closed his eyes, clawing the sheets. He writhed, and it looked a lot like pain. Shaw, who kept hitting the boy's hard prick with the back of his fist whenever he finished a rough downward stroke, knew exactly what it was. If he hadn't been holding himself away from the boy's ass with his weight awkwardly on his left arm, he would have reached down to help him out with that properly. Or, even better, he'd lie on his back with the boy riding his cock, and he could take care of himself. That image alone almost undid him.

Christ. This was high school shit. Mutual masturbation without the mutual. It had never felt so unsatisfying. He'd never wanted it to end so quickly.

Shaw fixed his eyes on Lee's mouth and imagined those lips stretched around his cock. He imagined Lee, on his knees, looking up at him with those brilliant green eyes through his dark lashes.

Lee swiped his tongue over his bottom lip, and Shaw came. His whole body jerked, and he pushed his hips forward. He felt Lee's cock straining between their stomachs and gripped it before he could remind himself it was a bad fucking idea. He fastened his fingers around Lee's hot shaft and stroked him once, twice, and that was all it took before Lee was jerking and shuddering and crying out as well. It sounded a lot less like pain this time.

Shaw fell sideways onto the bed, panting. He wiped his hand on the sheet. He could feel Lee trembling beside him and resisted the urge to pull him into an embrace.

He wondered what the fuck Vornis would make of the surprise ending to their little show. He wondered if Vornis had ever made the boy come. He glanced over at Lee and saw that he was crying now. Shaw felt guilt twist in his guts and shook it off.

Tears would look good for the cameras.

* * * * *

Shaw drew his laptop up onto the bed, turning onto his side so that it was shielded between his body and Lee's. He made a show of checking news sites first, and stock prices and exchange rates. Nothing to see here, move along.

Outside, the evening buzzed with insects. Shaw could hear the endless heavy roll of the ocean against the sand. God, it was so loud but so soothing at the same time. Everything here was contradictory. The island itself, so beautiful, so peaceful. So terrible. And Lee. Shaw couldn't see the bruises in moonlight and shadow. Chose not to. Shaw pulled his gaze away with difficulty, before he felt compelled to touch. Before he ran his fingers down Lee's gleaming torso. His fingers and his mouth, discovering Lee's skin, his pecs, his nipples; following the dip in his sternum all the way down to his abdomen. To touch, to taste. Shaw squeezed his eyes shut as his cock stirred again.

You're smarter than this.

There was only one way he could touch Lee in this place: want, force, take. That wasn't a place Shaw wanted to go. Not with anyone, not ever. He had to draw a line somewhere.

Focus.

There was no new e-mail from Callie, but Shaw composed one: *Lee Anderson. Info ASAP please.* He deleted the second sentence after he read it. He knew he could trust Callie to make whatever he wanted her first priority. She was dependable. She was more than dependable.

This strange world that they inhabited made their relationship even stranger. They were friends. They trusted one another implicitly. They shared custody of a dog. And they hardly saw one another.

If you weren't gay, Callie said all the time, and Shaw always followed up with, *If you were a man...*

Shaw had never had a friendship that had lasted. They were impractical in his line of work. They could be dangerous. But Callie had made the transition from trusted colleague to trusted friend. It was such a relief, he supposed, to have someone who knew all his worst secrets and liked him and supported him despite them. Because Shaw surrounded himself with monsters, he was afraid of becoming one. He knew Callie would never let it happen. Not without a fight.

Lee, sleeping, turned over on his side to face Shaw. Shaw took the opportunity to angle the laptop slightly and photograph him. Proof of life would go a long way. He sent the picture with the e-mail, and then deleted them both from the hard drive. His encryption levels took care of the rest, scrubbing everything clean. There was nothing on his laptop that Vornis could use to accuse him of breaching his trust. Because trust was all there was in this business, apart from force, and it was the most fragile of things.

He logged into a social media site next and checked his messages. There was a new one from Stuart: *Hi! Can't wait to see you! XOXO!*

Shaw smiled at that. Stuart sounded more like a flirt every time. He messaged back: *Hi Stuart. Great to hear from you. Love to catch up soon.* He logged off and closed his laptop. Shaw liked hearing from Stuart. Stuart was a sure thing, and there were so few sure things in Shaw's life.

He looked at Lee, who appeared even younger when he was asleep. His face was untroubled, and Shaw envied him that. He was no stranger to nightmares after six years in the business. He wondered why Lee didn't wake up screaming. Was it because he believed he was safe in Shaw's bed? Or were the drugs still flooding his system?

Lee shifted in his sleep and moved a hand up to his face.

Shaw looked at the raw skin and the bruises around Lee's wrist. He must have struggled at some point. Like an animal, Hanson had said. Shaw expected that Vornis had encouraged it. Vornis liked to break his enemies, and this one was well and truly broken. Shaw wondered if Lee knew that. Had he realized that Vornis was probably already bored with his dazed compliance and would kill him sooner rather than later? He wouldn't have let Shaw play with his toy if he still coveted it. And eight weeks, by all accounts, was a long time for Vornis to keep a prisoner. Lee's odds grew shorter every day.

Shaw rolled onto his back and watched the ceiling fan spinning lazily. There was that crazy fantasy again, poking at the edges of his mind: the boat, the ocean, and the salvation. *Focus.* He was about to sell a painting for ninety-five million dollars. He was about to meet a group of the world's most powerful men. And Shaw lived for moments like these. So why did he feel like shit? Why did he feel like he should be doing something more for Lee? Common sense and a sharp instinct for self-preservation told him there was nothing else he could do. Now was not the time to have a crisis of conscience.

Shaw rose from the bed and headed outside. The night was dark and peaceful, and the stars were brilliant. There was nothing like waves rolling endlessly on a beach to put things into perspective, like staring up at night into a timeless field of stars. The little things didn't matter anymore. Even the life-and-death things faded.

Shaw stood in the shallows for a while, letting the tiny waves crest and crash around his ankles. The water was cool, and Shaw sank deeper into the sand. He breathed for a while, just stood and breathed, and then turned and trudged back to the bungalow. Lee was still asleep.

Shaw realized he stank of sweat and cum. It wasn't the sort of scent that usually turned his stomach, but under these circumstances? Yeah, he needed to get clean. Running a hand through his hair, Shaw headed back down into the starlit bathroom and stripped off. He stepped back into the shower. His third shower in a day. That had to be some sort of a record.

He scrubbed his skin clean, looking up at the flawless sky. His bare toes sank into the crushed coral, and Shaw sighed. God, he'd love a place like this one day, without someone like Vornis breathing down his neck. Without the fucking complications.

The cool water stung his shoulders, and Shaw realized he'd burned earlier. Now that was the sort of distraction he could rely on. A few days of itchy, peeling skin would keep his mind off Lee.

He turned around to reach for his towel, and Lee was right in front of him. His eyes were clearer than Shaw had ever seen them.

He stepped into the shower before Shaw could turn it off. "My name is Lee Anderson," he said under the roar of the water. "I'm with the DEA."

Shaw raised his eyebrows at that. The DEA? Sure, Vornis had inherited his father-in-law's business, but drugs were, literally, the least of his sins. The DEA didn't know whom they'd gone up against. Whoever had supplied their intel had given them just enough rope to hang themselves.

"Fuck," Shaw said. "Vornis thinks you're CIA."

Lee stared at him. "And who are you?"

"Shaw," said Shaw. "And the less you know about my business, the better."

"Is that it?" Lee asked. "Is that all you'll say?"

"You should be thankful I don't break your neck," Shaw told him, narrowing his eyes in the gloom. "DEA, CIA, it's all the fucking same to me."

Lee's gaze faltered. "But you're not like him."

"I'm not a rapist," Shaw said, "but I'm a lot of other things. Look, you can either keep your questions to yourself, or you can go back to Vornis right now."

"Will you really tell them I'm here?" Lee asked.

Shaw frowned. He had that whole kicked-puppy look again. "I said I would. It's up to you if you believe it or not. I don't give a fuck what you think."

Lee flinched at his tone.

"But bring it up again," Shaw said, "and I *will* break your fucking neck."

Less shrank back. His chest rose and fell heavily.

The moon appeared from behind the drift of a

cloud, flooding the shower with silver light.

Shaw shook his head at Lee. "And what's this shit with following me in here? You're not supposed to think for yourself, mate."

Lee shook his head slightly. "No, he *um,* he — it's okay. He likes me to follow him."

"Yeah, I saw that," Shaw said. "You're a good little puppy. But I didn't whistle."

"Sometimes," Lee said, the words coming with difficulty, "sometimes I get a treat if I go to him without being called."

"What sort of treat?" Shaw asked with a frown, knowing he wouldn't like the answer and wondering why he'd been compelled to ask such a stupid fucking question.

Lee couldn't meet his eyes. "Sometimes he won't whip me after."

"Yeah," said Shaw in a low voice. His guts twisted. "Well, he's a sick fuck."

"Are you?" Lee asked, still looking at his feet.

"Jesus," Shaw muttered. "Just…just get out of here, okay?" He watched, astonished, as Lee went down onto his knees instead. "What the hell are you doing?"

Lee moved forward on his knees, the coral crunching. It must have hurt, but he didn't even wince. He was used to worse. "Just let me, please."

"Oh, fuck, kid," Shaw said, and then his voice hit another pitch as Lee reached out for his cock. "*Fuck.*"

One slender hand wrapped around his shaft. The other cupped his balls. Shaw jerked back and cracked his head on the wall of the shower recess.

"Don't," he said. "You don't have to do that. You're not my fucking toy."

Lee looked up at him, and it was as good as Shaw had imagined. Better, even, because rivulets of water ran

LISA HENRY

over his skin, and droplets caught on his lashes and his
lips. He gleamed in the moonlight. He was beautiful.

"I want to," he said and angled Shaw's cock toward
his mouth.

Shaw had a lot of reasons to push him away. He
didn't want to get any closer to the kid. He didn't want to
be the next man who used him. He didn't want to be like
Vornis in any way imaginable. And Jesus, he'd just
threatened Lee, and this was how he responded? That was
fucked-up. But every single protest died the second Shaw
felt those warm lips close over the head of his cock.

He'd drawn a line, he reminded himself, but
couldn't find it now.

Lee was good. His mouth was hot, and his tongue
was clever. It circled the head of Shaw's cock, pressing into
the tender underside, following the ridge of flesh all the
way around, and then pushing into the slit in the head.
And all the while his other hand worked Shaw's balls,
cupping them, squeezing them, teasing them. Every nerve
in Shaw's body began to sing. If Lee was straight, Vornis
had trained him well.

Shaw shook the thought away and tried to stay in
the moment. The last thing he needed was to think about
were the methods Vornis had used to break the kid. Don't
touch, don't touch, you don't have the *right* to touch, but
Shaw couldn't stop himself. He rested his hands on Lee's
dark hair, urging him gently forward but not wanting to
scare him. Lee moaned, and Shaw felt his mouth vibrate
around his cock.

"Fuck," Shaw murmured, wondering what this
made him.

No, not wondering. Knowing.

Lee slowly took Shaw's cock into his mouth until
Shaw could feel it pressing up against the back of the boy's

72

throat. He stroked Lee's head, and Lee looked up at him. His eyes were full of something Shaw hadn't seen there before. Was it pleasure? Couldn't be. Lee smiled around Shaw's cock, shifted forward, and swallowed.

Shaw groaned, feeling his cock slide into Lee's throat. All the doubts he'd had faded. Lee knew what he was doing. Shaw began to thrust his hips, listening to Lee time his breaths perfectly. His throat constricted around Shaw's cock.

Shaw bit his lip as he looked down at Lee's beautiful face, at his lips stretched around his cock. Lee's eyes were closed now, and he had a look of pleasure on his face that was impossible to fake. There was no way in hell that he'd been straight eight weeks ago. Nobody could deep throat like that without having a hell of a lot more experience. A novice would panic. A victim would choke. Lee, at this moment, wasn't a victim. And maybe that was why he'd wanted to do it.

Or maybe that's just what you're telling yourself because you want to come.

Shaw moaned. God. Lee was good. He was drawing this out too, just how Shaw liked it. A part of Shaw wanted it to last forever. A part of him needed to come right now. And that detached part of him that owned the voice in his head was telling him he should never have let this happen.

Where's that line you drew now?

Shaw's cock throbbed and ached, and his spine felt like liquid. His balls drew up tight under Lee's hand. He groaned. Time to give fair warning. "Gonna come."

He lifted his hands from Lee's head, giving him the chance to pull away. Instead Lee gripped the back of Shaw's thighs tightly and held them. Shaw came with a shout, shuddering. He felt his whole body spasm as he released. Gasping, he watched as Lee swallowed furiously.

Shaw leaned back against the shower wall.

Lee stood. His tongue flicked over his bottom lip, and Shaw had never seen anything so beautiful. "Thank you."

"Should be me thanking you," Shaw said. He reached out for Lee, prayed there was no camera trained on the shower, and pulled him close for a kiss.

What the fuck are you doing, Shaw? This is fucking dangerous!

Lee's tongue, so clever a minute ago, was suddenly shy. Shaw found it with his own at last and teased it for a moment. Lee's mouth tasted like cum and heat.

Shaw released him. "You weren't straight, were you?"

Lee smiled hesitantly and looked cautiously at Shaw through his dark lashes. "Not even for a second."

Shaw almost laughed at that, before he remembered he couldn't be Lee's friend or his savior. He'd do what he could, and that was it. "Next time when I tell you to leave the shower, I expect you to do it."

Lee's smile faded.

Shaw frowned at him. "Do you understand me? I'm not your friend. I'm the one in charge here."

Lee nodded.

"A blowjob doesn't change anything," Shaw said. Neither, he thought, does a kiss. "Go on, get the fuck out of here."

Lee nodded again, biting his lip. He turned and was gone before Shaw could be certain, but Shaw thought he was holding back tears.

Shaw felt like the biggest prick in the world, but that was what he needed to be for both their sakes. And if Lee looked as miserable as a whipped dog when he went back into the bungalow, even better.

CHAPTER SIX

In the beginning, in Colombia, Lee had been afraid to die.

That lasted about an hour.

Then he'd been afraid he wouldn't die, but the shock and the drugs took most of that away. Now, even when his mind was clear, he was rarely afraid. He was numb. Whatever happened would simply be inevitable. He'd been on this path from the moment the chopper landed in Colombia, and maybe even from the moment he'd been born. He just hadn't known it then.

Most of the time, he was beyond fear, and he knew it wasn't strength of mind or a philosophical decision he'd made. He was just too tired to fight anymore. He'd learned to shut his own mind down, even without the drug.

But now there was Shaw. Lee didn't know what to make of Shaw.

He sat on the beach and shivered despite the heat.

Coming down was always the worst. The drugs made him nauseated as his system fought against them. His hands shook, and his mouth tasted sour. But at least this time, he wasn't in the closet in the house, or anywhere near Vornis or Hanson or the guards. This time when his head had cleared, he was with Shaw. And he knew that was the safest place to be on the island. Shaw's touch was gentle, solicitous. He was different.

"When I'm off this island I'll get a message to your people."

That had shocked Lee. It had shocked him so much it had penetrated beyond the drug. It had stayed with him. He didn't know if he should trust it, but he held on to it because it was important. It was precious. It was like the painting Vornis had shown him.

"You like that, boy? Ninety-five million dollars. I could buy a thousand boys like you for that price and still have enough left over for a fleet of goddamn Lear Jets. That's a thing of fucking beauty, and you will thank Shaw on my behalf. Get on your knees."

The boy in the red vest looked tired, Lee had thought as he'd obeyed. Tired and unhappy.

Lee shivered at the memory and looked out at the ocean. Shaw had sold Vornis that painting. That made Shaw some sort of art dealer, he guessed. Probably not the sort who owned a gallery and filed tax returns, though. Shaw wasn't a good guy. There was no such thing on the island. But Shaw was different from the others.

Shaw had told him there were cameras in the bungalow. Shaw had told him he would make a call. And Shaw hadn't hurt him. Shaw hadn't hurt him, but he wanted it to look like he had. He denied he was different, but actions spoke louder than words. Lee didn't understand it, but that was okay. He didn't want to question his luck.

Lee watched Shaw swim. The sunlight reflected off the water and blinded him. He squinted, and shards of light stabbed his vision. He traced his hand along the edge of Shaw's beach towel, and his fingers came into contact with the arm of Shaw's sunglasses. He looked down at them and wished he could use them. But he knew it wouldn't be worth the trouble if Hanson or his men spotted him.

He closed his eyes.

Shaw, he thought, wouldn't care if he borrowed the sunglasses, but he didn't pick them up. He didn't want to be proved wrong. Hope was a fragile thing, and he needed to nurture it for a while before he put his trust in it.

He was certain Shaw was different, and not just because he didn't hurt him.

When Shaw looked at the ocean, Lee saw the change that came over him. He relaxed almost imperceptibly, and his hazel eyes let go of their sharpness. He wasn't Vornis's guest, then; he wasn't a criminal; he wasn't anything except a man looking at the ocean. The slight wistful smile that played on his lips made Lee wish he was seeing the same thing Shaw did whenever his gaze traveled the horizon, whatever it was.

Shaw hadn't hurt him, and Shaw had said he'd call the authorities once he was off the island—Lee replayed it in his mind just to be sure he hadn't imagined it. It was unprecedented, and he didn't understand it, but he wanted to believe it. And both of those things, the kindness and the promise, might have been enough to feed Lee's hope, but it was more than that. Lee had seen Shaw's face when he looked at the ocean, and it was the most human face Lee had seen in a long time.

That was that man Lee had gone onto his knees for in the shower the night before. He knew Shaw thought it was just gratitude or a behavior that had been beaten into him, but it was more than that. Shaw was the only man who had looked him in the eye for a long time, and he'd seen past the humiliation and degradation. He'd seen Lee. He'd given Lee his name back.

Lee traced his fingers through the sand.

Maybe some of it was gratitude, but most of it was because Shaw had looked him in the eye. The thrill Lee had felt as he'd gone down onto his knees had made him breathless. His body might have been his only currency on the island, but this was the first time since his capture that he had used it entirely on his own terms. Not bargaining, not begging, and not calculating.

If you go to him before he calls you, he won't hit you so hard.

If you make it good, he'll feed you.

If you don't struggle, maybe they won't cut you.

There was no shame in taking the path of least resistance, not with Vornis and Hanson and all the others, but with Shaw, it had felt different. It hadn't felt like a compromise.

If you get him off quickly, it'll be over sooner.

With Shaw, he had wanted it to last.

The thing with Shaw in the shower had been freely given, and Lee knew that Shaw didn't get that. His reaction had been confused: first a kiss, and then a harsh reprimand. He was a man used to showing affection to his sexual partners, Lee realized, and he had reasserted his dominance too late. It didn't matter. The blowjob had been as much for Lee's benefit as Shaw's, and he didn't regret doing it. Shaw had tasted good.

And it helped that he was hot. In his old life, Shaw would have been exactly Lee's type. There was no harm in acknowledging that, even though acting on the attraction had been frightening at first. Lee had been afraid that it might mean he had become an accomplice in his own torture, and that taking enjoyment in the act meant he had accepted everything that had come before, but Shaw was different. Shaw was someone he might have picked up in a club or at a party, back when he was allowed a choice. And so, in the shower, Lee had made that choice, because when would he be given the chance again?

It was okay to differentiate, wasn't it? He was in uncharted waters, and it made him nervous. But different had to mean better. It couldn't mean worse. Shaw wasn't like the others. His reaction in the shower had demonstrated that.

When you're with him, you're okay.

Lee nursed his secret hope anxiously.

He opened his eyes again and trailed his fingers through the warm sand. He found a sand dollar and turned it over in his palm.

Lee collected sand dollars. They were made by some sort of sea urchin, he guessed. They were light, flat, round shells, and whatever creature had once lived in them had left a pattern on each side that reminded Lee of a stylized flower or the first few turns on a Spirograph. He collected them because he liked the pattern, because they were abundant in the shallows, and because it gave him something to do.

It gave him some control.

He would take the sand dollars from the beach and wipe them clean with his thumb. He would slip them into his pockets and kept them until the end of the day. Some were too brittle and were crushed. Most of them ended up on the coral floor of the bungalow bathroom. He used them to while the days away. He used them to keep his focus.

One foot in front of the other. One sand dollar and then another.

In the beginning, he'd wanted to be dead. He'd wanted Vornis to just kill him and get it over with. Because nobody was coming for him. Nobody knew where he was. Shit, he didn't really know himself, except he knew it wasn't Colombia anymore. Fiji, Irina had said, and Lee couldn't even pick out Fiji on a map. It didn't matter. But now Shaw was here, and something had changed. Shaw was going to get off the island and make that call. For the first time in a long time, Lee allowed himself to think of the future.

It turned out the future looked exactly like the past. It looked like the house he'd grown up in. It looked like his parents' faces.

No. Don't think of them. Not yet.

He couldn't bear it if he never saw them again. Shaw had offered him a slim hope, but even if he was telling the truth, Lee couldn't trust that it would happen. He couldn't build himself up like that. He wouldn't. He could take some solace in his memories, but not too much. Searching his memories was like pulling at a scab and reopening a wound. He had learned to graze the surface, careful not to go too deep. A fine line, but practice had shown him how to walk it.

It was okay to think of places but not people. The memory of places gave him comfort. The memory of people was too raw. He liked to imagine that he was back in the house he'd grown up in, lying in his bed and looking at the ceiling. The walls were decorated with colorful pennants and posters of bands he'd liked growing up. When he'd been home at Christmas, he'd laughed at that. His mom kept the room like he was still a kid. Stepping through the door was like walking into the past. He'd laughed, but now there was nowhere he'd rather be than sleeping in that bed, wearing his old Vikings T-shirt and sweatpants. Home was the safest place in the world.

The next safest place was with Shaw.

Lee looked out at the water again and turned the sand dollar over and over in his palm.

One foot in front of the other, and don't get ahead of yourself.

*****

81

The stars were very different here. Lee wondered if he would have felt so lost if he could only look at the stars he knew. Or maybe that familiarity would have made it worse.

His dad loved hiking and camping. Lee couldn't remember the number of times they'd pitched a tent in the middle of nowhere and spent half the night staring up at the stars. He'd known the patterns of the constellations as a child, but he didn't recognize them half a world away.

Lee pressed his hands on the tiled wall of the shower and looked up at the stars.

Shaw was asleep upstairs.

Now, now was a good time.

Lee closed his eyes.

Mom, Dad, if I don't make it home I'm sorry it ended up like this.

His throat constricted with the tears he'd expected, and he fought them down.

I'm sorry you'll always wonder what happened.

Shaw had given him hope, but Lee didn't know what to do with it. He couldn't trust it, and he wasn't sure he even wanted it. It was all very well to want to live, but after this? He couldn't be the same person. He didn't know if he could look himself in the eye, let alone his parents and his colleagues, so maybe it would be better if —

No. Hold on to hope. Count the sand dollars, pass the time, wait and see.

Because if Shaw gave him hope, he had to take it. He had to believe in something, didn't he? Even though it would be easier not to. He wasn't certain he could believe in himself anymore, so maybe he could believe in Shaw.

Lee ran his fingers down the tiles and frowned.

But who the hell was Shaw anyway? Not a good

guy, not if he was friends with a man like Vornis. Shaw felt different, but that was probably just a matter of perspective, and Lee's perspective had been skewed since Colombia. He couldn't trust what he felt. Shaw had said it himself: *"I'm not a rapist, but I'm a lot of other things."* Shit, what the hell had happened to him that "not a rapist" had become a glowing fucking character reference?

God, he wanted to believe Shaw. He wanted to *trust* Shaw, and that was stupid. Just because the guy hadn't hurt him, and just because he'd said he'd make that call once he was off the island. And maybe just because Shaw was young and good-looking and had gazed at the ocean like it meant something to him.

And Shaw had trusted him first.

There were cameras in the bungalow. Why had Shaw warned him about that? Okay, so he wanted Lee to put on a good show at night and to keep his mouth shut. Wouldn't it have been easier just to hurt him? That was how everyone else got him to comply. So, Shaw wasn't a rapist, and he wasn't a sadist either. That only meant he was a good guy in comparison to Vornis, but who the hell wasn't? Lee couldn't trust his perspective.

Here on the island, the man he had become wanted to fling himself blindly into faith. But he knew the man he had been before would have been more guarded.

Careful, Lee, careful.

Then again, the man he'd been before the island had a hell of a lot to lose. What was he risking now, except his hope? And how much was hope worth? That was a philosophical question, and Lee didn't have the luxury of those anymore. Hope was worth nothing in practical terms. And in emotional terms, what did it matter if Shaw crushed his hope and his burgeoning trust? Lee had taken enough hits in the past eight weeks to know he could take more. They were always building him up just to break him again, with the drugs, the ill-treatment, and the unexpected kindnesses that it turned out hurt more than the torture. It was all about the juxtaposition, and Vornis was a fucking expert.

"There now, boy, you're okay. There now. Have a little drink of water."

Right before the next white flash of pain.

Shit, there'd been a time when he'd trusted Vornis as well.

"Come on, boy. Almost done. Not long now. Can you be a brave little soldier for me?"

Like they were on the same fucking side. And sometimes he still fell for it because he so desperately wanted it to be true. He wanted to be good, obedient, and compliant, and to believe Vornis would go easy on him for once. And he always ended up hating himself more than he hated Vornis. Vornis was clever like that.

Tears stung Lee's eyes as he looked up at the stars again. He'd slipped down into the bathroom just to see them. The shower was safe. Safe from the cameras, safe from the guards, and safe from Vornis. It was lonely, though, without Shaw.

Careful, Lee, careful.

Lee frowned.

So what? So what if I like being near him? If it turns out to be a lie, what's one more humiliation before they kill me? I have nothing to lose.

Just like he told himself when he wanted to believe the kindness in Vornis's voice. But Shaw was different, wasn't he?

Fuck, fuck, fuck!

He was going in fucking circles, and he knew he was. He just couldn't find a way to break free.

His throat ached. He bent down and picked up a

sand dollar he'd dropped there earlier. He held it up to the moonlight and traced the pattern with his thumb. Maybe it was just a new delusion, but he wanted to believe in it.

Hold on to hope. Count the sand dollars, pass the time, wait and see.

He dropped the sand dollar and left the shower. His bare feet creaked on the steps.

At first, he thought Shaw was awake. He turned his head on the pillow as Lee watched, but his eyes stayed closed. His fist was clenched around the sheet.

Lee looked at him for a moment.

He could kill him. He could, probably, even if he wasn't as strong as he had been. How much strength did it take to hold a pillow over a man's head until he suffocated? If it had been Vornis or Hanson or any of the guards, he would have done it. They'd kill him for it, but he had nothing to lose.

A knot of anxiety formed in his stomach.

That was what a captive should think, wasn't it? Always plotting, always planning, always looking for a chance to tip the balance of power if only for a moment. He could kill Shaw, and they would kill him, and it would all be over.

Shaw muttered something in his sleep, and a frown crossed his face.

Lee watched him. Shaw was having a bad dream. His conscience was biting back while he slept, and that, Lee realized breathlessly, might just be something big enough to put his faith in.

He didn't want to kill Shaw. Shaw had never hurt him. Shaw had promised to help him. And maybe there would come a time when he would regret trusting him, but at some point, he had to stop second-guessing himself and make a fucking decision.

His heart raced.

I have nothing left to lose. He is not *Vornis.*

He crossed the floor and lay down on the bed beside Shaw. He drew the sheet up, pulling it carefully from Shaw's grip, and ran his hand underneath it. He caught Shaw's hand in his own gently and held it until Shaw relaxed.

It was probably all bullshit, and he'd probably regret it, but right now, in the middle of the night, in the quiet, it felt like maybe they were in this together. Yeah, he was fucking crazy, but he wanted to believe it.

Careful, Lee, careful.

He closed his eyes.

Wait and see.

CHAPTER SEVEN

Shaw had the knack of always looking relaxed. It didn't matter that he was bouncing between being bored and nervous. Bored because there were only so many times a day he could check his e-mail, and nervous because in a matter of days he'd be meeting Vornis's other guests, and he'd wanted this for years.

He spent his days swimming, jogging, beachcombing, and watching. He knew now that there were at least sixteen armed security guards on the island. They lived in barracks in a building on the side of the island where the yacht was anchored. At first Shaw had thought the wooden building was a boathouse. It had been designed to look like one.

He knew that Hanson went swimming every morning at five, and running at dusk. He knew that Irina sometimes collected seashells off the beach, furtively, as though she was afraid she would be accused of stealing. And he knew that for all Vornis liked to be locked up in his air-conditioned glass house, every afternoon he strutted from the main house down the twisting paths that led to the bungalows and the beaches just to remind himself that he owned the place.

Shaw understood the rhythm of the island and its inhabitants now, just like he understood the rhythm of the ocean.

Shaw liked to listen to the dull roar of the ocean

from underneath it. He liked the push and pull of the water, the whirlpool of the waves breaking on the sand and rushing back again, and the low, white noise that drowned out the breathing world. The water was deep and cool.

He surfaced when his lungs began to burn, wiping his hair back. He was only about ten meters from the beach. He could see the roof of the main house from out here, shining like a mirror. He could see the palms swaying. He could see a security patrol trudging through the sand. One of the men was Hanson. And he could see Lee sitting below the high-tide line, tracing patterns in the wet sand with his fingers.

Shaw could have spent hours in the water, but he couldn't leave Lee waiting for him in the sun. The kid was used to a short leash, apparently. It hadn't even occurred to him to move farther up the beach into the shade. He'd be burned to a crisp before much longer.

Shaw let the gentle waves carry him toward the beach.

Lee looked up as he splashed out of the water and reached down for his towel. He seemed more alert today.

"Come on." Shaw nodded toward the closest shady palm. The sand burned the soles of his feet. He spread his towel under the palm and sat down. He rested his arms on his knees and looked out at the ocean. It was beautiful here.

He waited until Lee was settled beside him before he spoke in a low voice. "You seem better today."

Lee nodded slightly, scratching a tiny scab on the inside of his elbow. He didn't look at Shaw. "No needle today."

"Is that normal?" Shaw asked him, watching the breaking waves chase up the beach.

Lee nodded again. "He lets me remember, then starts it all over again."

Shaw heard the catch in Lee's voice and resisted the urge to reach out and stroke his hair. "Maybe it's better when you're drugged."

Lee bowed his head. "I don't even know how many times it's happened. I don't even know how many men it's been. There were men in Colombia, and then on the boat, and the guards here. I don't know."

This time Shaw couldn't help himself. He put a hand up onto Lee's shoulder and squeezed gently. Lee was shivering despite the heat.

"I'm not supposed to talk," Lee said. "Sorry, sir."

"You just have to remember who could be listening," Shaw told him. He felt Lee stiffen. "But we're okay here on the beach. It's windy on the beach. Full of fucking distortion. The beach and the shower, they're okay."

Lee relaxed slightly.

"So if you want to talk," Shaw said, "you talk."

Jesus, what was he thinking? He didn't need to open that floodgate. He already felt too sorry for the kid. He was too soft, that was the problem. It was why he'd let a Labrador puppy use a pair of Barker Black-Ostrich Cap Toe shoes as a chew toy, and it was why he'd told the kid he'd help him. It was his own fault the kid had latched on like a limpet.

"You said you're not my friend," Lee murmured.

Shaw sighed. "Yeah, and I'm not your friend. Not the sort of friend you need, anyway. But while I'm here, I won't rape you, and I won't hurt you for talking. That's the best I can do."

"Yeah," Lee said in a small voice. He cleared his throat and stared fixedly at the ocean. "Thanks. Um, I spent last Christmas with my parents back home. They're

89

good people."

Shaw had never seen a more ham-fisted attempt by a captive to humanize himself for his captor. It was straight out of *Hostage Situations for Dummies*. Jesus, was that what they taught the kids these days? Fucking pathetic. He shook his head and snorted with laughter. "Not subtle, are you?"

Lee's voice wavered, and his whole body tensed. "What do you mean?"

"You don't talk about your parents," Shaw told him. "Not like that. You bring shit in casually. Like I ask if you're hungry, or when I give you food, you say you could do with a plate of your mother's home-cooked whatever right about now. Don't even try it if you can't make it sound natural."

Lee swallowed.

"You look at the water for a while," Shaw said. He stared at the ocean and let the Pacific work its gentle magic. "This reminds me of when I was a kid. My parents had a place on the beach. We used to go there on weekends. My sister Emma, she's got kids of her own now, she used to build sandcastles." He let his voice sound wistful for a moment before he shook his head to break the spell. "You see what I did there?"

Lee tensed again. "I wasn't, um, I wasn't—"

"Of course you were," Shaw said. He rubbed his thumb against the top of Lee's spine, feeling the skin slide gently over the bone. "But it won't work on me, and it sure as hell won't work on Vornis."

"Sorry," Lee murmured. "What are your sister's kids' names?"

"I don't have a sister," Shaw said.

Lee relaxed under Shaw's gentle touch. "That feels

nice."

"You're wound tighter than a spring," Shaw said. He ran his hand lower and felt Lee hiss as he skirted over a small burn. The shape of it, like a fanged bite, made Shaw think of the cattle prod. "Sorry, mate."

"You're Australian," Lee said.

"Guilty," Shaw said.

Lee turned around to face him. "I thought so." He bit his lip.

Shaw didn't like it when Lee looked at him. So fucking trusting and hopeful, and so fucking broken. He reminded him of Molly in the early weeks. It made him feel guilty, even though he hadn't been the one to hurt him.

Lee dropped his eyes, and they widened as they took in the scars on Shaw's thigh. He raised his hand tentatively and traced them, hunching back as though he was afraid Shaw would push him away. "I saw them before."

He flushed then, and Shaw knew they were both thinking back to the blowjob in the shower.

"Did someone hurt you too?" Lee asked warily.

"No," Shaw said. "That's an Irukandji jellyfish sting I got as a kid."

He was eleven when it happened. He'd never felt pain as intense as he'd felt that day. He'd passed out in the ambulance on the way to the hospital. They told him later his heart had stopped. He'd never forgotten his stinger suit after that day.

Lee met his eyes, his hand still on Shaw's thigh. "And you still swim in the ocean?"

Shaw ran his fingers up Lee's forearm. He liked the way gooseflesh appeared and the fine hairs stood upright as his fingers grazed over them.

"I didn't, for a while," Shaw said, and then glanced

away. What was he going to say? *You have to overcome your fears? You can't let the pain beat you? You have to be strong?* Jesus, he'd told Lee he wasn't his friend, and now he was going all Dr. Phil on him. Maybe the kid was smarter than he thought, humanizing Shaw instead of himself. That was interesting.

Lee waited for a moment and then removed his hand and turned away again.

Shaw watched the ocean.

"He made them dig their own graves," Lee said suddenly. "In Colombia."

Shaw didn't say anything. There was nothing to say.

Lee closed his eyes briefly. "There were three of us alive at the end. And he made them dig their own graves, and then he made them watch when he fucked me. And then he made me watch when he shot them." He shivered.

The security patrol headed closer. Shaw stroked Lee's back quickly and then dropped his hand back onto the towel.

"And the whole time, all I could think was how strange it was he was using a condom," Lee murmured. "Seemed almost considerate. Then I realized it was because he was going to give me to whoever wanted a turn."

Shaw nodded at the security guards as they passed. Hanson smiled at him.

Lee watched them warily, waiting until they'd turned up the path that headed up to the bungalows and the main house before he spoke again. "And, you know, when those other two guys were watching, I could see they pitied me. They'd just dug their own graves, and they pitied *me*. How fucked-up is that?"

"That's fucked-up," Shaw agreed quietly.

Lee drew a deep breath. "Yeah. Maybe it is better when I'm drugged. Doesn't feel real then."

Shaw ran his fingers gently down the scars on Lee's back.

"I'm scared," Lee said in a low voice. "I don't wanna die here."

"I know," Shaw said. It wasn't the response that Lee needed. He was seeking reassurance, but Shaw couldn't give him that. It was out of his hands. "Come on back inside. I've got work to do."

* * * * *

Lunch was waiting on the veranda when they arrived back at the bungalow: coral trout on a bed of coconut rice, salad, and wine. Shaw sat and ate, saving a portion for Lee. Lee, sitting on the boards of the veranda at Shaw's feet, looked like he was going to cry with relief when Shaw passed him a piece of fish.

"Thank you," he murmured.

It struck Shaw as infinitely cruel that Lee still remembered his manners.

Lee was too thin, Shaw thought, and too pale. It was enough that he was probably going to die here. Shaw didn't see any point to make him suffer unnecessarily in the meantime. And that, he supposed, was the difference between him and Vornis.

"Go and get my laptop," he said, and Lee scurried to obey.

Shaw set it up so he had to squint in the light to see the screen. All the harder for the cameras to pick up a decent angle. Shaw appreciated Vornis's need for security but not when it encroached on his own need for privacy.

There was no reply from Callie yet, but Shaw hadn't expected one. Callie might be a miracle worker, but an inquiry this sensitive would take time.

Shaw was glad to be back at the bungalow. He shouldn't have told Lee it was okay to talk on the beach. He didn't need to get drawn in any further to the kid's misery. There was too much danger that he'd feel like doing something about it. And that was not why he was here. He had to remember that. Shaw couldn't be Lee's salvation. He couldn't be his anything. The danger in showing him any kindness at all was that Lee would misinterpret how far it could go.

Shaw flicked through the few photos on his laptop. Molly, of course, surrounded by the shredded cushions of his new lounge suite, looking up at the camera with her head on an angle. *What*, she seemed to say, *what did I do?* Molly at the beach, the first time they'd gone. She had no idea what was going on when Shaw had coaxed her into the shallows, and then, holy crap, the water was coming right at her! She'd been frightened at first, then confused, and by the time Shaw took her photo, she'd been frolicking like she'd been born in the water. The last photo was his favorite. Molly, sleeping on his bed, with her head on Shaw's pillow like she owned the place.

Shaw looked down at Lee. And that was the problem. You couldn't save every broken little animal in the world. You had to pick your battles.

This is a dangerous game, Shaw, he reminded himself, and you don't need the distraction.

Lee looked up at him through his brilliant green eyes, and Shaw saw something in them that he really wished he hadn't: trust.

* * * * *

94

Vornis sent Irina and a pair of guards down to Shaw's bungalow that night to borrow back his toy for an hour or two. He'd had an idea for something he wanted to try. Something new. Shaw hated to think what that might involve, but he shrugged like he didn't care either way and smiled when a security guard hauled Lee to his feet and Lee whimpered.

Irina's eyes widened at the sound, and Shaw looked at her curiously. Another soft touch? Maybe, but he wouldn't bet on it.

Shaw didn't watch as they led Lee away. He turned on the television instead and watched the news. He poured himself a glass of wine and leaned back on the bed and tried to look like he gave a damn about rioting in the Middle East. And he should, he supposed, because things like that always impacted on his work sooner or later, but he couldn't stop thinking about Lee.

What was *new*, to Vornis? Shaw's imagination was vivid.

Christ, what did it even matter? He couldn't have stopped it. He'd chosen not to try, but that was beside the point. He knew it wouldn't have made a difference. All he could do was count the minutes and hope to God that Lee didn't spill his guts about what he and Shaw had done. Or hadn't, as the case was.

The wine tasted sour in his mouth. Christ, but he dealt with some frightening fucking people. The thing he couldn't understand, that he would never understand, was that Vornis had a wife and kids, and he doted on them. Shaw had met them before, another indicator of Vornis's trust in him, and Carmina was beautiful and charming, and the kids were sweet and happy. And Vornis, when he was with them, was a different man. Shaw was no stranger to duality, but with men like Vornis, it worked on a whole different level. How could he help his daughter with her homework after he'd tortured a man? How could he ruffle his son's hair with the same hands that were so often steeped in blood? How could he make love to his wife when he was a rapist?

Shaw closed his eyes briefly and listened to the newsreader go on about the number of prodemocracy protesters killed. Prodemocracy in the Middle East, Shaw thought. If you lived long enough you saw everything. It was the staying alive that was the tricky part.

Almost three hours passed before Lee came back. Shaw heard the footsteps creaking on the veranda steps, and little exhalations of pain that matched the rhythm of the footsteps. Shaw was glad he heard them before he saw them. He wouldn't have been able to force a smile otherwise.

"Here you go, Mr. Shaw," Hanson said. "Mr. Vornis apologizes for the delay."

Lee was a mess. His lip was split, one eye was swollen shut, and when Hanson pushed him to his knees, Shaw saw that his back was covered in bloody welts. There was a nylon rope fastened around his neck like a noose, pulled snug. His hands were tied behind his back.

Shaw drank the last of his wine and looked at Lee like he didn't give a fuck. "No problem."

"Good night, sir," Hanson said. He grinned broadly as he looked at Lee.

"Good night." Shaw placed his wineglass down on the table. "Get in the shower, boy."

Lee couldn't stand, so Shaw helped him up and then helped him down the steps into the bathroom. His fingers worked at the knots around his raw wrists until the rope fell free, and then Shaw loosened the noose and drew it carefully over Lee's head. He unfastened Lee's pants and let them drop to the floor. He pushed him gently into the shower, following in his board shorts, and turned the water on.

The water was only cool, but Lee screamed when it hit his back. He tried to pull away, but Shaw held him there.

"Hurts!" Lee whimpered. "Hurts!"

"Gotta get it clean," Shaw told him, forcing him still. "You can handle it."

Lee dropped his head forward onto Shaw's shoulder. "Fuck. Hurts." His voice was raw.

"I know," Shaw told him. He took the bar of soap and began to work it very gently across Lee's back. Lee flinched. "Have to get it clean."

When he felt Lee could stand it, he turned up the hot tap.

Lee flinched again, but held himself still under Shaw's ministrations. "I thought he was gonna kill me. Why doesn't he just kill me?"

Shaw didn't answer that. He only knew it could take Vornis a lot longer than three hours to kill a man, if he had the inclination to draw it out. And he would, for Lee. He touched the ligature mark around Lee's throat. It was narrow and swollen. Shaw could see where the thin nylon had cut Lee's skin. Christ, Vornis was a monster.

"They strung me up," Lee said. "Couldn't breathe. God, it hurts."

"I know," Shaw said again. He turned Lee around gently and began to wash the soap off his back. Lee flinched as Shaw's hand slipped down to the crease of his buttocks. "Maybe you should clean yourself there."

"Yeah." Lee's face was a mask of humiliation as he turned back to face Shaw. He took the soap, lathered up his hand and winced as he moved it around behind himself.

Shaw didn't let his pity show. That was the last thing Lee needed right now.

"He made me beg for it," Lee said, dropping his eyes. "He likes that."

"Those are just words," Shaw told him, wondering when the shower had become the confessional, and wondering how desperate Lee was to unburden himself to a man he didn't even know. All Shaw had done was not rape him. That was how pitiful Lee was. He should have known Shaw wasn't that much better than Vornis, particularly after tonight, but he was too desperate to see it.

"I told him I wanted it," Lee said, his voice rasping. "*Begged* for it."

"Words are worthless." Shaw knew that better than most people. "It doesn't mean anything."

"What if it does?" Lee asked suddenly, his eyes wide.

Shaw shook his head. "I don't know what went on tonight, but it doesn't matter what you said in there. It doesn't matter if you begged for cock." He put a hand on Lee's shoulder. "And it doesn't even matter if you meant it."

Lee flushed with shame.

"So you meant it," Shaw said in an even voice. "Why wouldn't you, if it stops the beating?"

He wondered if Lee had seen it yet, or if he was so desperate to spill his guts to Shaw that he hadn't realized. Nothing he said had horrified Shaw, and nothing would. Shaw wasn't his salvation. Any consolation he offered was empty. Shaw lived comfortably in the hell where Lee had been tortured.

"Anyone would beg for it," Shaw told him. "That's

the point."

Lee frowned slightly. "Yeah," he said, and Shaw knew he didn't believe it. It was the truth, but it hadn't reached him. "Yeah."

Shaw remembered the way Lee's eyes had shone with hope that afternoon. Shaw wondered if he missed seeing it, but it wasn't a bad thing that it was gone. Lee needed to know where things stood. Shaw wouldn't hurt him, but he wouldn't prevent him from being hurt either. It wasn't much of a moral distinction, but Shaw had always operated in the gray areas. Shaw made decisions every day that would entangle ethicists for years in debate. Shaw didn't have the luxury of time. He made a decision, stuck to it, and stretched the morality to fit it later. Square pegs into round holes; everything could be made to fit in the end with a little mental dexterity.

Shaw was very good at that.

"We've all done things we're not proud of," Shaw said and regretted it at once. Lee looked so grateful that it made bile rise in Shaw's throat.

Lee's tears for the camera were real that night. Shaw positioned him on his hands and knees on the bed, and if he raked his fingers down the kid's back to make him cry out in pain, what did that matter? He was tired of rubbing himself against Lee like a dog in heat. He was tired of jerking off furtively and making it look like rape.

The longer Shaw stayed on the island, the more he lost his focus. The longer he stayed with Lee, same story. Why should Shaw be the only man on the island with a fucking conscience? Why shouldn't he take what was offered, the same as the rest of them? Shaw hated himself for what he was becoming, and he hated Lee for holding up a mirror to his ruthlessness. He wanted to punish Lee for that, just a bit.

Afterwards, when Lee was crying into the pillow,

Shaw took his hand under the cover of the sheets and held it.

He was no better than Vornis, probably. The small secret signs of affection were just another form of torture. Why didn't Lee see that he was nothing but a cold shell? It felt strange when Lee slept deeply that night and sighed when Shaw entwined his fingers with his own.

* * * * *

Shit.

Shaw stood at the edge of the water, his feet sinking into the wet sand. He stared out into the black Pacific, he listened to it, he demanded it work its magic. Nothing.

Shit.

He was at the end of his tether here. He hated his. He hated that Lee trusted him, because it came with a hopeful expectation that Shaw was in no position to fulfill.

"You're going to die here," he told the ocean, told Lee. Would have told him, except he'd left him sleeping in bed. "You're going to fucking die here."

Shaw was on his third beer, and that surprised him. He didn't usually drink much when he was working, but tonight he needed the buzz. He needed it to distract him from his guilt. His guilt. And where the fuck had that come from? He had nothing to be guilty about. He hadn't captured Lee. He hadn't tortured him. He hadn't raped him. He had nothing to be guilty about.

Fuck, fuck, fuck.

Except his complicity. He was complicit just by being here, just by letting it happen.

Jesus, the best thing he could do for Lee would be to go back into the bungalow and fucking smother him with a pillow. That would be the best thing, the kindest thing, but Shaw didn't even have the balls to do that. He didn't need a dead American DEA agent on his conscience. Or on a file somewhere in the Pentagon. Shaw had flown under the radar his whole career. He didn't need to start making waves now.

Shaw scowled. He didn't need any of this shit. He needed to go home. The thought caught him with a clarity that shocked him. Shit, he needed to go home.

So it was too fucking bad he was as much a captive on the island as Lee.

CHAPTER EIGHT

Vornis borrowed his toy back again the next night. Shaw tried to think of that as a positive. If Vornis wasn't bored yet, Lee still had half a chance. But it didn't look like a good thing when Lee whimpered as the men took him. When he was gone, Shaw watched television and tried not to count the hours. He fell asleep in the end and woke up when he heard footsteps on the bungalow steps. One of Vornis's men hauled Lee inside.

Lee came back with his hands cuffed behind his back and his eyes downcast. He winced at every step and looked too tired to even care. Vornis had given him to Shaw not as any strange sadist's welcoming present but as a way to prolong the boy's torture. He probably never got a rest between sessions. He'd just drop one day soon, Shaw thought, and never get up.

He was wearing the key to the cuffs on a string around his neck, like a bow on a birthday present. Shaw took it and turned him around.

His hands were swollen. The two smallest fingers of his right hand were taped, and when Shaw knocked his hand against them accidently, Lee flinched. When Shaw turned him around again he saw that Lee's eyes were filled with tears. It was reflexive. His body responded to the pain dumbly. His mind wasn't even in the game anymore.

He stank of blood, sweat, and cum, and it turned Shaw's guts. He drew Lee into the shower and stood him under the water. Lee's eyes were unfocused again. Not even the shock of the hot water brought him around.

When he was clean, Shaw wrapped him in a towel and laid him on the bed in the bungalow.

A knock on the door surprised him. He crossed to it and slid it open.

"I have tape," Irina said. Her pale eyes flicked to the bed and back to Shaw.

Shaw shrugged and let her in.

Irina crossed to the bed and sat on the mattress carefully. Her gaze slid down Lee's body. She took a small pair of scissors from her pocket and drew Lee's injured hand into her lap.

Two damaged things, Shaw thought suddenly, and they made a miserable tableau. Like the Pieta. Lee, brutalized and broken, and Irina, he saw for the first time, not much better.

Lee's eyes flickered open, and he stared up into Irina's plain face. His eyes shone with such sudden gratitude that Shaw guessed this wasn't the first time Irina had patched him up. As he watched, Irina murmured to him in a sing-song voice in a foreign language. A lullaby, Shaw realized. She was singing him a fucking lullaby. Shaw wondered if it was the most pitiful thing he'd ever seen.

Lee sighed and drifted back to sleep.

Irina began to cut off the tape. Whoever had taped Lee's fingers in the first place had made a mess of it. The fingers were broken. Irina re-taped them carefully, and the kid didn't even move. Shaw couldn't tell if it was shock or if they'd given him drugs again.

Irina lifted Lee's hand from her lap and stood again. There was something challenging in her eyes when she looked at Shaw. "Thank you for letting me do that," she said.

Shaw shrugged like he didn't care one way or another, and Irina left the bungalow.

He wondered what Vornis would make of Irina's Florence Nightingale routine. He didn't have long to wonder. He'd just thrown a blanket over Lee when Vornis himself appeared on the veranda of the bungalow.

"Shaw!" he exclaimed with a smile. "Have a drink with me."

They sat together at the table inside the bungalow.

Vornis lit a cigar. "So," he said, nodding at the bed, "what do you think of my toy?"

"You play rough," Shaw said with a smile.

Vornis laughed. "That's the only way to play."

Shaw had thought Lee was asleep but saw him tremble when Vornis spoke. Or maybe he was asleep, and Vornis was so far under his skin that he was manifesting as a nightmare.

"So I've heard," Shaw said.

Vornis's eyes gleamed. "But you don't practice it?"

Shaw shrugged and sipped his drink. "I like to be in charge, but I don't play at your level, Vornis. Why the broken fingers?"

Vornis leaned forward slightly. A look of satisfaction crossed his heavy features. "Because of the way it makes him *clench*, Shaw. Can you imagine?"

Shaw tasted bile and discovered that he could imagine. It could still surprise him how monstrous Vornis really was.

"You should try it," Vornis suggested, "instead of all your hot showers together."

Shaw laughed to show he wasn't offended about being spied on. "He still cries for me, don't worry! He knows his place all right."

"Right on the end of your cock." Vornis laughed.

The sly smile and the glint in Vornis's eyes made Shaw uneasy. He wondered if Vornis would attempt to use this little conversation as a way to invite Shaw to join his games. And, if that happened, Shaw knew he wouldn't like it. He doubted Vornis would try anything with him that he did with Lee, but it wouldn't be a candlelit dinner and spooning afterward either. Vornis was attracted to strong masculinity, but only so he could force it to submit. And there was no way in hell Shaw would get down on his knees for Vornis. No, he had to reestablish them as equals, or he'd lose any advantage he had.

"And yours," he said, raising his glass. "You've broken him in beautifully."

Vornis gazed at the boy. His lips curled proudly. "You approve?"

Shaw settled back in his chair. "I know an artist when I see one."

Vornis's eyes flicked to Shaw. "I suppose you do."

There was a question in Vornis's eyes that Shaw refused to answer. If Vornis wasn't going to ask directly why he'd let Irina tape Lee's fingers, Shaw wasn't going to tell him. It was dangerous to let him wonder, but no more dangerous than suddenly blurting out answers to an unasked question. That would be a sign of weakness to a man like Vornis, and Shaw couldn't afford to show weakness.

Shaw sipped his drink, feeling his stomach twist. Nothing to see here, move along. He smiled wistfully. "This place is paradise. You'd better watch out, Vornis. You might never be rid of me."

Vornis responded well to Shaw's joke, as Shaw had known he would. His face cracked with a grin. "You ought to show more respect, Shaw, to a man who has made you ninety-five million dollars richer!"

Shaw laughed. "Then let me get you another drink."

He stood and moved toward the bench. He glanced at Lee as he passed. No, there was no question. Lee was only pretending to sleep, but he was awake. He was too tense. His breathing was too shallow. His jaw was clenched.

Relax, Shaw willed him silently. *Relax, and maybe he'll forget about you.*

Shaw rattled around with the bottles on the bench to draw Vornis's attention away from the bed. It didn't work.

"So you like him?" Vornis asked when Shaw returned. "My little American toy?"

Shaw leaned back in his seat and raised his eyebrows. "What's not to like? He's pretty, and he's tight."

That seemed like the sort of thing a monster should say.

"Yes," Vornis said. "Not as tight as he was, but that's to be expected. I kept a tally in the beginning, you know, of how many times he'd been penetrated, but then I lost count." He frowned and then laughed. "By the end of the first week, we all got a little tired of him."

Shaw laughed as well, not daring to glance across at the bed.

Don't tell me, Vornis. Please don't tell me the fucking tally.

He hated the sound of his own laugh. Did Lee think he was a monster because he would laugh at something like that? The thought took Shaw by surprise. What the hell did it matter what Lee thought of him? It didn't matter at all. He had a job to do here.

It was a job he hated more and more by the minute.

"You let Irina tape his fingers," Vornis said at last.

Shaw was surprised how relaxed he sounded. "I assumed someone sent her. Anyway, I didn't want him whimpering all fucking night."

Was it enough, he wondered? Was it the right answer?

"She is too soft." Vornis drained his glass.

Shaw shrugged. "Women."

Vornis's laughed. "Ah, yes, women!" He set his glass on the table and rose to his feet. "I have calls to make. Good night."

"Good night."

Shaw walked with Vornis to the veranda and watched him disappear into the darkness of the path that led up to the main house. He was unaccompanied, and that was interesting. Vornis had let his guard down with Shaw. He trusted him. A glow of cautious satisfaction spread through him. He could do this. He could really do it.

When he went back inside, Lee's eyes were open. They were more focused than the last time. He was running his hands over his flesh, searching carefully for fresh injuries. His eyes widened when he saw Shaw, and he froze.

Shaw picked up his towel from the back of a chair. "I'm going for a swim," he said. "Come on."

He wondered if Lee thought he was cruel, or if he suspected the truth. Shaw didn't want to hurt him by making him move, but he didn't want to leave him alone in the bungalow either. They'd drugged him before when Shaw wasn't there. They'd taken him before. Shaw didn't want Lee to just vanish.

Lee drew himself carefully up from the bed. He winced, and a hand went straight to his ribs. Shaw stepped toward him and then remembered the cameras. He leaned in the doorway instead and waited as Lee shuffled toward him.

Shaw stripped off his shirt and headed down the steps. There was torchlight on the beach as they headed for the water, but it was a fair distance away.

Shaw touched Lee's shoulder gently, glad of the darkness. "You okay, kid?"

"Yes," Lee said in a dull tone.

It was such a blatant lie that Shaw wanted to laugh at the absurdity of it.

"Wait for me here," he told Lee, and Lee nodded and sank into the sand.

Shaw waded into the dark ocean. He didn't go too far out. It was too easy to get turned around at night, and he already had a few drinks in him. Alcohol and night swimming: a dangerous combination Shaw had never been able to resist. It took him right back to high school. To simpler times.

He was homesick, Shaw realized as he let the swell of the ocean lift him. He was homesick, and not for Sydney or Los Angeles. He was homesick for a beach shack and a small country town, and for the kid he'd been then. Before he'd known that men like Vornis existed. Before he'd known that boys like Lee suffered. The kid he'd been back then wouldn't recognize the adult he'd become. The adult who laughed with Vornis when he said he'd kept a tally.

But that was the price of ambition. You sacrificed things for ambition. Time or relationships or maybe even human decency itself. Ambition demanded it. If you weren't serious about your sacrifices, you didn't deserve to succeed.

A part of Shaw wondered if that was really true or if it was just a convenient philosophy he'd picked up somewhere as a crutch. And it didn't really matter. He was here now. He was already committed.

Shaw looked at where Lee was sitting obediently on the beach. He couldn't make out his face in the darkness. He could only see the pale, lean shape of him as he sat with his arms hugging his drawn-up knees.

A beautiful boy, a beautiful beach, a beautiful moonlit night, and it was a travesty.

It was none of his business what Vornis did with the kid, Shaw told himself. He couldn't even tell if he believed it anymore. It was none of his business, it was not his responsibility, and the kiss in the shower had meant nothing.

Yeah, bullshit.

He should never have let it come to this. Should never have let Lee under his defenses. He'd known the second he saw him standing in the rain that Lee was fucking dangerous. Beautiful and dangerous, just like the island itself, and Shaw had let it happen anyway. What the hell was wrong with him?

Shaw sighed and let the waves carry him back toward the beach.

* * * * *

Lee was a fucking mystery. Two nights in a row, Shaw had sent him off without a complaint to Vornis, and two nights in a row he'd come back racked with pain, and now, for some crazy reason, he was following Shaw up a fucking hill like a loyal dog.

The island had one hill, and, that morning, Shaw decided to climb it. He was bored, he supposed, and looking for an excuse not to be confined to the bungalow with Lee, so he asked Hanson if there was a way up. There was a path, Hanson told him, that the guards sometimes ran for training. But it was a hell of a climb, and it would be slippery after the overnight rain. From the top, though, Hanson said with a smile, scrubbing his scarred knuckles over his buzz cut, the view went on forever.

It was difficult to remember that Hanson was probably one of those who had raped Lee the night before.

Shaw put on his trainers, shoved a water bottle in his pack, and headed for the hill. And Lee followed him.

Shaw didn't have the heart to tell him to go back to the bungalow. Because if Lee followed him, Shaw reasoned, then he wouldn't be in a position to be abused. And that was probably what Lee figured as well. He was eager enough to keep up at the beginning, but a few hundred meters later, as the path began to incline steeply, he lost ground.

Shaw slowed down for him. His trainers were caked in mud, and Lee was struggling in his bare feet. The day was hot. The air was humid under the thick canopy of trees. The mud was black, and the air buzzed with insects.

They weren't even halfway up when Shaw made the decision to turn around.

"Come on," he said to Lee.

Lee was too weak for this. Eight weeks of malnourishment and torture had stripped his strength. He was gasping for breath.

Shaw took his water bottle out of his pack, unscrewed the cap, and passed it to him.

"Thank you, sir," Lee murmured and swallowed gratefully.

"When we get back," Shaw told him, "you're going to walk up and down in the shallows until your feet are clean. Any cuts, you make sure you get salt into them."

It wasn't exactly first aid, Shaw knew, but it was better than nothing. And he had some antiseptic cream

110

somewhere in his suitcase.

Lee's green eyes flashed with fear. "I don't want to go back!"

Shaw raised his eyebrows. "And what's your alternative?"

He hadn't meant for it to sound that harsh, and he was afraid Lee would react badly. It surprised him when Lee only frowned slightly, squared his shoulders, and nodded.

"Good boy," Shaw told him.

And then Lee ran.

Shaw was surprised by the suddenness of it but only for a second. Then he barreled off the path as well, chasing him down.

Lee couldn't go up hill, wouldn't go downhill, so he headed across it. Shaw could hear him just ahead, thrashing away, but couldn't see him. The bush was too thick. Snappy branches whipped Shaw in the face. Vines tangled around his legs. Thick undergrowth obscured the ground. Shaw was afraid he'd snap an ankle at every step.

He didn't shout. There might be guards nearby, and he didn't want them to catch Lee instead. He didn't even want them to know this had happened. He had to find Lee and return him before anyone found out, because it was hopeless. He had no strength and no shoes and he was on an *island*. How far did he really think he'd get?

No more than about fifty meters, as it turned out. Lee was tangled in a vine when Shaw stumbled across him. He was whimpering and thrashing.

"Don't move!" Shaw recognized the vine. He'd had run-ins with it, or a variation, in his youth. It had barbs. "Christ, Lee, don't move."

Lee froze.

Shaw couldn't see the main clump of the palm, but didn't need to. Lee was caught in the chaotic tangle of vinelike stems that sprouted from the palm like flagella. Both the leaves and the tendrils were covered in backward-facing hooks to enable the tendrils to reach the canopy. Many of these hooks were caught in Lee's thin pants. Some were digging into his flesh. One tendril raked across his face. It drew tiny pinpricks of blood from his right cheek that coalesced into a single droplet. The blood slipped down Lee's pale face like a tear.

Shaw hissed in sympathy. "Don't panic. Don't move."

"I'm sorry," Lee said, squeezing his eyes shut. "I'm sorry!"

For running, Shaw wondered, or for getting caught?

Shaw approached him carefully. He caught one of the tendrils between his fingers, avoiding the barbs, and drew it away from Lee's face. "Okay, put your arm up. This one's going to spring back. It'll sting, but you don't want it on your face again."

"I'm sorry." Lee squeezed his eyes shut. His chest heaved. "God, so sorry. I try not to. I try not to!"

Shaw rubbed the small of his back. "Try not to what, Lee?"

Lee sucked in a breath. "I try not to panic!"

Shaw rubbed Lee's back again. Around them, insects chirped in the dense rainforest. It was almost tranquil. Might have been, except for the adrenaline still flooding Shaw's body.

The island is beautiful. It's dangerous. It's a trap.

Difference is, Lee knows he's caught.

"Keep your arm up," Shaw murmured.

Lee obeyed, wincing as Shaw carefully repositioned the tendril against his bruised forearm.

"Okay?" Shaw asked him, and Lee nodded.

Shaw couldn't see the ocean or the white beach from here. He couldn't see the glass-and-steel house either. This was the real island. This was the island that had been thrown up from under the sea by a volcanic eruption a million years ago. It teemed with life; it stank of decay. Insects and spiders devoured one another. Vines strangled the trees they climbed. The rainforest consumed itself endlessly.

Shaw flicked a green ant off Lee's hip before it stung, and began to work on the vines caught around Lee's legs. He eased each hook free, careful to hold the tendril away as he worked so it couldn't reattach.

"They have these at home," he told Lee. "They're called wait-a-whiles."

Lee didn't answer.

Shaw moved around behind Lee, feeling a tendril snag in his shorts. He didn't pull on it, only moved back the way he'd come to get free. He tried the other side, working the vine slowly free from Lee's pants.

"You shouldn't have run. It's dangerous." The words were out before Shaw realized how absurd they were. *Dangerous?* Shit, he was losing it.

"Couldn't help it," Lee said, his voice no higher than a whisper. "I'm sorry."

"You will be by the time we're finished here."

Lee tensed.

"Because of the wait-a-while," Shaw said, shaking his head. But, Jesus, of course Lee was confused. How could he know what to expect from Shaw, when Shaw blew hot and cold? When Shaw had listened to him in private, reviled him in company, promised to call his people, threatened to break his neck, and held his hand at night under the sheets? Shaw had never hurt him, but, if he had, at least Lee would know where they stood. This was just another form of torture.

Shaw worked another hook free, pulling threads as he did.

"I'm sorry," Lee whispered again.

Shaw rubbed his back as he worked. "I know."

Me too.

It took over twenty minutes to free Lee, but at last Shaw was able to take him by the hand and guide him out of the thorny tangle. He was bleeding from a multitude of tiny puncture wounds. Death by a thousand cuts, Shaw remembered, and it seemed apt.

All the fight had gone out of Lee by that time. His head down, he followed Shaw meekly back to the path that led down the hill to the bungalow.

* * * * *

It wasn't a bad thing in the end, Shaw realized, that Lee got tangled in the wait-a-while. His back and chest were covered in angry welts because of it. Even his face was swollen. In the end, it looked like Shaw had taken Vornis's advice and played harder. Vornis was full of praise when he'd borrowed Lee again for an hour that afternoon.

Irina, when she brought Shaw his dinner, couldn't look him in the eye. So now she thought he was as monstrous as Vornis. So what?

Shaw checked his watch. It was only an hour. What could happen in an hour?

Shaw wanted to know and didn't want to know. He couldn't offer Lee any comfort, he couldn't empathize, so what was the point? He was just glad Lee had no more broken fingers when he was returned.

When night fell, Shaw took Lee down to the beach, and they sat together below the high-tide mark and looked at the stars. Shaw rubbed antiseptic cream on Lee's back and chest, on the marks left by the wait-a-while and by Vornis, careful to keep watch for security patrols.

Lee's breathing was shallow. He was trembling despite the warmth of the Pacific night. Shaw hated that. He hated not being able to fix it, and he hated the part he was stuck playing in this sick game. He wasn't even sure himself what the hell he was doing. Christ only knew what Lee thought of him.

Small waves washed onto the beach and back again, a gentle, endless murmur. Shaw looked up at the moon and thought of the pull of the tides and a boat and an imaginary escape he couldn't offer Lee.

"Thank you for looking after me," Lee said at last. It was the first thing he'd said since being returned.

Shaw didn't answer. Lee's quiet gratitude turned his stomach.

Lee surprised him by turning around to face him. "Thank you."

Shaw opened his mouth to say something — he didn't know what — and suddenly Lee's warm lips were pressing against his. Shaw jolted with surprise. He put his hands against Lee's shoulders, mindful of the welts, and pushed him away gently.

"Don't do that," he said. Surprise made his tone harsher than he intended.

Lee hunched his shoulders. "I'm sorry."

Shaw shook his head. "Christ. Just don't, all right?"

"I'm sorry," Lee whispered miserably. "I thought you wanted it."

"I don't," Shaw told him brusquely. Jesus, in any other situation he'd be begging Lee to get closer, but this was beyond wrong. This was Lee responding to the unexpected kindness of a monster, and Shaw didn't want that. He didn't want to be that. Not for anyone.

"You're the only one who looks me in the eye," Lee said. He turned away again. His breath hitched.

Shaw sighed and ran his fingers down Lee's spine. "Don't be upset."

Lee hunkered down farther. "Sorry."

"And don't fucking apologize," Shaw murmured. "It is what it is, Lee."

"I know," Lee whispered.

They watched the black ocean together.

CHAPTER NINE

Another night and he was on his knees again. Another night in the room he hated. He couldn't hear the ocean from here.

"And how is Shaw treating you, boy?"

Lee winced as Vornis gripped his jaw tightly and twisted his head to face him.

"Please," he murmured. "Oh, please."

Vornis gave an exasperated sigh.

Lee lowered his eyes quickly, his heart racing. He'd miscalculated. It was too early for begging. He wondered how many more broken fingers that mistake would earn him. He tasted bile, and his stomach clenched. Every nerve in his body screamed at him to fight or to run, but experience was a better teacher than adrenaline. He struggled not to move.

"I asked how Shaw is treating you, boy," Vornis said. His eyes were dark, almost black. Like a shark's. "Tell me what happens when he takes you into the shower."

Lee tried to swallow. "I give him blowjobs, sir." His voice cracked.

Vornis raised his eyebrows and released Lee's jaw. "How very adolescent. Is that all?"

Every instinct in Lee warned him to lie. He owed it to Shaw to lie, but it wasn't all about gratitude. It was about self-preservation as well. Because whatever game

117

Shaw was playing, he'd made Lee play along, and Vornis would punish him for that.

Shaw trusts *you. Don't fuck it up.*

"He, um, he pulls my head back under the water, and I can't breathe." Lee fixed his eyes on the floor, hoping that was enough. He prayed he hadn't given Vornis any new ideas. A shudder ran through him.

"Ha!" Vornis sounded pleased. "I told you Shaw has potential."

Lee closed his eyes briefly.

Hanson laughed from somewhere behind him.

Lee hated sessions like these. He preferred it when he was drugged. He'd hoped they'd drug him tonight — the cabinet where the syringes were kept was open, but so far neither of the men had made a move toward it. He always panicked when he was lucid, but sometimes that was just what Vornis wanted.

Sometimes he wanted the drug-fucked Lee, dazed and compliant, but sometimes he wanted to see real fear. When he was drugged, Lee whimpered from the pain but didn't understand its cause. When he was lucid, he screamed and begged when he saw it coming, his eyes rolling in his head and every muscle straining, and that made Vornis laugh.

He'd been drugged last night and the night before. That meant tonight they wanted his every reaction.

Oh God. He needed something. He couldn't do this. Not again.

"Please," he gasped, his fear breaking him like it always did in this room. He shuffled forward on his knees, his cuffed hands making it difficult. He bent toward Vornis like a supplicant. "*Please.*"

Vornis reached down and stroked Lee's hair with

his blunt fingers.

Lee responded to the gentle touch gratefully. He pushed his face against Vornis's trouser leg. Like a fucking dog. He hated himself, but he was too desperate not to beg.

Vornis's voice was soft and beguiling. "That's a good boy. Show me how well behaved you are."

Lee shivered.

He hated this. He hated to see himself as Vornis must have: on his knees, begging, nuzzling the man's trouser leg. He wished he could say he didn't recognize himself, but who was he kidding? Every time he entered this room, they turned him into a fucking slave. *Yes, sir. No, sir. Anything you want, sir.*

He'd played games like this once. Just games. Cuffs and blindfolds and pretending to be master or slave without laughing too hard. Tim, his boyfriend from college, had been more into it than him. He'd ended up getting into leather and discipline and the whole deal. It had been a little too weird for Lee. Playing was fine, but he could never do it with a straight face. He couldn't beg a man and make it sound real. He couldn't have imagined it would be one day.

"Please, sir, please don't hurt me!"

It turned out the only thing holding him back had been his consent. Take that away and he was a fucking natural. On his knees, bending toward Vornis and begging with every fiber of his being for mercy he knew he wouldn't get. And later, of course, he'd beg for pain as well. Just because Vornis wanted to hear him do it and had the ability to make it happen.

He choked back a sob.

Oh God, oh God.

He skated close to the edge of mindless panic.

No.

119

Fishing for gar and green sunfish at Round Lake.

Counting the cracks in the sidewalk on the way home from school.

The Vikings pennant on his bedroom wall.

Hold on to that. Hold on to what you were. What you are. You're not nothing. And when this is done, Shaw will look after you.

Shaw looked him in the eye, and Lee had never seen anything like disgust there, and that was something else to hold on to. Vornis could try to make him forget the man he'd been, but Shaw wouldn't let that happen.

Hope was so fragile and easily crushed, but Lee took as much as he could. He had tried to show Shaw what that hope meant to him, using the only currency he had left, but Shaw always rebuffed him. He wanted Shaw. He wanted to remember what it was like to have a choice, but that was one choice Shaw wouldn't let him make. Lee wished he would, because Shaw would look him in the eye if they fucked, and it wouldn't hurt. Lee wanted that. He needed it. It wasn't just about lust. Shit, nothing much was these days, but he couldn't deny the spark he felt when Shaw touched him. It was about remembering who he had been and maybe reclaiming just a fraction of it. Just enough to hold on to at times like these, because he was so afraid these were the only times he had left.

Lee drew a shaking breath.

No. Shaw won't let you die here.

"Good boy," Vornis said in that soothing tone Lee didn't want to trust. He stroked his head.

Lee stared at the floor and at Vornis's shoes. God, he hated this room. He hated it because it always broke him, and he hated it so much that he started to look for his salvation anywhere, even in Vornis. *Please, sir, please.*

"We ought to bring Shaw here and let him play," Vornis said.

Lee shuddered. No, not that.

Hanson laughed again.

Lee had seen the security feeds from the bungalow. And it looked so real. Vornis had liked it a lot, and Lee realized it wasn't just about him. It was about Shaw as well. Vornis wanted Shaw, and Lee wondered if Shaw knew it. Maybe he did. He seemed clever. But if Vornis brought Shaw to this room, it wouldn't be a charade anymore.

They can't bring Shaw here. Shaw is my sanctuary. I don't want him to see what this room makes me.

Shaw knew because Lee had told him, but knowing wasn't the same as seeing. What if he looked at Lee differently afterward? Shaw had lied for him. Shaw had tried to preserve what little dignity Lee had left. Shaw saw the man he was before, or at least the memory of him. Lee couldn't have Shaw here, because Shaw was his hope.

You have to pick a side in this room, and he couldn't pick me.

Lee felt Hanson unfasten the cuffs. They fell free with a rattle, but he kept his hands behind his back until he was told different.

How many sand dollars today? Twelve today. Twelve was a good number. One of them had been almost green. That was from algae, maybe. He'd liked the color of it. He'd held it up to the sunlight, and it had appeared as translucent as stained glass. So many colors on the island.

Lee closed his eyes and tried to regulate his breathing.

He hated the way the anticipation alone made him tremble. And every time it happened, he told his body not to react. He told himself it was pointless. He told himself to be insensible, but it never really worked. Every time he thought he must have used up his last reserves of fear, he surprised himself. Fear, like pain, turned out to be a bottomless pit.

Lee heard Hanson's footsteps behind him.

Lee didn't have to open his eyes to see the room. Every detail of it was burned onto his retinas and had been since the first time they'd brought him here. The walls were hung with instruments of torture, and there wasn't a single one Vornis hadn't used on him. Pain was such a strange thing, made up of a thousand different variations of rhythm and pitch, and Vornis knew how to play an entire symphony on his body.

Don't think about it. Just breathe.

Somewhere on the other side of the world, it is spring. Somewhere, fresh blades of grass are breaking through the cold crust of the earth and the streams are running full as the last of the snow melts. Somewhere on the other side of the world, your room is waiting for you. Somewhere on the other side of the world, your parents buried an empty box.

No. Think of something else.

He was breathing so quickly his lungs ached, and he still couldn't get enough air.

Fishing for gar and green sunfish at Round Lake.

Counting the cracks in the sidewalk on the way home from school.

The Vikings pennant on his bedroom wall.

It wasn't enough. It wouldn't be enough.

He heard movement behind him, and Hanson pulled him to his feet. Then he was being pushed toward the frame in the corner.

"Oh please, please no." He struggled for breath. "Please!"

Later, when he thought back, he realized he'd

started screaming even before they tied him down.

* * * * *

A knock on the door.

"Honey?"

It took him a moment to realize where he was. Then he saw the sunlight slanting through the gap in his curtains and falling across his desk. He'd left his computer on from last night, and the screen saver was swirling across the screen. God, he'd had a nightmare or something, and his tears had soaked his pillow. The taste of it was still sour in his throat. His heart was beating fast.

"Honey? You'll be late for school."

He mumbled something into his pillow and closed his eyes again.

He could hear sparrows trilling outside, and the sound of Mr. Keller's old truck grinding through the gears as he headed off to work. Seven sharp, every morning. Mr. Keller was more reliable than an alarm clock.

His door squeaked open. "Lee, honey, get out of bed!"

He heard his mother's footsteps recede down the hall. She'd be going downstairs now, to start breakfast. Very soon the aroma of sausages and pancakes would fill the house.

Tears stung his eyes.

Now what the hell was that about? Just the hangover from some stupid nightmare. He had to get up and get ready for school. Was it the SAT practice today, or was it the game? It was something important. Why couldn't he remember? He struggled to think.

Don't.

His bed was warm. It would be nice to stay in it all

123

day, caught in this pleasant drowsiness, but he had to get up and get moving. He had that important thing.

Don't!

His breath caught in his throat.

No, he was okay here. This was the safest place in the world.

That was a weird thing to think.

He sighed and stretched, and couldn't move his arms. Why couldn't he move his arms? He had to get out of bed, get in the shower, get dressed, and go downstairs for breakfast. There were things he had to do today, places he had to be. But he couldn't move his arms.

Fear chilled him. "Mom? Mom, I can't get up. Please come back, Mom. I think I need help."

He shifted, but he was tangled in the sheets or something. He couldn't pull free.

"Mom?"

Realization caught him in a sickening rush.

Oh no, oh no. It's not real. It's not fucking real. This never happened. You were never stuck. You got out of bed, and you got ready for school, and you had your breakfast, and you did it over and over again for years. And you went to college, and you met Tim, and it didn't last, but it ended okay, and you graduated, and you moved to Denver and you joined the DEA, and your boss suggested you for an assignment with the Miami office, and you went in a chopper, and you landed in Colombia, and you hadn't even learned those guys' names properly before Vornis killed them. How the fuck could you ever forget any of that?

Lee moaned. *Mom?*

You're not there. Open your eyes and see.

No. No. Keep them closed.

A low laugh close to his ear brought him around.

Hanson.

Lee's eyes snapped open. He was bound over the frame, his arms and legs splayed. He could see blood on the floor. Couldn't feel it yet, though. His body was numb, or the pain had been so intense that his mind had cut itself off from it. Cut itself off and run straight back home.

"He's crying for his mommy." Hanson laughed. He caught Lee's hair and twisted his head around. He bent down and put his face close to Lee's. "Are you back, bitch?"

Lee nodded through his tears.

How many sand dollars?

Twelve.

Which was your favorite?

The green one. Never saw one that color before.

Find another one tomorrow.

"That's my brave little man," Vornis said. Lee could hear the amusement in his voice. "Tilt your head and have a drink."

Lee opened his mouth and Hanson tilted a plastic bottle of water toward him. Most of the water spilled out onto the floor, but Lee managed a few shallow gulps. "Thank you, sir."

He let his stinging eyes close again.

How much longer?

There was a tiny rock pool in the shallows at the bottom of the path that led up the hill. He'd seen it before. When Shaw went for a jog tomorrow, maybe Lee would be strong enough to go with him or at least trail along behind him. And maybe he could inspect that rock pool then. There might be hundreds of sand dollars in there.

Lee always walked with his eyes down, and the island revealed all its secrets to him. Sand dollars, tiny holes inhabited by translucent crabs, glittering shells built like spiral towers, and sand that turned from brilliant white to warm caramel when the ocean caressed it.

Lee wasn't allowed to swim, but he could wade. He'd seen starfish lying in the shallows. He'd never seen a real starfish before in his life, and now he'd seen hundreds. Some of them were small and sand-colored, and he was afraid of hurting them if he stood on them, but some were larger than his hand and deep orange. The water was so clear that Lee could see them laid out like strings of lanterns all the way from the shallows to where the waves broke on the reef. The large starfish were too far out for Lee to touch, but he wondered if they felt as velvety as they looked.

Which was stupid. They were probably poisonous. What the hell did a guy from Minnesota know about reef creatures? Almost everything from the reef was either poisonous or venomous, wasn't it? Shaw had scars on his thigh from some unpronounceable jellyfish. The reef was beautiful and dangerous.

Shaw had scars, but he still swam in the ocean. Lee didn't know if that was brave or stupid.

Shaw looks you in the eye.

His breathing slowly calmed.

How many sand dollars today?

Twelve.

"Tell me what you want, boy." Vornis laid his hand on Lee's trembling shoulder.

In the beginning, Lee remembered, he'd recoiled from Vornis's touch. Now he didn't bother.

He kept his eyes closed, not knowing how to respond. "Please, sir."

"Please what, boy?"

Lee felt a part of his mind retreat. "Anything, sir."

Vornis dug his fingers in, and suddenly that

sensation joined in with others; all the pain he'd held off until now ripped back through him. His body was on fire, and he was glad, so fucking glad, that he couldn't see the welts on his back. Some of them had bled, maybe all of them, but Lee couldn't differentiate between them. Everything hurt. That was the clever thing about the whip: even those parts of him untouched by its tails screamed in agony. Every muscle hurt from trying to hold himself together, from trying to distribute the pain into something manageable.

A cry tore out of his raw throat, and Vornis and Hanson laughed.

How many sand dollars?

Twelve.

He bucked against the restraints uselessly.

"Please, sir!"

"Please what, boy?"

Lee tensed as another wave of pain crested over him. "Please give me the needle, sir! It hurts so much!"

Vornis's breath was warm against his ear. "I'm not sure if you deserve the needle tonight."

Lee bit his lip and shook his head. Hot tears escaped him.

"Maybe you can show me how much you want it," Vornis said. "Maybe you can change my mind."

"Yes, sir," Lee agreed desperately. "Please!"

He hated the sound of Vornis's laugh almost as much as he hated himself.

He thought he might have blacked out when Hanson pulled him off the frame, because he couldn't remember it happening. One minute he was strapped there, and the next minute he was on his knees trying to keep his balance while the stench of his own blood threatened to overwhelm him. He burned. He fucking *burned.*

He looked up at Vornis through his tears, and the man smiled back down at him.

"Go on, then. Show me."

Lee wet his lips with his tongue and bent his protesting body toward Vornis.

Another night and he was on his knees again. It didn't matter. He only had to hold himself together until it was over. He only had to hold on to hope.

Shaw will look after you when this is done, and tomorrow you're gonna find another green sand dollar.

CHAPTER TEN

The e-mail from Callie confirmed what Lee had already told Shaw. Lee was DEA. And, rumor had it, it hadn't been a strike on Vornis's Colombian compound at all. It had been surveillance, and they'd fucked it up completely. The DEA would be very interested to know that one of their men had survived. Callie would make the call for Shaw as soon as he gave the word. Her only reply to the photograph of Lee, taken when he was naked and sleeping in Shaw's bed, had been short and sharp: *WTF?*

So now Shaw was committed. As soon as he'd finished his business here, he'd have Callie make the call, and some strike force or another would descend on the island, turn it into a bloodbath, and probably kill Lee during extraction. Or Vornis would save them the trouble.

The difficulty was that he actually liked Lee, more and more each day. Their little peepshows were becoming tiresome for both of them, and their sessions in the shower more awkward. It was getting harder and harder not to touch, and Lee wasn't making it any easier.

"I wouldn't mind," Lee whispered that morning.

"Wouldn't mind what?" Shaw asked him and was sorry he did.

"I wouldn't mind if you fucked me," Lee said, blushing. "For the camera, I mean, to make it look real."

And the worst part, Shaw realized, was that if he

really thought Lee was as good as dead he'd do it. That was the sort of man he'd become. But if Lee somehow survived this, and Shaw hoped he did, the last thing he wanted was to have his picture on a wall somewhere in the Pentagon with a target on it.

"I'm not going to fuck you," Shaw said. The sight of Lee's welts made his stomach turn. "I'm not a rapist."

"Wouldn't be," Lee whispered.

"You're a fucking prisoner," Shaw said. "What else could it be? Shut up about it."

And he liked Lee. He liked having him around, even if all he did was sit quietly with his head bowed. Shaw found his presence comforting and suspected it was mutual. He wished he could talk to Lee, to find out what was going on in his head — *"I wouldn't mind if you fucked me,"* he'd said, like it was something he *wanted* — but it was what it was.

And the worst thing had happened when Shaw had walked out of the bathroom after lunch. He'd left the television on, just for background noise, and there was some stupid American sitcom playing when he'd walked back up the stairs. That's when he'd seen it: Lee, sitting on the floor looking up at the screen, smiling at some dumb joke. He'd heard Shaw and bowed his head quickly, but it was already too late. Shaw had seen Lee as a human being, a guy who liked dumb jokes, and it was more horrible than he'd imagined. He'd wanted to throw up. His mouth had flooded with saliva, and he'd tasted bile, and it was all he could do not to stumble back down the bathroom steps to the sink.

Oh shit. The last thing Shaw had needed was to look the real Lee Anderson in the face — the human being instead of the thing — and, now that he had, Shaw couldn't forget it. The knowledge of it twisted in his guts. It hurt.

On his fifth day on the island, Shaw heard the sound of the choppers approaching in the early afternoon. At least two, he thought, from the noise. He was on the beach at the time, with Lee lying next to him, and the way the kid had lifted his hopeful face to the sky was heartbreaking. Shaw could have told him, just from the way that Vornis's security guards weren't worried, that it wasn't a rescue. Nobody knew he was here except Shaw and Callie, and they were holding those cards very close.

"More guests," Shaw said in a low voice.

Lee had tears in his eyes. He nodded and rested his chin on his arms again. Shaw watched as he cried silently. Hope was the kid's worst enemy. It would build him up only to throw him down again. And Shaw hadn't helped any.

Shaw watched as the choppers came in. Two of them, private charters from Suva. They landed on the far side of the island and left again. Less than an hour later, Vornis was showing his friends around.

Shaw stood as the men emerged from the shaded path onto the beach. Such a peaceful, beautiful setting for a meeting with monsters. He pushed Lee out of his mind. This was what he'd come for. This was everything he'd worked for.

"This is Shaw," Vornis told them. "A useful man with useful contacts. We have a close association."

Not as close as Vornis wanted, but Shaw smiled anyway and waited for him to introduce the others. He shook their hands, repeated their names, and ran through what he knew.

Pieter Guterman. The man Shaw had wanted so desperately to meet. He was in his fifties, tall, solid, and physically impressive. A silver fox. He wasn't unattractive with it.

"Mr. Guterman," Shaw said, shaking his hand

firmly. "Good to meet you."

"Shaw," Guterman said, testing the name. "How *succinct*."

Shaw laughed. "Adam Shaw, Mr. Guterman."

The next was Sudomo Atmadja. A small man, dark and sharp-eyed. The sponsor, Shaw knew, of several terrorist organizations currently operating out of Indonesia. More dangerous than all his hate-filled clerics combined, because Atmadja had longevity. He'd been in the business for almost thirty years. Martyrs came and went.

"Mr. Atmadja," Shaw said, shaking his hand.

Shaw hadn't been expecting the third man, but he wasn't entirely surprised to find him in this company. Franco Bertoni, mob boss. He was shorter than the others, and rotund. He was sweating in the heat and kept wiping his round face with a handkerchief. He wasn't a terrorist, but like Vornis and Shaw, he knew where the future lay.

"Mr. Bertoni," Shaw said, and Bertoni wiped his face and shook his hand.

The fourth man was introduced as Ali Ibn Usayd. Interesting. The last time Shaw had met the man, he had been using a different name. Neither of them showed any recognition as they shook hands. Usayd was tall and swarthy with narrow features.

"Mr. Usayd," he said.

"Mr. Shaw." Usayd's eyes fell to Lee, lying on his stomach on the sand. "And who is your friend?"

Vornis laughed. "Not his friend, Ali! This is my new pet. Shaw was just borrowing him."

Was. Shaw tried not to react to the vile implications of word. Of course Vornis would offer Lee to his new guests. They were all more important than Shaw. He looked down at Lee's scarred back and saw his shoulders stiffen. He was listening.

"He is wearing interesting pants," Usayd said.

It had been the first thing Shaw had noticed as well: the military fatigues. Usayd was clever.

Vornis swaggered over to Lee, standing above him. "American. He and his team attacked my Colombian compound two months ago. This one survived, and I am making sure he is sorry for it."

Lee flinched as Vornis drove his shoe into his ribs.

Shaw forced a smile as he caught Usayd's eye. He wondered which of the men would take Lee if Vornis offered. Guterman, probably. He was cut from the same cloth as Vornis. Atmadja, maybe. Shaw didn't know enough about Bertoni to hazard a guess. And Usayd? Shaw had seen him torture a man before, but he didn't get off on it. Usayd was all business.

Vornis kicked Lee again, and Lee yelped like a dog. This time they all laughed, except the pale, middle-aged man who was lingering at the back of the group. He looked completely out of his depth in this crowd and couldn't disguise his horror as his eyes flickered from Vornis to Lee. He blinked rapidly behind his glasses.

"And this is John Gatehouse," Vornis said, remembering the little man at last. "He is an expert on Cézanne."

And on nothing else, probably, Shaw thought as he held out his hand. For a moment, he thought Gatehouse would recoil, but self-preservation was a strong motivator. He'd already seen enough to know he didn't want to be on the receiving end of Vornis's temper. Had he seen enough to know he was a dead man? He gripped Shaw's hand at last, nervously, and mumbled something.

"Bring the kid to the house for dinner, Shaw," Vornis said. "We'll have some fun then."

"See you then." Shaw nodded. He watched the men walk away and sat back down in the sand. There was nothing to say. There never was. He stared out at the endless blue ocean and waited for it to work its magic, and nothing happened.

Great. Now Vornis had stolen that from him as well. And it was no more than he deserved. What the fuck was he doing here? Was it worth it? Shit, he'd worked so hard for this. So many years, and so many sleepless nights. It had to be worth it. He had to keep believing that.

There is nothing you won't do for this. This is worth any price.

Shaw fixed his eyes on the horizon and ran his hand down Lee's trembling back.

It's okay. It's okay. It's okay.

And Shaw smiled at his own hateful delusion.

Lee buried his face in the crook of his arm.

* * * * *

Sitting on the veranda, Shaw took a swig from a bottle of beer and wondered idly when it had become so fucking easy to compartmentalize. Because at that very moment, Lee was sitting inside on the floor of the bungalow with his arms wrapped around his knees, rocking back and forth. He was in shock, maybe. And Shaw had looked at him, helped himself to a beer from the fridge, and gone to sit on the veranda and watch the ocean.

Out of sight, out of mind.

Except, not exactly. He wasn't thinking of Lee, but he was thinking about his own curious reaction to Lee's obvious distress. Thinking about, because he didn't *feel* it. Reason told him that there was more at stake here, there always had been, but it shouldn't have felt so easy to ignore him, should it?

Shaw drew a hand through his hair. Fuck. Maybe he was just tired of the fucking drama. Shaw wasn't a knight in shining armor. He didn't need this shit. This wasn't his fault. He had more to worry about now.

Guterman was here. The man Shaw had wanted to meet for years. The rest were just icing on the cake. There wasn't a thing Shaw wouldn't do to get into Guterman's inner circle. His mind drifted back to Lee for a moment. No, not a thing.

Guterman was here. Better than fucking Christmas.

Shaw looked up as a man picked his way slowly along the beach. His trousers were rolled up to his calves, and he was glowering at the ocean as though it had personally offended him. Shaw almost laughed. It was Bertoni. He was out of his element here. He belonged in the concrete jungle.

Shaw slipped back inside for a moment, ignoring Lee as he headed for the fridge. Lee didn't even look up. He probably didn't know Shaw was there. Wherever he'd gone now, how far into the dark recesses of his memory, Shaw didn't need to know. He was quiet. That was enough.

Shaw grabbed another beer and headed back outside.

The sand burned his feet as he made his way down to the water. "Mr. Bertoni, good afternoon. Beer?"

Bertoni wiped his face with a handkerchief and then shoved it back into his pocket. "What sort of fucking place is this anyway? It's too hot," he grizzled, taking the beer.

It's a tropical island, you fucking tool. What did you expect?

Shaw nodded. "I know."

Bertoni took a long swig from his beer. The back of his shirt and his underarms were stained with sweat. "And what are you doin' here, Mr. Shaw? Apart from fucking Vornis's boy."

"I came here to sell a painting," Shaw told him evenly. "Fucking Vornis's boy is just a sweet bonus."

Bertoni curled his lip in disgust. Not at Shaw's admission of rape, of course, but at the admission he'd liked fucking a boy.

"What are you?" Bertoni growled. "Some kind of faggot?"

Shaw stood his ground. "There's only one kind, Mr. Bertoni, as far as I'm aware."

Bertoni's sneer was caught somewhere between disgust and respect, and it hovered there uncertainly for a while before he finally shrugged it away. "Yeah, Vornis said you had balls, Shaw."

Shaw smiled at that.

Bertoni glared out at the ocean. "So, you sell paintings?"

"No," Shaw told him. "I'm a facilitator. I put buyers and sellers in touch with one another, for a percentage. I can find whatever it is you need."

Bertoni narrowed his eyes. "I don't outsource."

Bullshit he didn't.

Shaw shrugged. "Your presence here suggests to me that you're in the process of expanding your operations. It's a new world, Mr. Bertoni, with new challenges. Your former business associates might not be up to the task."

"What do you mean?" Bertoni asked. "You mean like weapons? Because I can get fucking weapons!"

Trust a mob boss to get straight to the point.

"Weapons, absolutely," Shaw said. "Or maybe certain chemical compounds."

Bertoni narrowed his eyes.

"I don't just deal in art, Mr. Bertoni. I deal in *anything*. And my reputation speaks for itself."

"Yeah, well," Bertoni snorted, "I'm not looking to build a fucking biological weapon or nothin', you understand? That's more Usayd's style, the fucking rag head."

"Of course it is," Shaw agreed. "It was just an example. I can get you whatever you want."

Bertoni scowled at that. He turned his red face to Shaw's and sneered. "And how the fuck do you know what I want?"

Shaw allowed himself a smile. "I got you that beer, didn't I?"

For a moment, it could have gone either way, and then Bertoni laughed. It was a big, deep laugh that rose above the gentle roar of the ocean, boomed out across the beach, and startled a solitary seagull into flight.

Shaw's smile grew.

He could do this. He could actually pull this off.

* * * * *

And now, Shaw thought, the moment we've all been waiting for . . .

Breathe, Shaw. Just breathe.

Pieter Guterman was walking up toward the bungalow.

Guterman was a good-looking man. He wasn't young, but he wore his age well. He was still in good shape, and his graying hair made him look distinguished. He had a strong jaw, a wide mouth, and eyes that shone with cleverness. He exuded authority. He looked like the poster-boy CEO of a Fortune 500 company. *Trust me*, his handsome face said, but Shaw knew better. Guterman was as much a monster as Vornis. He just wore a more attractive mask.

Guterman looked just as comfortable in chinos and a casual shirt as he would in a suit and tie. He didn't have to dress to impress. He would have looked impressive in anything. Self-confidence rolled off him in waves.

"Shaw," he said when he walked up the steps. His eyes crinkled as he reached out his hand.

"Mr. Guterman," Shaw said. Guterman had a strong, firm handshake. Shaw wouldn't have expected anything less. "Come in, please."

Lee was still sitting on the floor, exactly where Shaw had left him. He'd stopped rocking, at least. The lack of movement made it easier for Shaw to ignore him.

"I do love Fiji," Guterman said as he sat down at the table. "So far removed from the real world, don't you find?"

No, Shaw thought. The Pacific had always felt like home to him.

"It's certainly remote," he said instead. "Drink?"

"Gin and tonic."

Shaw moved over to the bench, aware that Guterman's gaze was on him. And that was okay. That was exactly where it should be.

Nothing he wouldn't do.

Shaw had waited a long time for this, and he'd run through every scenario he could imagine, just to see how far he'd really go. Just so he wouldn't be surprised. And, in every one, he'd do whatever Guterman asked. Shaw knew enough about Guterman to know there probably wasn't much off the table. Shaw was good-looking, and Guterman was responding to that. Guterman was a good-looking man as well. Not Shaw's usual type—he preferred guys who weren't old enough to have been voting when Shaw was still in kindergarten—but that was a small concession to make. Shaw didn't have daddy issues or daddy fantasies either, but if Guterman wanted to play that game, Shaw would make an exception. Because Guterman was rich and powerful, and governments rose and fell because he made it happen. And Shaw wanted in. He wanted to be in Guterman's inner circle; he needed to be there. He burned for it. And there was nothing he wouldn't do to make it happen.

Not that his scenarios had included Lee. Shaw had come to terms with the fact that he'd let Guterman do whatever the hell he wanted to his body, but where was Lee's choice?

More to the point, Shaw wondered as he prepared Guterman's drink, why did it suddenly matter? He'd seen people tortured, raped, and killed before. He did business with some seriously scary assholes, and those were the things they did. Shaw had once seen Vornis's head of security back in the States shoot a man in the head because he was skimming profits. And Shaw hadn't even blinked.

Well, he'd blinked. But only because he'd been sitting next to the man at the time and not expecting the sudden hot spray of blood and brain matter on his face. And Vornis had laughed so much that Shaw had laughed as well and accepted a towel and a change of clothes like it was nothing more than a spilled drink.

Shaw had taken the execution in the spirit Vornis had intended, as both punishment for the thief and a demonstration to Shaw of his iron will. Shaw knew the accountant had deserved it. The fool had practically begged for it the first time he'd put his hand in the kitty. Shaw understood that. Of course, Vornis thought Lee deserved it as well. Maybe that was the difference. Vornis thought that Lee had wronged him. Shaw saw a kid who'd just been doing his job. And maybe in this world that deserved a bullet in the head but not rape and torture. Because, shit, nobody deserved that.

And if Vornis played hard, everything Shaw had ever heard said that Guterman played harder.

Lee hadn't featured in any of Shaw's scenarios, but it didn't make any difference. Because here Shaw was, and he was going to stand back and let it happen. Again.

When Shaw returned to the table, Guterman was watching Lee.

"Thank you," he said as Shaw passed him his drink. His gaze slid to Lee again. "He's nice."

Lee was sitting beside the bed. He had his arms wrapped around his knees and his face buried in his arms. His breathing was shallow, and he was trembling. He was teetering on the edge of panic. Shaw could almost taste his fear.

"Very nice," Shaw agreed, sitting down.

Guterman sipped his drink and set it on the table. "You know who I am."

Shaw raised his eyebrows slightly. "I know your reputation, Mr. Guterman."

Guterman smiled. "And you want to know more?"

Shaw allowed himself to return the smile. "Let me put all my cards on the table, Mr. Guterman. You're an influential man. You're a wealthy man. It would be a privilege to have the opportunity to work with you. Of course I'm interested."

He gave Guterman a moment to process that, along with all the implications. What wouldn't Shaw do? Shaw guessed that Guterman was the sort of man who would relish the challenge of finding out. And that was exactly how Shaw had intended it. He was young, he was good-looking, and he didn't mind a challenge himself. He would do this and worry about his conscience later. There would be plenty of time to soothe it once he was out of here.

Fingers crossed.

"How much do you want it?" Guterman asked.

Shaw's gaze lingered for a moment on Guterman's mouth. He smiled and shrugged. "Try me and see."

Shaw could play the tease for the right reward.

Guterman regarded him evenly. "What would you say if I told you I came here for a blowjob?"

Careful, Shaw cautioned himself; draw your boundaries.

He considered his answer for a moment.

"I'd say that I'm nobody's bitch, and you'd have to make it worth my while." He leaned back in his chair and flashed his cockiest grin at Guterman. "I'd also say it's a great way to get over jetlag."

Guterman needed to know he'd do it, but he also needed to know nothing was for free.

Guterman dropped a hand to his crotch and began to rub himself through the fabric of his trousers. "Did you put those marks on the kid?"

Shaw looked at the narrow welts on Lee's arms and back from where he'd gotten caught in the wait-a-while. "Some of them."

"Not a lot of artistry," Guterman commented, "but some enthusiasm."

Shaw couldn't tell if that was a compliment or not. "Maybe I need some more practice."

Guterman's eyes narrowed. "Have you ever been whipped?"

"No," Shaw said, and it was the truth.

Guterman's lips quirked. "What would that privilege cost me?"

Shaw raised his eyebrows and wondered if he would ever be willing to put himself under Guterman's control. Restrained. Shit, no. Because how could he trust Guterman to release him? It wasn't worth his life.

It was worth Lee's, apparently, but not his own. *Coward.*

Shaw took a sip of his drink before he answered. "Now, you see, that's a show of trust. And I don't even know you, Mr. Guterman, and my mother always told me not to go off with strangers."

He smiled, and the amusement wasn't entirely feigned. *Actually, your mother told you a stranger was just a friend you hadn't met yet.* But she didn't mix in Shaw's circles.

Guterman raised his eyebrows. "And when we're no longer strangers, Shaw?"

Shaw shrugged. "Then we'll discuss it."

Guterman laughed. "I look forward to it. And maybe I'll use the boy tonight to show you what you can expect."

Shaw ran his finger along the rim of his glass and resisted the urge to look at Lee.

Guterman lowered his voice. "One day you'll scream for me as well. And bleed."

Shaw's eyes widened. Was that meant to turn him on? Because the chill that ran down his spine had nothing to do with pleasure.

"Really?" he murmured. His stomach churned.

Guterman smiled again. Light danced in his slate-gray eyes. "Oh, I do enjoy a challenge."

Shaw forced a smile. At least he'd been right about

that.

CHAPTER ELEVEN

Guterman left without his blowjob in the end. Thank Christ, Shaw thought and was almost overwhelmed with relief. Because there was no use pretending any different—Guterman scared the hell out of him. *One day you'll scream for me as well. And bleed.* And there was no doubt in Shaw's mind that Guterman believed it. He almost believed it himself. He knew Guterman was hardcore, but the man's audacity was unbelievable. Like he could have Shaw strung up in a dungeon within minutes if he wanted. And, fuck, maybe he could.

Shaw felt sick at the thought of it. There was no way in hell Guterman knew the meaning of the word consent. No way in hell he'd respect boundaries or safe words. So there was no way in hell that Shaw could allow that to happen. He had to keep his head. He had to stay focused. He was balanced on a knife's edge with Guterman, and he couldn't afford a misstep.

Shaw had met with Guterman expecting that he had something to offer the man. A blowjob or a fuck, those had always been negotiable. But now he wasn't sure. Guterman had thrown him off balance. He'd been in over his head before he even realized. So it was too fucking bad he'd already as good as sold himself.

Shaw sat on the bed and stared out the window at

the Pacific. His hands were shaking. He wanted a cigarette, and he hadn't smoked in years.

On the floor, Lee shifted. He raised his head and looked up at Shaw. His face was drawn, but something like malice shone in his eyes. *The shoe is on the other foot now, asshole.*

No, Shaw thought as he studied Lee's face, he'd misread that. It wasn't malice at all. It was empathy. And that was even more sickening.

"Come on," he said, hating the sound of his own flat voice. "Let's get you cleaned up for tonight."

Lee rose awkwardly to his feet and headed down the steps to the bathroom.

Shaw undressed slowly and followed Lee into the shower.

Lee leaned against the wall, his hands hanging slackly at his sides. He looked up at Shaw, his brilliant green eyes wide with hope and fear. "Please, I don't want that man to hurt me."

That makes two of us, Shaw thought, but he couldn't say it. He kept his voice even, and it almost snagged in his throat. "Too bad."

That broke him. "Please, no, please! I've tried, I've *tried*, but I can't do it anymore!"

Lee had allowed his terror overtake him. He was disconsolate, shaking and crying, and in the end, Shaw pushed him face-first against the wall, crooked an arm around his throat, and held him like that. It wasn't the embrace Lee needed, and it wasn't the one Shaw wanted to give, but it was all Shaw could do. Lee responded to domination. Vornis had trained him so well.

"Settle down," Shaw said into Lee's ear, because there was nothing else to say.

"Oh, fuck," Lee managed, shaking in Shaw's grasp. "Oh, fuck. Help me, please. Please! No more, please!"

Shaw hated himself. "I've told you what I can do for you. In the meantime, you have to take it."

"Please," Lee whimpered. "Please, Adam!"

Shaw felt a jolt of surprise at hearing his name come from Lee's mouth. Guilt washed over him, followed by self-recrimination. He shouldn't have let it come to this. The kid had no right to expect any help at all, and he somehow thought Shaw could magically stop what was going to happen tonight? Even when he hadn't stopped it the last time or the time before that. He hadn't raised an objection or lifted a finger, so why the hell did Lee think it would be any different now?

What could he say? *Listen, mate, realistically you're a dead man. Vornis is going to kill you just like he killed your team, and just like he's going to kill Gatehouse. Maybe I'll get out of this alive and maybe I won't, but if I do, I'll make that call. And it will probably be too late to help you at all. Don't you get that?*

"We're not friends," Shaw reminded him in a harsh tone.

"Please," Lee whispered. "Jesus Christ, please! Whatever you're doing here, they'll pay more. My government will pay more if you get me out of here!"

Shaw shook his head. He rested his chin on Lee's shoulder. "No, mate. Maybe they would and maybe they wouldn't, but we'll never know. You're not worth it. And I'm sorry, but that's the truth."

Lee tried to struggle, but Shaw held him against the wall. "You're just as bad as them." He pushed backward. "You've got a hard-on for this!"

A hard-on for you, Shaw wanted to say, not this.

"I never said I was better than them," Shaw growled. "I'm just not a rapist."

"I thought you liked me," Lee whispered. "Fuck."

Shaw's guts twisted, and he smiled at that. Wasn't Lee supposed to be the one feeling the sting of betrayal? Except it wasn't betrayal, because Shaw hadn't broken any promises. It was what it was, and it didn't matter how he felt about Lee. He couldn't risk everything he'd worked for. He wouldn't. This was the culmination of six years of hard work. Shaw could taste it now. He only had to reach out and take it. There was nothing that would prevent him from doing it. Probably not even Guterman, Shaw realized with a sick sense of foreboding. Shaw had bled for less, hadn't he? And if he was prepared to sacrifice Lee, he had to be prepared to sacrifice himself.

We could find a boat. We could get out of here. Both of us. But that wasn't why Shaw had come to Vornis's island. He'd come for Guterman, and he had to do whatever it took. He knew that.

Jesus, six years. He couldn't throw that away. He couldn't, not when he was so close.

He turned off the shower, and Lee fell silent. So well trained, Shaw thought again. He allowed Shaw to lead him back up the steps to the bungalow.

"Get on your knees," Shaw said.

Not looking at him, Lee obeyed.

Shaw took the cuffs from the table and moved around behind Lee. He clipped one cuff around a raw wrist, and Lee began to moan and shake his head. "Please, please don't. I won't run, I promise. Please don't."

You'll run, Lee, just like you did on the hill. Even when there's nowhere to go, how can you not try?

Shaw felt sick. He twisted Lee's other arm back and cuffed his wrist. "Shut up."

Lee began to cry.

Shaw ignored him. He dressed and sat at the table with his laptop.

There was no news from Callie. Shaw e-mailed her

the details of Vornis's guests. The most important one was Guterman. Shaw had been trying to arrange a meeting with Guterman for years. The others were just the icing on the cake.

He tried not to look at Lee as he worked. He could hear him struggling to choke back his tears, and the sound was awful. *At what point,* he asked Callie, *am I a fucking monster?* He knew she'd know the answer.

There was another message from Stuart as well. *Call me when you want to get together, babe.*

Babe? That was new, and it almost raised a smile in Shaw. He removed his phone from his laptop bag and plugged it in to charge it. There were no new messages, and he hadn't expected any. Shaw did all of his correspondence on his laptop. But he had Stuart's number somewhere in the phone, and the temptation to send a text was there.

No, not yet. He needed to do his job first. He needed to keep his head straight and worry about everything else later.

Callie must have been online: *You're not a monster. Stay strong.*

Shaw looked across at Lee. His scarred back was bowed, and his shoulders were still shaking. Shaw didn't know if he could trust Callie's assessment at all. Maybe they were both monsters and just didn't know it. What would he tell himself when this was all over, if he actually made it out alive? *I left that kid to die. But I didn't rape him.* That was no consolation at all, not to himself and sure as hell not to Lee.

Shaw sent a reply: *Feel like one. They're gonna torture him tonight.*

He closed his eyes, feeling a headache begin to pound at his temples. Was he really leaving Lee to die? He didn't *know* that Vornis would kill him anytime soon. He didn't *know* that he wouldn't be rescued. But whatever happened, if Lee died, Shaw would always know he'd had an opportunity to save him, and he hadn't taken it. He didn't know if that was a decision he could reconcile himself with.

Shit, shit, shit.

Callie's reply was just what he'd expected, and exactly what he needed to hear: *It's not your job to give a fuck.*

I know, he sent back, feeling his resolve strengthen once more. *Thanks.*

And Callie answered: *Good luck.*

Shaw waited for his phone to charge and then slipped it into his pocket.

* * * * *

Dusk was softening into darkness when Shaw dressed Lee and led him by the cuffs up toward the main house. The air was heavy with perfume; frangipani blossoms littered the ground. Shaw could hear the endless roar of the ocean, but it didn't calm his nerves tonight. Nothing could.

Lee was silent, trembling, and his breath caught in his throat as he shuffled along in front of Shaw. His whole body was tensed, flooded with fear and adrenaline. Fight or flight, and he couldn't do either.

The breeze sighed. The palm fronds shivered. From somewhere close by, Shaw heard a bird calling; a low, mournful note in the night. The air smelled too sweet tonight, too warm, too sickly, and too much like decay. Shaw hated it.

The main house was illuminated from inside, a shining beacon in the soft darkness. Shaw had never seen anything so terrible. He felt like he was leading a lamb to the slaughter and probably was.

He hated himself for this, really hated himself. But all the self-loathing in the world didn't stop him from leading Lee up that path. And that, Shaw supposed, was what made him so fucking good at his work. It also made him a monster, but such a clever monster.

"Please," Lee murmured as they headed up the path. "Oh, please. *Oh.*"

Such a tiny exhalation of breath but it spoke to Shaw of regret and fear and the elegy of all Lee's dreams. Dreams, Shaw thought, that had been formed on a different side of the world, under a different field of stars. Wherever Lee came from, the boy he'd been could never have imagined it would come to this.

And neither did the boy Shaw had been. Shaw caught a glimpse of himself in his mind's eye: a gangly teenager with braces, still growing into his own limbs. Sitting on the bag racks at Ayr State High School, the metal burning the backs of his thighs, and trading friendly punches with his best mate Paul.

Shaw drew a deep breath. *Holy fuck.* He didn't know that kid anymore. And that kid would be scared shitless of him now, for all his adolescent bluster and bullshit. Shaw had owned the world when he was fifteen. Stupid, ignorant kid.

Shaw looked up at the house and remembered the first time he'd seen it from the chopper as he came in to land. He'd gone straight back to high school then as well, straight back to Year Nine English. *My name is Ozymandias, king of kings: Look on my works, ye Mighty, and despair!*

The irony, Shaw thought, and that was the point. But it didn't matter that the great statue of Ozymandias was ruins in the future. Not to those whose lives had been sacrificed to the king of kings, because nobody remembered them at all.

Shaw tightened his grip on Lee's cuffs and pressed the buzzer on the front door.

Irina admitted him with a smile that didn't quite reach her eyes. "Mr. Vornis is in his study."

"Thank you." Shaw kept his hand on Lee's cuffs and walked him up the stairs.

"Art?" He heard a familiar voice sneer as he approached the door. "Art is for fucking faggots!"

"Mr. Bertoni," Shaw said as he stepped inside. "Nice to see you again."

Bertoni was standing with Vornis at his desk, looking down at *Jeune garçon au gilet rouge* as John Gatehouse inspected it carefully. Gatehouse looked up when Shaw spoke, saw Lee, and almost dropped his magnifying glass.

Usayd was standing at the cabinet, decanter in hand. "Drink, Mr. Shaw?"

"Thank you," Shaw said. He pressed a hand on Lee's shoulder, and Lee sank, shivering, onto his knees.

"It is beautiful here," Usayd said.

"Yes," said Shaw.

Usayd looked at Lee and back to Shaw, his dark eyes curious.

Vornis was nervous, Shaw realized. He was watching everything Gatehouse did as though he was half afraid the man would suddenly seize the canvas, hold it up, and scream forgery. Shaw tried not to let his surprise show. Vornis really did love his art after all.

Shaw sat in one of the leather armchairs, nursing his drink, and waited for Gatehouse to pass judgment. He kept his eyes off Lee.

Out of sight, out of mind.

Gatehouse straightened up at last, clearing his throat nervously.

Shaw wondered what sort of man Gatehouse was. He clearly hadn't dealt much with people like Vornis before, but that didn't make him morally pure. He must have known it was a stolen painting he'd been asked to evaluate. He was here for the money, the same as everyone else. No better and no worse than the monsters around him.

"It's astonishing, Mr. Vornis," he managed at last. "Astonishing. I have no doubt it is genuine. It is the *Jeune garçon au gilet rouge.*"

Shaw had known the painting would pass scrutiny. It already had, no less than seven times in the last year and by better experts than Gatehouse. Ninety-five million for a bit of paint on a bit of canvas. It was ridiculous, even if it had been the real thing. And it wasn't. Shaw had met the man who'd painted it.

It was so much more honest than the real thing, Shaw felt. Any man who bought a painting knowing it was stolen deserved a forgery. And at least this *Jeune garçon au gilet rouge* wasn't tainted with the smell of Nazi death camps.

Shaw sipped his drink. He'd expected this moment of secret triumph to be more gratifying. Getting one over on Vornis? Gold. But it wasn't how he'd imagined, and Shaw knew it had everything to do with the boy kneeling by the door. Shaw wanted to look at him, and couldn't. He wanted to comfort him, which was worse.

"So you have connections with the art world, Mr. Shaw?" Usayd asked him, giving Shaw the opening he'd been waiting for.

"I have more connections than that," Shaw said. He felt Bertoni looking at him, appraising him as carefully as

Gatehouse had appraised the painting. He allowed himself a glow of satisfaction at that. This was why he was here.

Usayd raised his eyebrows. "Weapons?"

"Depends what you're after," Shaw said. "I know a lot of people."

Usayd smiled. "I think we have a lot to talk about, Mr. Shaw."

"I look forward to it," Shaw said.

Vornis clapped him on the shoulder. "Shaw, I didn't doubt you for a second."

You should have, Shaw thought but laughed instead. "A sensible precaution, Vornis. Anyone would have done the same."

Vornis didn't move his hand. "Of course."

Shaw forced himself to relax under the heavy touch.

Vornis released him at last. "Well, gentlemen, shall we eat?"

Vornis shepherded the others out of the office, holding up a hand to stop Shaw as he went to move past. He looked down at Lee and back to Shaw. "You hardly touched him, my friend. I don't see any new marks on him."

Shaw raised his eyebrows. "I was always taught, Vornis, that it's the height of bad manners to return something in worse condition than when it was borrowed."

Vornis's mouth twisted into a smile. "But the bag?"

Shaw thought back to the contents of the bag, untouched except for the condoms and lube he'd used as props for Vornis's sick little peepshow. "Very thoughtful of you. And if I'd known your other guests were arriving so soon, I might have played a bit harder. Got my money's worth, as it were."

Vornis's smile grew. "Well, we will make up for it tonight, yes?"

Shaw pretended not to hear the strangled whimper from the floor. He returned the smile. "That sounds promising."

He always knew the right thing to say to monsters. He spoke their language too well to pretend it was a coincidence. He was no better than any of them.

They walked out of the room.

* * * * *

The dining room was open to the landscaped gardens behind the main house. From the top of the slight hill, Shaw could see over to the far bay where Vornis anchored his yacht. The lights of the yacht glittered on the dark ocean, and put Shaw in mind of that old fantasy: a boat, Lee, and escape. It was far too late for any of that now, he thought half-regretfully. Only half. Shaw was enough of a hypocrite to realize he was almost glad the choice was now out of his hands. He'd finish what he'd come for, he'd get off the island, and he'd make that call for Lee. That was all he could offer. It was more than Lee had any right to expect.

I'm so sorry, Lee.

Shaw ate his dinner, made polite conversation that didn't stray too much into business, and wondered which of the other men were players. Which of them would join Vornis in his games with Lee tonight?

Not Bertoni. He hated faggots, although it wasn't unthinkable that he was one of those men who could fuck another man and believe he was straight. Rape wasn't about sexual preference, and men like Bertoni knew it. But

Shaw had the feeling Bertoni wouldn't use Lee in that way. He would probably still torture him, though, given the choice.

Atmadja, Shaw still didn't know. He didn't look like the sort of man who liked bloodshed. He could order it, sponsor it, and support it, but only from a clinical distance. If Shaw was right, that made him the biggest hypocrite at the table.

Guterman, no doubt. Shaw knew his reputation. Money, violence, power, sex. Guterman liked to get his manicured hands dirty.

Usayd, no way. He wouldn't get too involved, but he wouldn't protest either. He was too clever for that.

That left Gatehouse. Gatehouse would probably be dead before Lee. He was wearing a look like a deer caught in the headlights. He stank of fear, and that would amuse them when they killed him.

"Eight weeks," Vornis said in response to something Usayd asked. "He fought like an animal before we drugged him. Now he opens his mouth for cock without being asked."

"That's a shame," said Guterman.

Vornis raised an eyebrow.

Guterman snapped his lobster claw. "I do like it when the pretty things fight."

Bertoni laughed, but Atmadja didn't. Shaw was right about him.

"He still makes all the right noises," Vornis said, "given encouragement."

Rape and torture. Charming fucking subjects for the dinner table. Shaw leaned forward and poured himself a glass of water.

It was Usayd who brought the discussion back to business, and Shaw was grateful for it. It gave him the chance to make an impression on these men. And Vornis was only too happy to back up everything he said. Shaw had procured for him what he thought was a genuine Cézanne, and Vornis was glad to return the favor. He talked Shaw up like he was the Second Coming.

"I'm impressed, Mr. Shaw," Usayd said, and Shaw knew it was the only genuine thing he'd said since he'd arrived on the island.

Meanwhile, Gatehouse was trembling so much that he was playing a samba on his dinner plate with his cutlery.

Shaw looked at him sideways, and Gatehouse almost shit himself.

Dinner was good. They ate and talked and listened to the dry rustle of the breeze stroking the palm fronds. As the talk drifted away from business, Shaw found that the company was almost pleasant. He embraced the delusion. Anything to stop thinking about Lee.

"Trust," Vornis announced over dessert, "is not an easy commodity to deal in."

His guests murmured their agreement.

"So, a proposition," Vornis said. His dark eyes gleamed. "Tonight I am going to kill my prisoner. As a gesture of my trust, you will bear witness."

Shaw felt his heart skip a beat. He caught Usayd's eye across the table for a brief moment. Everyone had fallen silent. Even Gatehouse was too shocked to tremble.

Oh shit. Oh, Lee. Shaw reined in his wild thoughts with difficulty and silently castigated himself. He'd always known this was a possibility. He should have been more prepared, because killing Lee tonight was the logical thing to do. Shaw was enough of a realist to recognize that and to admit to himself that, in Vornis's position, he would have done exactly the same thing.

It was an audacious move, Shaw thought, but a smart one. Any one of these men could one day use Lee's life as a bargaining tool with the U.S. authorities, if it came to that. Shit, it was exactly what Shaw had been intending. Lee had to die sooner rather than later. He had to be made worthless, and the only way that could happen was if he was dead. Vornis called it a gesture of trust, but it wasn't just that. It was a demonstration of his ruthlessness. Such a demonstration would go further in present company than any empty gesture. With one single act, Vornis could impress upon all of them his brutality, rid himself of a thing they might one day use against him, and make them all accomplices as well. It was perfect.

And it was too late now to make that call like Shaw had promised Lee. Jesus, was that actually relief that washed over him? He had become a monster after all.

Shaw sipped his water and wondered when that had happened. It must have been a gradual process, he supposed. He'd always been so worried about it, and it turned out he'd never seen it coming.

Usayd spoke first. He raised his eyebrows. "Well, dinner and a show. How nice."

Shaw laughed.

CHAPTER TWELVE

Hanson had brought him into the room and forced him down onto the floor by applying pressure to the back of his neck. He'd squeezed as well, even though Lee had been compliant, and grinned when Lee winced.

"Good puppy. Stay."

It felt like hours had passed, but time always lost its meaning in this room. A minute could be drawn out to last a lifetime in this place. An hour could vanish in the blink of an eye as consciousness fled. There was no time here. There was only sensation.

Lee's body ached from kneeling, from his neck all the way down his spine. The muscles in his thighs had already cramped once, and he'd swayed from side to side to try and alleviate the pain and soothe the muscles. The cuffs dug into his wrists and scraped against the wounds from last time.

And none of it mattered.

My soul is unbreakable.

Whatever happened here, they wouldn't get that. Not Vornis, not Hanson, and none of the other men. If this was the end, and Lee knew that the stakes had never been higher, he was free to delve into his memories now. Free to take what he needed from them, and screw it if it hurt.

He studied the small grate in the floor and wondered where it led.

Regrets, Lee, count 'em up.

In eighth grade, he'd cheated on a math test. Which wouldn't have been a regret at all, except he'd gotten caught. Two weeks of detention, and it had gone on his permanent record. They always said that, didn't they? *This will go on your permanent record.* Somehow Lee had expected it to come back and bite him on the ass when he was applying for colleges: *Oh, now, we can't possibly have a cheater here,* but maybe that permanent record thing was just bullshit, because nothing had ever come of it.

In eighth grade, you cheated. They can't take that from you.

Troy Faulkner was a regret, a real one. A tenth grade regret. They'd been friends. They'd hung out in each other's houses all one summer. It started because Troy's folks had a pool and it had been a hot summer, but it turned out they had a lot in common. Troy was one of the weird kids. He liked music nobody else had ever heard of, he read books in the school cafeteria at lunch, and he made short films and dressed in thrift-shop clothes by choice. He was weird but cool, and nobody gave him too much shit.

He was also gay, but Lee had never done anything about it. All summer long, they'd bullshitted about all the girls they thought were hot and which of them they'd like to fuck, and they both knew they were lying. It was plain as anything in their eyes, but they both kept up the pretense. They were fifteen-year-old boys in a small town, each one of them terrified to make the first move in case the other one called him out as a faggot. Then Troy's dad got another job out of state. On Troy's last night in Andover, Lee had slept over at his place in a sleeping bag on a floor covered in packing boxes.

It had been before dawn.

"*Lee?*"

"*What?*" He'd struggled up from sleep.

And Troy had pressed his lips against Lee's, quickly, urgently, and Lee had felt his heart race and his breath quicken. And that was it; a single kiss, almost chaste, and the next morning Troy had left, and that whole long, hot summer had suddenly felt like a waste. They'd been best friends all summer. They could have been something more if only they hadn't both been so scared.

In tenth grade, Troy Faulkner kissed you. That's yours forever.

Lee shifted on his knees.

When he was seventeen, he had used a fake ID to go to his first gay bar. And when he'd drunk too much and was on his way home with a guy, he'd let it slip that he was underage. And the guy had called him jailbait, punched him, and told him to fuck off. Even now he didn't know if he'd accidentally let it slip or if he'd just been too scared to go through with it. He'd hated that guy, even though in his place Lee knew he'd do exactly the same thing. It was still a regret, though. He ruined that guy's night and his own.

You were a dumb kid. All yours.

He'd once thrown up on the Gravitron at the county fair. He shouldn't have been drinking beer before going on it, but if he hadn't been drinking beer, he wouldn't have gone on for a fourth turn when Shaun had dared him. It was the most disgusting thing ever. Because the vomit had gone out and then come straight back and hit him and the people on either side of him. And everyone screamed, and it stank, and it hit them again every time they came back around, like being caught in a blender.

You once vomited on a whole bunch of people at the

county fair. They'll never forget you.

He smiled at the floor, and tears stung his eyes.

He took Chastity to the prom. The name didn't suit her. He'd thought it would be okay since she was still hung up on Shaun, but it was prom night, and she expected to get laid. His first and last time with a girl. It had been weird, and he'd only been able to get an erection by thinking about the time he'd walked in on her and Shaun at a party, and she'd been doing the reverse cowgirl. And it wasn't her he thought about. It was Shaun, the muscles cording in his arms as he held her hips, the sweat on his chest, and his hairy legs sticking out from underneath Chastity. It was still a disaster. Chastity had told him in no uncertain terms how unfavorably he stacked up against Shaun, which he supposed was justified. He'd been terrible.

He should have gone to prom with Dean. Dean had asked, but in a joking sort of way: *"So, dude, if you don't have a date, do you want to go together? Just for a joke, you know."*

He'd seen the same lie in Dean's eyes as he'd seen in Troy's during that long summer years before, and it had freaked him out.

Prom had sucked. His, Chastity's, and Dean's.

Chastity hated you because of prom. They can't have that.

In college, she'd once banged on his door in the middle of the night. *"I know you're in there, Anderson! Open the fucking door!"* Then, seeing him and Tim scramble for their clothes, she'd arched a perfectly sculpted brow and tossed her blonde hair back over her shoulders. *"Hello,"* she'd said to Tim, *"I'm the slutty cheerleader he fucked on prom night. You can blame me for any feelings of inadequacy he displays."*

It made him smile, even now. Even here.

Chastity was your best friend in college. They can't take her away from you.

When he was nine, he came off his bike and broke his arm. And because his mom had told him he was grounded and he'd gone out anyway, he'd tried to keep it a secret. He'd wrapped his arm in ice for a whole day, hiding the swelling under long sleeves and hoping it would magically disappear by the morning. In the middle of the night, suddenly panicking that his arm would swell up so bad it would turn black and fall off—that was what Shaun said would happen—he'd woken his parents and confessed to everything. And after they got back from the hospital, his mom had written *You're still grounded* on his cast.

He smiled at the floor and shifted his aching shoulders as much as he could.

You broke your arm and didn't tell anyone for ten hours. You were stupid and stubborn, and they can't take that.

He had those memories and a million others.

The cuffs were digging into his wrists, scraping against the broken skin.

He didn't look up. Not in here, not unless he was told. It wasn't just obedience, but because the anticipation was difficult enough to manage with his gaze on the floor. There was a reason they made him wait in this room. The walls were hung with the instruments of his torture, and Lee couldn't look at them. He knew from experience that if he let himself dwell on them, to speculate what order they might be used in tonight or what inventive variations Vornis had thought of for their use, he'd be a mess before it even began. And tonight he needed to hold himself together for as long as he could.

Something bad was going to happen tonight. Something *worse*. And this room would break him—it always did — but at least he could hold himself together until then.

Whatever happens in here, you know Shaw can't help you.

Whatever game Shaw was playing, whatever he'd promised, and whatever Lee had believed, he knew Shaw wouldn't help. Couldn't help. He'd have to take a side when he came into this room, and that was okay. He'd given Lee more than he'd had any right to hope for, hadn't he?

I know. I know he can't help.

Lee closed his eyes briefly. Seven sand dollars today. Not a great haul, but they'd been good ones. Round and white and fragile. Lee always fought the compulsion to crush them when he was holding them in his hand, to turn them to sand and let the wind take them.

Whatever happens here, your soul's unbreakable.

He kept his eyes closed.

It's a shame the rest of me is made of fucking glass.

* * * * *

"*Ukochany*," Irina whispered.

Lee lifted his head, and pain ripped down his spine.

Irina knelt down in front of him and held out a cup of water. She held it carefully while he drank and wiped his mouth with a handkerchief.

When had water become such a luxury?

"Thank you," he murmured and saw that her pale eyes were filled with tears. He forced a smile and didn't know whose benefit it was really for. "I'm okay. I'll be okay."

My soul is unbreakable.

She raised a hand to his cheek and touched it
gently.

Lee closed his eyes and leaned into the touch. She
had always been so kind to him. He heard the rustle of her
clothing, and then the touch was withdrawn, and she was
gone. The door opened — he heard laughter from
somewhere in the house — and then closed again.

"One foot in front of the other," he told himself,
and the sound of his voice washed to the walls and back
again to where he knelt.

In the chopper, John had shown him a photograph
of his wife and kids. So it could have been worse. What
would Lee leave behind when the time came? His parents
and a few friends and an empty desk in the Denver office.
No little kids wondering when Daddy was coming home,
so it could have been worse.

He hadn't known any of those guys, not really. Not
beyond their names. He'd been the new guy, the
interloper, but they'd made him welcome. He hadn't
known them enough to mourn them. So it could have been
worse.

Tonight it would be worse. Tonight this room
would break him again, every part of him. It always did. It
wasn't a surprise anymore. It was almost a relief when
they ratcheted up his fear and pain as far as it could go,
and it crashed over him and broke him. Because at least
then he could let go, until next time. He could scream and
not care, and cry and not care. He could call them *sir* and
do what they told him and not care. He wanted to be in a
place where he didn't care. He always told himself that the
waiting was the worst, and some crazy part of him always
believed it until the torture began.

Tonight would be the worst yet because those other
men would be here, and Vornis would want to put on a

good show for them, and Shaw would be here as well. And Shaw would see him break, and Shaw would have a hand in breaking him because you had to pick a side in this room.

Lee shifted on his knees and wondered why Vornis had chosen him. He'd been the youngest guy on the chopper, and maybe he was just unlucky enough to be Vornis's type. He would have thought a man like that would have got more satisfaction out of breaking Ramon, though. Ramon was big, and Ramon had been in charge. Shit, not that he'd wish this on anyone else. He just wondered, that was all.

He thought of the boy in the red vest with his tired eyes and his unsmiling face. Vornis had called the painting a thing of beauty. Lee had thought the boy looked sad. Those tired eyes looked like they had seen too much. They wanted to close.

Two tired boys, but Vornis would only destroy the one with a heartbeat. One was a work of art, and the other was nothing.

Lee fixed his gaze on the grate in the floor.

Ramon was one of the guys who had dug his own grave in Colombia. One of the guys who'd looked at Lee and pitied him. Ramon had been rotting in the shallow ground for eight weeks now, and Lee envied him that. Wherever he was now, whatever he believed—Ramon had worn a silver crucifix, he remembered now, that had glinted in the sun when he'd been digging—at least the worst was over for him. It was never over for Lee.

In the beginning, he'd wanted to die. That had changed. Now he wanted to survive as long as he could, and that was down to Shaw. Shaw and the tiny thread of hope he'd spun.

Shaw won't let you die here. He'll get off the island, and he'll make the call.

LISA HENRY

Lee sighed and closed his eyes again.

Maybe. But he'll be here tonight. And he'll hurt me.

Lee wondered if it would be all right as long as
Shaw looked after him when it was over. Would Shaw's
hands feel different on his flesh if he was the one who had
made it burn with pain? Because it wasn't really a betrayal.
The fragile trust he'd nursed since Shaw came to the island
was his own creation. Shaw hadn't forced him to believe.
That had been his own choice, and he'd always known
how it would end.

Shaw won't hurt you.

He thought of the way that Shaw's face changed
when he looked out at the brilliant blue Pacific. Shaw
wasn't like the others. Shaw saw something beyond the
horizon. Shaw looked him in the eye and saw a human
being looking back.

Shaw won't hurt you.

Except he will. He has to.

It was still there, though, that stupid, insistent voice
in the back of his head that clung to hope: *Shaw won't hurt
you.*

Lee bowed his head and wished it were true.

When it was over, maybe they would go and sit on
the beach and listen to the ocean, and Shaw would clean
him up and rub antiseptic lotion into his wounds and say,
"It is what it is, Lee. Don't cry." And in that strange stillness
after the pain, when his body was numb with shock and
flooded with endorphins, when he could feel his skin
glowing with pain that didn't quite reach his mind, maybe
he'd believe it. *It is what it is.* Maybe he'd even take some
comfort in it, because Shaw's voice was so calm. *It is what
it is.*

One foot in front of the other.

One sand dollar and then another.

Time would pass. It always did.

And one day it would end, one way or another.

He had hope, and they could take that in a heartbeat. But he could build more. Wasn't that his strength? In some corner of his mind, wasn't he still resisting? And wouldn't he always? There was a part of him they couldn't touch in a million years. It had always been there, but Shaw had unknowingly given him the means to find it. That shining thread of hope; Lee had followed it like Theseus in the labyrinth and discovered that it led to freedom. They didn't own him. They didn't even fucking know him. He'd had a whole life beyond this island. He was a human being.

In eighth grade, you cheated. They can't take that from you.

In tenth grade, Troy Faulkner kissed you. That's yours forever.

You were a dumb kid. All yours.

You once vomited on a whole bunch of people at the county fair. They'll never forget you.

Chastity hated you because of prom. They can't have that.

Chastity was your best friend in college. They can't take her away from you.

You broke your arm and didn't tell anyone for nine hours. You were stupid and stubborn, and they can't take that.

Even on the island, he had kept his secrets from them.

Today you found seven sand dollars, and they were all beautiful and fragile, and you didn't crush them.

Shaw won't hurt you.

He swayed on his aching knees and tried to believe it.

Whatever happens tonight, your soul's unbreakable.

LISA HENRY

CHAPTER THIRTEEN

Shaw had always had the ability to mask his emotions. It was essential in his line of work, given the people he dealt with and the situations he found himself in. It also made him a hell of a poker player. But when Vornis led his guests into the room after dinner, even a consummate professional like Shaw couldn't stop his eyebrows from shooting up in surprise.

Holy shit.

It wasn't a dungeon, exactly, but its purpose was clear. There were shackles hanging from the ceiling, racks of equipment and accessories on the wall, and a padded bench in the middle of the floor. The room was in the center of the main house. There were no glass walls here that looked out to the endless ocean; the room was solid, secure, and soundproofed.

Guterman looked around the walls approvingly, and then his gaze fell on Shaw. Appraising him? Shaw curled his mouth into a smile.

Lee was kneeling on the floor, his hands still shackled behind his back the way Shaw had left them. Shaw knew that made him an accessory to whatever happened here. *Well, I didn't rape him, and I didn't kill him, but I did cuff his hands behind his back and deliver him to*

Vornis and Guterman. Christ, where was Callie with her no-bullshit advice when he needed her?

Lee looked up as the men crowded into the room, his face already streaked with tears, and then lowered his head again. Shaw could see his chest heaving with quick breaths.

"I don't," Gatehouse stammered, "I really don't think I . . ."

Vornis looked at him, and Gatehouse snapped his mouth shut.

"Shaw, get his pants off him," Vornis said.

Shaw moved forward. Another little show for Vornis, he supposed. His favorite boy stripping his favorite toy. Vornis had always liked Shaw, always wanted him, and every performance Shaw had staged back in the bungalow must have added more fuel to that nasty little fire. Vornis had probably jerked off when he'd watched the security feed.

Shaw stood behind Lee and pulled him up by the cuffs. Lee staggered back against him and Shaw put a hand on his back to steady him. He reached round in front of Lee's hips and found his fly. He popped the button and pulled the zip open. Lee whimpered, and Shaw wrenched the pants down.

Any minute now. Any minute now the other shoe will drop.

"And the cuffs," Vornis said.

Shaw felt in his pocket for the key. Lee's hands shook as Shaw released them and dropped the cuffs on the floor.

Vornis laughed, and Lee glanced up at him fearfully.

"I'm gonna fuck you until you scream," Vornis said, his voice low and amused. "And then anyone else who wants is going to fuck you."

Lee's jaw trembled.

Shaw drew a deep breath. *He's going to give me up. He's going to scream at me to save him. He's going to get us both killed. And why shouldn't he? He's got nothing to lose.*

Vornis leaned in toward Lee, his dark eyes gleaming. He reached out and traced a blunt finger down Lee's chest. "And then we're going to kill you."

The strangled gasp didn't come from Lee. Shaw turned his head sharply. Gatehouse. Gatehouse had lost his nerve at last and was scrambling for the door. Bertoni pulled the little man back by his shirt and laughed when he squealed.

There was a knife hanging on the wall. Shaw didn't see Vornis reach for it. He didn't even see Vornis move, but suddenly Gatehouse was squashed between Bertoni and Vornis, and when they stepped away, he was on the floor. He jerked and gaped like a landed fish.

Shaw watched as the blood slowly trickled toward the drain in the center of the room. The floor was sloped, like an abattoir's. How clever.

Shaw heard Lee's slow intake of breath. He could feel Lee shaking against him. He could feel the warmth of his flesh, the fluttering of his heart. He lowered his head and brushed his lips against Lee's shoulder. He tasted of sweat and fear, but he didn't pull away from Shaw. Jesus Christ! He still trusted him, after everything. He would trust him, Shaw realized, even as he died. His head swam. What the hell had he done to earn that amount of trust? Stupid fucking kid.

Usayd was watching them.

Guterman was watching them as well. Untroubled by the man dying on the floor, he rubbed his crotch through his trousers and stepped toward them. Even when he was standing in front of them, even when he reached down to grip Lee's cock in his meaty hand, Lee didn't flinch. He leaned his head back against Shaw's shoulder and squeezed his eyes shut.

Guterman's eyes were dark with desire. He grinned at Shaw. "Bend him over the bench for me, Shaw."

Shaw couldn't breathe. The blood pounded in his skull. He heard Bertoni and Vornis laughing as they stood over Gatehouse's body. And that was *his* responsibility, Shaw thought. He'd brought art to Vornis, so Vornis had brought an art expert. Gatehouse was his responsibility. And so was Lee.

"Hurry up," Guterman said, unzipping his fly. "Bend the little bitch over."

Shaw began to move toward the bench. He raked his gaze over the wall. Vornis was nothing if not prepared. There was another cattle prod there, and it was almost in his reach.

"You're okay," he murmured to Lee, pushing him down onto the bench. It made him sick how Lee immediately knew where to put his arms, how far to spread his knees.

Jesus, Shaw, what are you going to do? Are you really gonna let this happen? Really?

Shaw heard the blood roaring in his skull, as loud as the ocean.

The ocean.

Guterman ignored Shaw now. He fumbled in his pants for his cock. A look of bliss crossed his face when he found it, and then he was spitting into his hand and pressing his fingers into Lee's anus. Lee whimpered and pressed his forehead against the leather padding.

Shaw looked at Usayd and reached for the cattle prod.

"Guterman," he said. "Who's the little bitch now?"

Guterman screamed and fell back when Shaw

pressed the prod into his neck, and then all hell broke loose.

It was fucking chaos, but Shaw liked chaos. He *knew* chaos. Guterman, slipping around on his back in Gatehouse's blood, screamed and cursed, and Shaw took the opportunity to hit him again. As close to the balls as he could manage this time.

Guterman didn't scare him now. None of them did. Shaw was in his element.

Bertoni stood there like a sack of shit, gaping. Then he went for Shaw with the knife. Shaw dodged him, and then his back was against the wall.

Vornis, his face distorted with rage and disbelief, went straight for the alarm. His mistake. He'd thought it was four against one, but that was before Usayd caught him around the neck and forced him to the floor. Usayd knelt over him, one arm tensed around his throat, choking him out.

Shaw felt the knife slide against his ribs and glance off. He got an elbow in Bertoni's fat face and felt the man's nose crack. It felt good. Bertoni reeled away, clutching his face. Shaw hit him with the cattle prod, and he went down. Shaw hit Guterman again. Just so the prick really felt it.

He heard the dull thud as Vornis hit the floor.

Usayd looked up, his eyes black.

Atmadja edged carefully around the wall, his delicate hands fluttering anxiously.

Shaw reached down and retrieved the knife. "Get up, Lee."

Lee was pale and shaking. He hitched his pants up and fastened them with trembling fingers.

Usayd didn't take his eyes off Atmadja. Shaw advanced on him. The man pressed back against the wall.

He tried to disappear into it as Shaw held out the cattle prod. He didn't scream when it hit him. He only jerked, his eyes rolled back, and he dropped to the floor.

"All this waste for a pretty face?" Usayd asked him and wrinkled his nose at Lee. "No offense."

Lee trembled.

Usayd held out his hand, and Shaw gave him the knife.

"You don't have to watch," Shaw said to Lee.

"I want to," Lee whispered, and Shaw put a hand on his shoulder.

Lee flinched as Usayd moved through the room like a predator, crouching over the trembling or unconscious men, pulling their heads back by the hair and cutting their throats. He worked quickly and silently, and when he was finished, he turned back to Shaw.

"Let's get out of here."

Shaw nodded. "Ready when you are."

Lee didn't speak as they slipped out of the room. He was trembling. Not even Shaw's hand on his shoulder calmed him now, and why would it? The men who killed your monsters weren't heroes. They were even more frightening.

They walked quietly through the house, heading for the front door, and then Irina saw them. Saw them, saw the blood, and saw exactly what had happened. Her hands fluttered to her mouth.

Fuck. Shaw exchanged a glance with Usayd.

Irina's gaze traveled over Lee's bruised and scarred body, and then she looked Shaw in the eye.

"Where?" she murmured.

"Away from this," Shaw said, willing her to believe it.

He saw the doubt cross her plain face, the

suspicion. But, like Lee, she clung to useless hope. She needed to believe it, and so she did. As simple as that. How had Vornis not beaten it out of her? Shaw thought that he would never understand hope as simple and pure as that. He was too much of a realist, and maybe he'd been lucky enough never to have needed it. Leaps of faith were for the desperate. Shaw had never been desperate.

Even now he wasn't there. The advantage was theirs. Usayd still had the knife. Whether or not he used it was Irina's decision, even if she didn't know it.

Her gaze shifted from Shaw's face and back to Lee. Tears glistened in her pale eyes.

"One minute," she whispered, her thin hand hovering over an alarm on the wall. "One minute."

They ran out of the house, heading for the beach. It was the longest sixty seconds of his life, Shaw thought, and the shortest. They'd hardly cleared the house when the alarm started blaring.

"Have you got a boat?" Usayd gasped as they pounded down the path toward the guest bungalows. "Tell me you've got a boat!"

"Not exactly," Shaw managed, his lungs burning. He pulled his phone out of his pocket. "Have you?"

"No!"

Lee was lagging. Two months of imprisonment and torture had weakened him, and Shaw was afraid he wouldn't make it. He was too slow. He was stumbling. Shaw heard shouting behind them now and gripped Lee's good hand to pull him along.

They hit the beach and headed straight into a pair of security guards responding to the house alarm. One of them was Hanson, the head of security. The big man's face twisted into a mask of rage as he saw them, and then the moon slipped behind a cloud.

Shaw heard a burst of static from the man's radio.

A part of him had wondered from the moment he'd met Hanson and sized him up if it would end in a confrontation. At the moment, he still had surprise on his side, but not for long.

Shaw pushed Lee into the sand. "Stay down!"

Usayd lunged, and he had Hanson's sidearm pointed into his stomach before Hanson knew it. Shaw heard the shot before he'd even reached the men, and then a second and then a third. Shaw saw bodies tumble into the sand, a tangle of limbs in the darkness.

"Fuck." That was Usayd. "Fucking got me."

But he was already back on his feet.

Shit. Shaw wasn't often surprised, but Usayd was something else. The man was a killing machine. He reached down and hauled Lee to his feet again.

"Let's go, come on." Shaw pulled Lee toward the water.

"This is your plan?" Usayd asked as he splashed into the shallows. He was holding his arm across his body, gripping his shoulder. "I'm fucking shark bait now."

They waded deeper.

"The boats are on the other side," Shaw said, tasting saltwater on his lips. "They won't get them around in time. Just go with the tide."

He could see torchlight on the beach now and hear shouting, but they were far enough out to stop splashing and move quietly through the water. It was warm and dark, and maybe it would be safe enough.

Shaw turned his phone on, praying the case was as waterproof as he'd been promised. He sent the text message he'd typed out that afternoon before dinner: *Where are u? Need you, babe.* And he activated the GPS.

175

* * * * *

They drifted for hours. Usayd was losing blood, and he wasn't happy about it. "When the sharks come, I hope they eat you first. You're a fucking disaster zone, *Shaw*."

Shaw was worried about Lee as well. They all floated together, Shaw in the middle, and held hands to stay close. Usayd's grip, despite the wound in his shoulder, was strong. Lee's wasn't. At one point, he let his hand slip out of Shaw's entirely, and Shaw caught him by the wrist to stop him drifting away.

He couldn't lose him, not now, not in the warm embrace of the black Pacific. Not after everything.

Shaw swallowed. The saltwater was already swelling his throat painfully. Beside him, he heard Usayd spit out a mouthful. Lee was too quiet. He was sinking into shock. His flesh was cold.

"If the sharks don't get us, the sun will in the morning," Usayd said after a while. "We'll die of exposure by tomorrow night."

"You're such a fucking optimist," Shaw told him, but he knew Lee wouldn't even last that long. He needed to get out of the water soon.

"Fuck you," Usayd returned.

Shaw wanted to ask Lee if he was okay, but this wasn't the time. Not with Usayd listening in, ready to offer a sarcastic comment at the drop of a hat.

"Stay with me, Lee," he said instead. He adjusted his grip and felt Lee's fingers grip his own again.

The Pacific and the stars. It wouldn't be so bad to die here. The black water reflected the field of stars above them. They drifted in the Milky Way. Shaw fixed his eyes on the Southern Cross and fought sleep.

He became aware that Lee was mumbling something; humming something. It took Shaw a moment to realize it was the lullaby Irina had sung to him the night she'd taped his broken fingers.

"Lee," he said. "You're okay."

You are not *slipping away. You are* not *going quietly into the dark. Stay with me.*

It felt like hours again before they heard the drone of a boat. Shaw hoped to God that the tide hadn't pushed them back toward the island. But he couldn't see any lights, except for those on the boat. No, this was good. This was the plan.

"Wake up, Usayd," he said. "Our ride's here."

"About fucking time," Usayd growled. His voice was weaker now.

The drone of the boat's engines grew louder, and Shaw flinched as a spotlight hit him in the face. Familiar accents called out to them. Hands reached for them.

"Careful," Shaw said. "They're injured."

Shaw felt himself pulled over into the inflatable. He landed badly and didn't care, and then someone was holding a bottle of water up to his lips. Shaw washed the first mouthful around to get rid of the taste of salt and then spat it into the black ocean. The saltwater had shriveled his lips and his skin. He drank deeply and looked around for Usayd and Lee. Usayd, hunched over with a blanket around his shoulders, actually managed a wan smile.

Lee sat blinking in the torchlight. One of their rescuers wrapped a blanket around him, and he looked like he didn't even notice. Shaw shuffled over to him on his knees and put an arm around his shoulders.

"Have some water," he said. "It's okay."

Lee focused his eyes with difficulty. He looked as frightened now as any time Shaw had known him, and that was fucking unfair. He should have been jubilant. Instead, he stayed silent as the boat began to move again.

"Wash your mouth out," Shaw told him and angled the plastic bottle against Lee's lips.

Lee obeyed, shaking, before Shaw allowed him to drink.

"We might need a sling," Shaw told one of their rescuers. "He's weak."

"No problem," the man said. He relayed the message into his radio. "Ten minutes."

Ten minutes, Shaw thought with relief, ten minutes. He allowed himself to close his eyes for a moment. They stung.

It was almost dawn. There was a softening of the night, a faint glow on the horizon, but it was still dark when they approached the ship. It was running with lights out, and it seemed to loom suddenly out of the darkness above them.

Lee shrank back when the ladder was dropped down. "Where are we?" he whispered, his voice cracking. "What is this?"

Shaw helped him stand. "This is the HMAS *Stuart*," he said. He gripped the ladder and splayed his fingers against the metal hull. "Good to see you, babe."

"Babe?" Usayd grizzled.

"Private joke," Shaw said, "between me and *Stuart*."

CHAPTER FOURTEEN

It was like being reborn. It always was. As soon as he was onboard, Shaw was almost overcome by a rush of relief that fought with the adrenaline still coursing through his system. He felt like his heart could discover its regular rhythm for the first time in months, if he let it. He felt like his muscles could relax at last, his eyes could close, and his brain could switch off, if he let them. He could breathe again. He didn't have to be that guy for a while, and his whole body sagged with gratitude. Thank Christ, Shaw breathed, thank Christ. He hadn't realized how heavy the weight of his fear was until it was lifted from him. He'd suppressed it for too long.

His body shook, now that it had the chance. He sat in the sickbay with a blanket around his shoulders, his heels beating a tattoo on the side of the examination bed.

Thank Christ.

When the medical officer cleared him, Shaw made the call to Callie.

"I'm okay," he said. It took all his concentration to run through what had happened. He was tired. He wanted sleep. His voice was a monotone as he recounted the escape to Callie.

"Are you sure?" she asked him softly.

Shaw drew a shaking breath. "We're okay. The operation's all fucked-up, though."

A six-year op. Six years of gathering intel, six years of establishing his cover, six years of doing business with men who scared the living crap out of him. He'd been so close, and he'd thrown it all away in a heartbeat to save the life of someone whose government thought he was already dead. Someone who didn't count for anything in the big picture. Jesus, on paper this would look like the worst decision anyone could have made. And it was, of course it was, but at least Lee was off that fucking island. At least they both were.

"It's good to hear your voice," Callie said. "And we've weathered worse shit storms."

"Yeah." Shaw summoned the ghost of a smile. "I'll see you soon."

"I'll be waiting at the dock with Molly," Callie said. "We'll both have bells on."

Shaw knew she wasn't kidding.

The hot shower was the best thing, followed by the hot meal. Shaw felt almost human again at the end of it. Almost.

He headed back to the sickbay to check on Lee and Usayd. Usayd was already up and about, testing his sling and asking for cigarettes. It would take more than a single bullet to put Usayd down; at least that was the impression he liked to give.

"I'm going to find cigarettes," he said to Shaw.

"You'll need an escort, sir," the nurse told him.

"Then get me an escort," Usayd said and left anyway.

Lee was lying in a bed. His eyes were closed, but Shaw knew he wasn't really asleep. His hands, lying on top of his blankets, were shaking. As Shaw watched, the doctor lifted one.

"It's okay," the doctor said, glancing at Shaw. "It's okay, son."

The doctor was a small, narrow man. He was balding and wore glasses. His hands were deceptively large. He applied ointment to Lee's raw wrist and began to wind a crepe bandage around the broken skin.

"Just patching you up," the doctor murmured as Lee flinched. He saw Shaw watching and turned his head away.

Shaw left and headed back to his cabin.

Jesus, the week he'd had. His bosses would question every word of it, he supposed, ripping it apart to find every mistake, but he began to write his report anyway. He used a borrowed laptop. That was fucking typical as well. He'd just gotten used to the old one.

His fingers trembled as he typed. Adrenaline again. A part of him was still caught in that room, still fighting. It would take a long time before he could really relax. More sleepless nights. More nightmares. He was used to it.

He looked up when the door to the cabin opened, and Lee stepped through. He raised his brilliant green eyes to meet Shaw's gaze, and then dropped them again. Shaw waited, and eventually Lee looked at him again. This time he didn't look away.

Shaw felt as though Lee was looking at him, properly looking for the first time, and he really wasn't sure what he was seeing. Shaw had seen that wary expression in a lot of people before. It always ended badly.

"Can I come in?" Lee was wearing a T-shirt, sweatpants, and joggers. It was strange to see him fully clothed. No stranger, Shaw supposed, than what Lee was seeing. Whatever the hell that was. Jesus, sometimes he didn't know himself.

"Yeah, of course," Shaw said. Lee closed the door. The cabin was small, and Shaw had the only chair, so Lee hesitated for a moment before sitting on the bunk. He had crepe bandages around his wrists and clean tape around his broken fingers.

Shaw closed the laptop. "Has the doctor cleared you?"

Lee nodded and bit his lip. "I, *um,* I have to take some pills and see him tomorrow."

Shaw wondered what the examination must have felt like for Lee, having to show his scars and bruises to strangers and to have them all *know.* He wondered if Lee wished he had died with the rest of his team, or if that would only come later when he tried to pull the torn fabric of his life back together.

"I, *um,*" Lee managed. He cleared his throat. "I don't know where we are, and I don't know what's going on."

"You're okay now, Lee," Shaw said. "I promise."

Lee looked at him warily. "Was anything you told me the truth?"

His eyes said it all: *liar.*

Shaw shrugged wearily. He was too tired for this shit. Not now. He needed sleep. He needed time. He needed to feel comfortable in his own skin again before he could begin to dissect it all for Lee. "I dunno. Does it matter?"

Lee leaned forward, watching Shaw's face closely. "You're not a bad guy, are you?"

"I don't know anymore," Shaw said, surprised. He'd expected recriminations. "No, I suppose I'm not a bad guy."

Lee frowned, trying to gather his thoughts. "Why did we get picked up in the middle of the ocean by an Australian navy ship?"

"Frigate," Shaw corrected him. "Anzac class. The crew gets shitty when you call it the wrong thing."

"Whatever," Lee said. He drew his brows together. "What are you?"

"I work for ASIO," Shaw said. "Do you know what that is?"

Lee shook his head.

Typical insular American, Shaw thought, his old prejudices showing. "It's kind of like your CIA. But smaller." He smiled. "But better."

Lee managed a slight smile at that, but it didn't reach his eyes. "You're a spy," he said.

"I'm a spy." It felt strange to say it aloud. It sounded wooden, like a lie. The first honest thing he'd said to Lee, and it sounded like a fucking lie. Typical.

Lee's gaze slid away and back again. "And who is that Arab guy?"

"Oh, don't call him that," Shaw said. He fought to keep his smile. *Keep it light, keep it easy. Let him see you're not that guy. Show him you can smile. Show him it's okay.* "He hates that. His name's Zev. Zev Rosenberg."

"Is he Mossad?" Lee asked, his brows arching.

"Not that he'll ever admit," Shaw said.

"Will he be okay?" Lee asked.

"He's had worse."

Lee lowered his eyes. "Were you sent there to kill all those men?"

"No," said Shaw, his smile fading, and Lee's eyes flicked up again. "I was sent there to make friends with those men. To infiltrate their groups. And I fucked up. I couldn't, *um* . . . "

Lee swallowed.

"Well," said Shaw. "I couldn't let them do it."

Lee nodded.

"Look," Shaw said, drawing a deep breath. "Look, I have to write a report on what happened, and we probably won't get a chance to talk much back on dry land. Is there anything you want me to leave out?"

Lee looked up sharply, flushing. "You mean in the shower?"

"Yeah," said Shaw. "I mean, they're gonna find out what was done to you. And that wasn't your fault, you have to remember that. And that shit for the cameras, well, they'll let that slide, I suppose. But maybe it would be a good idea, for both of us, if we shut up about that blowjob."

He wondered if Lee would question which one of them he was trying to protect. He wasn't sure himself.

Lee frowned again. "I don't regret that."

"Christ, me neither," Shaw said too quickly. "But maybe you don't want your boss reading about it."

"Yeah, maybe. Okay." Lee looked at his bandaged wrists. "Is this for real?" he asked in a quiet voice.

Shaw watched him closely.

Lee raised his eyes again. "Or am I still in that room? Maybe I just went crazy." He shrugged. "Maybe he's killing me right now."

"You're okay now," Shaw said.

"Maybe you're not even real," Lee said. "Maybe I just imagined someone there who wouldn't hurt me."

Shaw sighed. Was it Voltaire who said that if God didn't exist, it would be necessary to invent Him? How could Lee trust anything anymore? Jesus, he'd been teetering on the line between drug-fucked and complete psychological breakdown for months now. Maybe he really thought he'd finally just slipped.

"You're okay," he repeated, wondering how many

times he'd have to say it until Lee believed it. "I promise."

And there was the look of desperate trust in Lee's eyes again. "You saved me."

"Yeah," Shaw murmured uncomfortably. He didn't regret it, he couldn't, but he'd waited long enough to do it.

Lee bit his lip and looked at Shaw through his dark lashes. "When does your report end?"

Shaw shook his head. "What?"

"Your report," Lee said. "Does it end when we got rescued?"

"Yeah," said Shaw. "I suppose."

Lee moistened his lips with his tongue. "Then do you wanna fuck?"

Shaw's jaw dropped. "What?"

Lee stood and moved to stand beside him. He raised his hand and touched Shaw's cheek gently. "Do you wanna fuck?"

The intensity in Lee's green eyes shocked him. Shaw felt a jolt of electricity go straight to his balls. His mouth was suddenly dry. "That's, *ah,* that's probably not a good idea, Lee."

"Don't you want to?" Lee asked him. "I want to."

Shaw didn't know how to answer that. Of course he wanted it. He'd wanted it for a week, and it had been a long fucking week. "You've been through hell, Lee, and I, I don't want to be the guy who takes advantage of that."

"You're not that guy," Lee said. He leaned down, his lips close to Shaw's ear. "You're the guy who saved my life."

Shaw leaned away from the brush of lips on his ear. "Yeah, well, I don't want to be that guy either, Lee. Because I don't want you to feel like you owe me."

"But I do," Lee breathed.

Shaw closed his eyes. "Doesn't matter. This isn't

the time or the place." He heard the faint crumple of foil and opened his eyes to find Lee holding out a fistful of condoms. "Christ!"

"I took 'em from the infirmary," Lee said. His eyes sparkled with mischief, and Shaw discovered that he liked that. He liked naughty Lee a hell of a lot more than frightened Lee, even if he knew it was false bravado. "Let's not waste 'em."

Shaw snorted with laughter, wiped a hand across his aching eyes, and wondered how long he'd be tasting saltwater. God, he was too tired to be having this conversation with Lee. He had his report to write and his job to worry about. This was a complete shit fight. No, what was the term he'd heard Callie use once? A goat-fuck. This was a complete goat-fuck. Shaw needed to write his report and get some sleep. He did not need Lee standing there, holding out a handful of condoms, offering himself.

"Do you want to?" Lee asked him again. He chewed his lip.

Shaw's smile faded. "It's not a good idea."

"That's not what I asked you," Lee said in a steady voice. He fixed his gaze on Shaw's. "Do you want to?"

Shaw's breath caught in his throat. Couldn't lie. Not now. Not a moral decision; Shaw just knew that Lee would see right through the deception if he tried.

"Yeah," Shaw said, and that tiny admission felt momentous. A shiver ran through him. Adrenaline. Surrender. Something. "Lock the door."

Lee moved quickly to obey, pulling his shirt over his head. He was stripping off his sweatpants before Shaw had even stood. He slid them down over his narrow hips, exposing an erection that was already throbbing against his stomach.

Shaw began to strip and was surprised to find his hands were shaking.

Lee looked at him hungrily. "I want to go on top. Can I?"

"Whatever you want," Shaw breathed, pulling him close for a kiss. So good. So good to touch him without worrying about who was watching. Not taking, sharing. *Want you, want this,* need *this,* but he couldn't say it.

No pressure, no obligation. Just, fuck, just whatever the hell this was.

Adrenaline? Closure? Fuck knows.

Just for once, Shaw tried to lose himself in a moment. Lee's mouth was eager, greedy, and he moaned under the kiss. His hands slid up Shaw's sides, following his ribs, his fingers kneading his flesh. Their cocks strained against one another, and Shaw reluctantly pushed Lee away before the friction undid him completely.

He climbed onto the narrow bunk, lying back. "You sure?" he asked.

"Yeah," Lee said, but Shaw saw the flicker of fear that crossed his brilliant green eyes.

"We don't have to do this," Shaw told him, reaching out and encircling Lee's bandaged wrist with his fingers. "We can get off another way."

"How long do we have on the ship?" Lee asked him and wrinkled his nose. "Frigate, I mean."

"Two days until Sydney," Shaw told him.

Lee nodded and set his jaw. "Then we do this now."

He climbed up onto the bunk.

"We don't have to," Shaw said. "Not if you're not ready."

Lee straddled Shaw's hips and ran his hands up and down his chest. "I want to," he said. "Before it's too late."

Shaw nodded. He was the rebound guy. The rebound guy after the rapists. Lee needed to exorcise those other men. Maybe he'd have to exorcise Shaw as well when he'd done that, his last reminder of that terrible place. Shaw was the bookend to his nightmares. It was enough.

Lee leaned down and kissed him, and Shaw sighed. It was enough.

Lee's hands fumbled with the condom packet. He grew frustrated and scowled. "Fuck!"

"Take your time," Shaw murmured. He lifted a hand to touch Lee's. "It's okay."

Lee met his eyes, nodded, and finally managed to rip the packet open. He shifted back, straddling Shaw's thighs. Shaw groaned as Lee's trembling hands rolled the condom over his cock. Then Lee was fumbling again, with a bottle of lube this time, applying it to Shaw's cock and then reaching around to prepare himself.

He was breathing heavily. Shaw stroked his thighs. "It's okay, Lee."

"Yeah." Lee flashed him a nervous smile and raised himself up onto his knees. He gripped Shaw's cock, angled it, and notched it against his anus. He drew a few quick breaths and began to lower himself.

Shaw bit his lip as he felt the head of his cock push past Lee's tight entrance. He gripped the sides of the bunk to stop himself from thrusting and stared up at Lee. His stomach twisted. "You okay?"

Lee was crying. He scrubbed at his face furiously with his hands.

"Stop, if it hurts," Shaw said, trying to lift him off.

"No!" Lee gripped Shaw's hands and sank lower.

"Don't move, please, don't move."

"Lee?" Shaw gripped his hands tightly, mindful of his injured fingers, feeling Lee impale himself fully on his throbbing cock. He was so hot, so tight, but his face was screwed up with pain, and his tears were flowing freely now. "Lee, get off. Get off me."

"Shut up," Lee said through gritted teeth. "I'm sorry, I'm sorry. Fuck!"

It was torture not to move. Shaw felt every muscle in his body tense with the effort. "Lee, just get off, okay? I don't want to hurt you."

"No." Lee pulled his hands free and scrubbed his face again. "Gonna do this."

Jesus. Enough was enough. Shaw caught his hands again. "Look at me. You don't have to prove anything here, okay? If it hurts, just get off. Come on." He tempered his voice. "Come on, it's okay. We'll do something else."

Sudoku was probably the safest thing.

"Don't touch me!" There was real panic in Lee's voice as he pushed Shaw's hands away. "Don't fucking touch me!"

Shaw frowned. "Lee, get up. Get up now!"

Lee groaned in pain, squeezing his eyes shut. "No, I'm sorry. Just stay still, please. I'm sorry."

"This was a mistake." Shaw tried to roll away, but Lee held him down. Fuck, he'd throw him off in a minute, and screw his feelings. "Come on, why are you torturing yourself?"

Lee's eyes flashed open. "Got no one else to do it for me now."

"*Oh*, shit, Lee," Shaw said. "Come on, get off."

"No," Lee said. He drew a deep breath and began to rock his hips.

Fuck. Shaw gasped and dropped back onto the

mattress. That was fucking good. Lee was so tight, so hot, and he was clenching around Shaw's cock now. Clenching and rocking, even though he was still crying.

"Fuck me," Lee whispered. "Fuck me, Shaw."

Shaw gripped his hips, changed his angle, and pulled back. He felt Lee tremble and thrust gently again. That was it. That was the spot. Lee's eyes rolled back in his head.

Exorcism, Shaw thought. You had to call up the evil thing before you killed it. And Lee needed to know he was the one in control.

"We'll stop," he managed, "if you want to."

Lee shook his head, swallowing. "Don't want to."

Christ, that was a relief, because Shaw was worried it might have been a lie. He'd dreamed of this, of fucking Lee, but never in any of those fantasies had Lee been crying. Which was the real difference, he supposed, between him and men like Vornis and Guterman. When was the last time Lee had been fucked without tears? How long would it take him?

"Lee," he whispered. "Lee."

Shaw drew him closer, leaning up to kiss him, to kiss his lips and his wet cheeks and eyelashes.

"Oh, Jesus," Lee moaned. "Will you touch my cock, Shaw?"

"Anything you want," Shaw said, sliding his hand down into the sweaty heat between their bodies. Lee jerked and cried out as Shaw's fingers closed around his hot shaft. "*Shh. Shh.*"

Lee struggled for breath as Shaw began to stroke him in time to his own thrusts. His cock pulsed. It was slippery with precum.

"Haven't been hard like this in forever," he

whimpered. "Not with someone . . . someone fucking me."

"I know," Shaw said, licking his jawline. "I know."

It wasn't a fuck Lee needed, Shaw realized too late; it was a psychologist. It probably wouldn't matter in the end even if it did feel good for him; Lee would only hate himself for it. This was a mistake. He'd just be one more regret for Lee in the end. Maybe not a horror like Vornis, but a regret.

"Shaw," Lee moaned. "Oh, fuck, Shaw."

Shaw thrust again, picking up the pace now. He could feel the muscles in Lee's thighs trembling. Fatigue or pleasure, he didn't know. He couldn't even tell if Lee was enjoying it. His cock was hard, but his face was a mask of pain. Shaw closed his eyes. He didn't want to see the same expressions Vornis must have.

Shaw thrust quickly now, hating himself every time.

He felt Lee's balls draw up. His cock pulsed, and Shaw shafted it in his fist as Lee came. Lee arched up, cried out again, and Shaw came as well. It was quick, furious, and he was afraid it wasn't what Lee needed.

Lee fell forward, and Shaw encircled him with his arms. He rolled them over in the narrow bunk, his cock sliding out of Lee's tight passage. Shaw reached down for the blanket and drew it up over Lee's trembling body.

He sat up, and Lee tensed.

"It's okay," he said. "I'm just going to clean up. I'll come back, if you want."

Lee twisted his neck to look at him. He nodded.

Shaw disposed of the condom and wet a washcloth under the tap in the corner basin. At least he didn't have to walk all the way to the head. He pulled on his sweatpants again and picked Lee's up from the floor.

He returned to the bunk and drew the blanket back. Lee lay there quietly as Shaw gently wiped him down with the washcloth. He tilted his hips obediently as Shaw pulled his sweats back on.

Shaw climbed back into the bunk. "You okay?"

"Yeah." Lee was facing away from him, but Shaw heard the uncertainty in his voice.

Shaw drew him closer and wrapped his arms around him. "You'll be okay."

Lee sniffed. "Yeah."

Shaw stroked his dark hair.

Lee's breath caught in his throat. "I don't know what happened there. I don't know what that was. I'm sorry."

"Don't apologize," Shaw said. "It's okay. It'll take time, that's all."

"We don't have time," Lee whispered.

"No, we don't," Shaw said. He forced a smile, needing Lee to hear it in his voice. "But you do, Lee. You've got all the time in the world. You'll get better."

"I'm sorry," Lee said. "I didn't want it to be like that."

"It's okay," Shaw said again. "It's okay."

He moved his hand down Lee's body and caught his hand. He remembered their first night in the bungalow together and wondered if Lee did. He wondered if he could win back that trust. He turned Lee's palm over and rubbed his thumb against it. Back and forth, back and forth, back and forth, until he could feel the tension draining slowly from Lee's body.

"It's okay," he whispered, even when he thought Lee was asleep. "It'll be okay for you."

Lee sighed in his sleep.

CHAPTER FIFTEEN

"For fuck's sake, Zev," Shaw snapped. "Eat your own fucking dinner!"

"I like yours better," Zev said.

"It's the same fucking thing," Shaw said.

"Yours seems a little more kosher," Zev said.

"I've seen you eat lobster," Shaw said, slapping his hand away. "I saw you eat lobster two nights ago."

"*Mmm*," Zev said. "That wasn't me. That was someone else."

They were bickering like kids, and the captain and his officers had no idea what to make of them. Neither did Lee, who was eating everything put in front of him quietly and politely.

"We can do kosher," the captain said. He looked at the XO. "Can't we?"

The XO shrugged her shoulders. "It's never come up, sir."

Shaw had an idea the captain would be very glad to see the back of the lot of them.

"Movie night tonight," the captain said. "If you're interested."

"What's on?" Zev asked.

"*You Don't Mess With the Zohan*," Shaw suggested.

Someone farther down the table almost choked.

Shaw glanced across at Lee and saw that he was smiling. Zev saw it too and bit back whatever acerbic reply he'd had ready. He reached across and filched Shaw's chicken instead.

Zev could be a clown in public. He liked to be a clown. But when he worked, he was dangerous. He had a level of professionalism that Shaw both admired and feared. He killed men in cold blood, and, as far as Shaw could tell, he didn't lose sleep over it. Shaw didn't know if he aspired to be like that or not.

After dinner, Shaw saw Lee back to his cabin, and he and Zev headed up onto the deck. The crew who passed them in the narrow corridors looked at them curiously.

The crew gave all three of them a wide berth on the ship. They knew, Shaw supposed, that he was ASIO. They suspected Zev was Mossad. They had no idea where Lee fitted in. And what the three of them had been doing floating in the ocean off a Fijian island would remain a topic of speculation. Shaw had heard the lower ranks speculating since they'd been picked up.

The sea air was invigorating. Shaw and Zev headed over to the rails, where Zev lit a cigarette.

"What are you doing?" Zev asked him. His voice was low, serious. The joker was gone.

"What do you mean?" Shaw leaned on the rail.

"I mean with that American," Zev said. "You threw away your mission. Fuck, you threw away mine as well, even if I'm glad the bastards are dead."

"Thanks for backing me," Shaw said. "I didn't know if you would."

Zev only shrugged.

"I mean that," Shaw said. "Thanks."

Zev inhaled, and his narrow face was illuminated by the ember of his cigarette. "Did you fuck him?"

"What?" Shaw felt guilt rise in his gut.

"On the island," Zev said. "Did you fuck him?"

"No," Shaw said, glad it was the truth. Glad Zev had clarified the question.

There's the loophole, and there's Shaw slipping through it.

"Good," said Zev. "The Americans might not have liked that."

"I'm not an idiot," Shaw said.

Zev shrugged again. "I saw the way you looked at him. He's been thinking with his cock, I told myself. I knew you wouldn't let him die."

"Would you have let him die?" Shaw asked curiously.

Zev didn't answer that. "When my superiors ask why I'm not plotting atrocities with terrorists, I can just blame the whole fucking mess on you, of course." He shrugged his narrow shoulders. "And I expect I will. I just wonder who you're going to blame."

Shaw didn't know how to answer.

"But, for what it's worth, I'm glad you did what you did," Zev said.

"Are you really?"

"Of course," Zev said. "You saved me from having to make the decision."

Shaw smiled slightly and watched the black ocean.

* * * * *

Shaw woke up when the door to his cabin opened.

"Are you awake?" Lee whispered.

Shaw sighed. "Yeah. What's up?"

Lee crossed to the bunk. "Couldn't sleep. Can I stay with you?"

I'm not your savior, Shaw wanted to say. *You cried when we fucked, remember?* But it was less than two days until Sydney, and he was the closest thing to a friend that Lee had. He needed someone, Shaw supposed, to tell him it was okay now.

"Yeah," Shaw said, shifting across to make some room in the narrow bunk.

Lee slid in beside him with a sigh, his arms going around Shaw's body. He rested his head on Shaw's chest and sighed again. "Thanks."

"It's okay," Shaw said. His fingers found the scars and welts on Lee's back and brushed over them gently. "Just try and get some sleep, okay?"

"Okay," Lee whispered.

Shaw thought about what Zev had said earlier on deck. He was wrong. Shaw hadn't been thinking with his cock. It had always been more than that. From the moment he'd seen Lee, Shaw had wanted to rescue him. He'd fought the instinct as far as he could, but in the end, it hadn't made any difference. He'd fucked everything up, but he was relieved as well. He'd spent so long pretending to be somebody else, somebody ruthless and cold, that he was afraid he'd forgotten how to be anything else. Lee had shown him there was still a scrap of human decency left in him after all. It wouldn't save his career, but it was good to know.

"I had an iPod," Lee said.

Shaw frowned slightly in the darkness. "What?"

"I had an iPod in my pack," Lee said. "Vornis took it. I thought of it a lot, you know. I really wanted it back.

Out of everything, I thought that was the worst thing he could do — take my fucking iPod. Do you think that's weird?"

"I don't know," Shaw said. He stroked the soft hair at the nape of Lee's neck. It would be curls soon, Shaw thought. What a shame he'd never see that. "What sort of music do you like?"

"Everything," Lee murmured. "I just missed it. I thought it would be better if I had somewhere to go in my head. I needed it, yeah? I needed to go somewhere apart from the sedatives, I mean. I think they were sedatives. I never saw them prepare the syringe."

Shaw stroked his hair.

"What if it was something else?" Lee asked. "What if it was something worse? What if it was heroin?"

"Heroin isn't all it's cracked up to be," Shaw said, which might have been the wrong track to take with a DEA agent. "I mean, if they made you an addict, Lee, you'd know by now, wouldn't you? Come on, you know you would."

"I guess," Lee said.

"Anyway," Shaw said, "I'll bet the DEA has access to the best rehab programs in the world, if it comes to that. Right? I mean, given the undercover work you guys do."

"I guess," Lee murmured.

"Of course they do," Shaw said. Lee should have been more worried about disease than addiction, Shaw thought. And maybe that was something Shaw should have given some thought to before fucking him, protection or not. But it had been an act of trust in the good people at Durex, and Shaw had put his trust in a lot less before. It was meant to have been an act of trust between him and Lee as well, but so much for that.

Shaw couldn't resent it. What had he expected, exactly? That he'd magic Lee off the island and *ta-da*, he'd be a real boy? Shaw was too old and too clever to believe in fairy tales. The real miracle was that they were both still alive. Shaw had no right to hope for anything more than that.

He knew it would hurt when he had to let Lee go.

Lee exhaled slowly. "Thanks for looking after me."

"That's okay." Shaw tried to disguise the waver in his voice. "You just sleep now, okay?"

"Okay." Lee sighed.

The sound of Lee's breathing, the drone of the engines, the swell of the ocean; it all conspired against Shaw in the end. He slept.

* * * * *

Shaw woke up with Lee's mouth around his cock.

"Fuck!" It was still the middle of the night. Shaw reached out, searching for the light switch. "What are you doing, Lee?"

Lee didn't answer. Shaw had forgotten how good that hot mouth felt around his cock. That tongue that knew all the tricks. Those clever fingers that teased his balls.

Shaw pushed him away with one hand at the same moment his other one found the switch. "No," he said firmly. "No, we're not doing this again."

Lee blinked in the sudden light. "Why not?"

Holy shit! When had Lee slipped out of his clothes? The light gleamed on his naked body.

"Jesus, Lee, because you *cried!*" Shaw hitched his sweatpants up again. "You're not ready for this."

"Will you hold me, then?" Lee asked him. "Will you please just hold me?"

"Yeah, okay," Shaw said. There wasn't much room to maneuver in the narrow bunk, but he ended up on his back with Lee lying in the crook of his arm. And, unless he was imagining it, Lee's cock poking into his hip.

Shaw closed his eyes and tried to ignore it. He could feel Lee's breath against his throat. The closeness felt good. It felt comfortable. He hoped Lee would fall asleep again.

"I got scared last time," Lee said quietly in the darkness.

"That's normal," Shaw told him, even if he had no idea.

"It felt good," Lee said. "That's what scared me."

Shaw stroked the back of his head. "You'll be okay."

He wondered how long it would take before Lee was healed. He wondered if it was even possible. Even once the fear was gone, what then? Would he feel sick every time sex felt good? A part of him would always be the victim, terrified of the pain and afraid that accepting pleasure meant he'd asked for it. And he had the physical scars as well. Would every potential new partner ask him about them? And what could he say?

Shaw wished he'd been the one to cut Vornis's throat instead of leaving it for Zev. He wished Vornis had been conscious. He could have really made it hurt. He could have made it last for hours. And he would have told him that painting was a forgery as well, just to see the look on the bastard's face.

Maybe he was a monster after all.

Lee drew his hand down Shaw's chest gently, spreading his fingers wide.

"Don't," Shaw murmured. "Just sleep. Can you reach the light?"

Lee didn't move.

"When you got stung by the jellyfish, how long before you got back in the ocean?" Lee asked him quietly.

Shaw tried to remember. "It was a long time ago. I was in hospital for two days. Maybe a week?"

"That's brave," Lee said. "Will you help me do that?"

"It's different," Shaw said, closing his eyes as Lee's fingers caught his nipple gently. The jolt of pleasure shot straight to his balls, and he hissed. Now, now was the time to get some space between them. Right now, before it went further, but Shaw didn't move.

"Did you like it the first time you went back in?" Lee asked him. His mouth was close to Shaw's ear now. Shaw could feel his hot breath.

"I was terrified." Shaw remembered.

"Did it still feel good?" Lee asked him.

"I don't know," Shaw said. "It probably did, but I was too scared to realize. I kept thinking it would happen again, any second now. I had to force myself to stay in the water." He felt Lee's tongue against his ear and jerked his head away. "But it's different."

"I think it would be okay," Lee said, "if you were on top. I think I like it when you're in charge. You know what's right for me. I got scared when I had to be in control before."

"That's why it's wrong," Shaw said.

Lee slid his hand farther down, tracing his fingertips over Shaw's abdomen. "I trust you. When's that going to happen for me again?"

"I don't want to hurt you," Shaw said. He should have kicked him out when he'd first turned up, but Lee had needed this closeness. Why couldn't they just leave it at that? Why couldn't Lee just sleep?

"Can't we pretend there's a camera?" Lee asked. "Can't we pretend someone's watching? I liked it when I got to look up at you. It made me feel safe."

"You are safe," Shaw told him. "We don't have to pretend anymore."

Lee shifted suddenly, rolling onto his back and pulling Shaw on top of him. "Please. Just jerk off if you want." He drew his legs up and spread his knees.

Shaw pushed off him and straightened up, and then he was in exactly the same position that had become so familiar to them both: on his knees between Lee's spread thighs, looking down at Lee's erect cock. He felt the same hunger he always had, and none of the caution. He didn't have to pretend here. And he didn't have to resist.

And he didn't even care that Lee had manipulated him into it.

Shaw shifted back, looked Lee in the eye, and bent forward. Lee squirmed as he felt Shaw's warm breath on his cock. His whole body undulated in need before Shaw even flicked out his tongue to claim the droplet of clear fluid already glistening on the head.

"Oh, Jesus," Lee whispered. His hands clenched into fists at his sides.

Shaw licked him again. He tasted good. He drew the head slowly into his mouth, loving the small sounds of pleasure that Lee made. There was no pain in this and no fear yet. This was good. Lee's cock was so smooth, so hard. It felt almost velvety under Shaw's tongue. The skin was so soft and sensitive, but the flesh was rigid and straining underneath.

And this, Shaw knew, was something Vornis would never have done for Lee. Jerked him off, maybe, just to make him hate himself for coming, but Vornis would never have taken Lee's cock gently into his mouth.

Shaw circled his fingers around Lee's shaft, feeling

it twitch under his touch. He slowly fed it into his mouth. He'd owed Lee this since the blowjob in the shower, but it wasn't just about reciprocity. Shaw wanted this as much as Lee did. He wanted to give Lee this. He needed to. Needed to give Lee something that nobody else on the island had. Needed not to be a monster.

Stop it. It's not about you. Focus.

Shaw worked his tongue around the head of Lee's cock.

"Oh, oh Jesus," Lee whispered again, his hips trembling. "I'm gonna come!"

Shaw lifted his head quickly, and Lee squirmed with disappointment. "Not yet."

"Please," Lee whispered, still holding his fists at his sides.

That was interesting, Shaw thought as he drew Lee's cock into his mouth again. He really had given Shaw all the control. Shaw circled the base of Lee's cock with his fingers to prevent him from coming and ran his tongue along the thick vein on the underside of Lee's shaft. Lee trembled and writhed.

"Please," he whispered again.

Shaw moved away again. He leaned forward and ran his tongue along Lee's bottom lip. Lee jerked forward, opening his mouth and trying to follow Shaw's face as he moved back again. He was panting.

"Do you still want me to fuck you, Lee?" Shaw asked him. He rolled his hips, bringing his cock into contact with Lee's through the thin material of his sweatpants.

"Yes," Lee breathed. "Please, yes."

Shaw shucked his sweatpants off and reached for a condom. This time he wouldn't let Lee prepare himself. He was in charge here, and not because he was stronger but because Lee wanted it that way, and that was reason enough. They could both worry about the psychology later.

"Lie back," Shaw said. He squirted lube onto his fingers and reached down between Lee's buttocks.

And there was that look again. Fear flashed in Lee's eyes as Shaw's fingers found his anus and pressed gently against the entrance.

"We're going to do this," Shaw said firmly. He hoped it wasn't the wrong path to take and was relieved when Lee clenched his jaw and nodded.

Lee drew a shaking breath as Shaw slipped a finger inside him.

"You're okay," Shaw said, and it wasn't a question.

Lee nodded.

Shaw withdrew his finger and then pushed back inside with two. He twisted them slowly in the tight heat, looking for that sweet spot. Lee shuddered as he found it, rocking his hips.

Shaw scissored his fingers, stretching Lee slowly as he watched his face. The fear was still there, but it was only weak. There was discomfort now, but pleasure as well. And there was trust. Lee hadn't been kidding about that. Shaw bet it was the only thing keeping him from panicking.

Shaw withdrew his fingers and notched his cock against Lee's tight hole. Lee's cock was still hard. He still wanted this. Shaw hesitated for a moment. He opened his mouth to speak, and nothing came. Relax? Let it happen? You can handle it? There was nothing he could say that didn't sound like coercion or, worse, that wouldn't sound like an echo of a hundred different things Lee had been told on the island, so Shaw held Lee's gaze and didn't say anything.

Lee gasped as Shaw entered him, and his fists unclenched as his hands fluttered anxiously.

"You're okay," Shaw told him again. He withdrew slightly and pushed again, feeling Lee open up underneath him.

Shaw hoped he was doing the right thing. Jesus, it was too late now for regrets, they were already fucking. Shaw had trained his conscience well. It didn't make itself heard until he was already on the home stretch. He wasn't the good guy Lee believed he was.

He heard Lee's shaky intake of breath.

"You're okay," Shaw told him, willing him to believe it. He pushed forward again, and then he was all the way in. "Look at me, Lee."

Lee opened his eyes. There were no tears yet, but Lee blinked rapidly as though he was trying to hold them at bay.

Shaw leaned forward and kissed him. Lee's mouth opened slightly. Too fucking passive, Shaw thought. He tilted his hips. Lee gasped, and Shaw pushed his tongue into his mouth. He found Lee's tongue and teased it until Lee was groaning underneath him. He wriggled, and Shaw moved his mouth to his throat. He mapped Lee's skin with his lips and his teeth, gently sucking and nipping until every one of Lee's breaths was a tiny gasp instead, and Lee was arching his back toward him.

Shaw wanted more. He flicked his tongue against Lee's nipple and, half afraid of the consequences, bit down quickly.

Lee cried out and arched farther against him. Surprise flashed through his eyes.

"You like that," Shaw said before Lee's brain jumped to unpleasant associations. "Feels good."

Lee dropped back, trembling. "Fuck me, Shaw, please."

There it was. A breathy demand. Lee *wanted*, and it was beautiful.

Shaw licked Lee's throat and nipped at the muscle between his neck and shoulder. This time Lee's gasp was all pleasure, and at last his hands knew where they were supposed to be. They slipped around Shaw, his fingers digging so hard into his back that Shaw knew he'd have bruises in the morning. And it would be totally fucking worth it.

Shaw felt the moment that Lee gave himself fully. His body pushed against Shaw's, desperate for skin-on-skin contact. His legs hooked around Shaw. He began to raise himself up to meet each thrust. And he pulled Shaw's head down and gasped into his ear: *Fuck. Oh, Shaw. Fuck."*

Shaw knew he wouldn't last much longer. He reached between them and gripped Lee's cock. It pulsed as soon as he touched it, and Shaw felt Lee shudder as he came. He threw his head back, clenched convulsively around Shaw's cock, and Shaw laved his throat with his tongue. Lee's whole body shook, but he didn't let go.

Shaw thrust again and felt his balls contract. His muscles tensed, froze, and then he came as well. He sagged down onto Lee, and their sweaty bodies slid against one another as they carefully disengaged.

Shaw lay on his side and pulled Lee into his embrace. Lee was slippery with sweat and cum, and his skin was flushed. Shaw slipped his arms around his back and kissed him gently.

"That was good," Lee murmured.

Shaw ran his tongue across Lee's bottom lip. "It was."

"Thank you," Lee said.

Shaw smiled slightly, thinking of that time in the shower. "Should be me thanking you."

Lee tilted his chin and kissed Shaw's jawline. "Can we do that again?"

"Give me a minute," Shaw murmured.

Lee laughed softly and poked him in the ribs. "I mean before we get to Sydney?"

Try and stop me, Shaw wanted to say but couldn't. There was too much off limits with Lee, and most of it was Shaw's favorite dirty talk: I want to fuck you senseless. I can make you beg. I can make you *scream.*

He squeezed Lee's hand as regret spread through him. "That's probably not a great idea, Lee, is it?"

Lee's face was unreadable in the darkness. "Oh. Okay."

Shaw held Lee as he drifted off to sleep at last, and wondered what the hell he was thinking.

* * * * *

One step forward and two steps back. Lee was never far from breaking.

Lee winced as the doctor unwound the bandages around his wrists, and clamped his mouth tightly shut.

Shaw, leaning in the doorway, wondered how long it would take until Lee unlearned what Vornis had taught him. How long until he stopped forcing down his pain responses? How long until he realized that allowing himself to show weakness didn't mean inviting more pain?

You're an asshole, Shaw. You shouldn't have touched him. Not when he's still a broken thing.

Shaw thought of Molly. Kind words, gentle touches, and whispered endearments were all very good, but just because it had worked on a Labrador didn't mean it would work on a human being. It just meant that he was as bad as Vornis. It just meant he thought of Lee as a dumb animal as well.

But then Lee looked up at him, and his eyes shone with the same helpless trust that Shaw had seen so many times back on the island. He was submitting to the doctor's examination because Shaw had told him he had to, just as he'd gone quietly up to the main house on that last night. Shaw hated himself for that. It wasn't Lee's fault that he needed someone to trust, but it was Shaw's fault for being a monster after all. He'd exploited Lee, just like everyone else.

I didn't let him die. He's grateful for that, but how long until he realizes I could have saved him at any time? I just chose not to.

"This is healing well," the doctor said, turning Lee's left wrist. "It's still infected, so we'll put some antiseptic cream on it and bind it up again. Have you been taking your antibiotics?"

Lee looked at Shaw before he answered. "Yes, sir."

The doctor raised his eyebrows. "Now, we've talked about that, son."

Lee flushed. "Sorry. Yes, doc."

Shaw liked the doc. He had a good bedside manner, and not just with Lee. None of the crew addressed him by his rank inside the medical bay. He was just the doc. And Lee, whether he realized it or not, responded well to the man.

"Okay," the doc said. "Take your shirt off please, Lee."

Lee's fingers fumbled along the hemline of his shirt for a moment, before he drew it over his head. He hunched over slightly on the examination table, swinging his legs restlessly. He squeezed his eyes shut as the doc began to inspect the marks and bruises on his torso.

The harsh fluorescent light did him no favors. Shaw remembered the first time he'd seen Lee, his skin shining in the rain. He hadn't noticed the bruises then, and now they were all he could see. He watched as the doc's gloved fingers moved gently across Lee's skin.

Shaw saw the raised puncture marks left by the wait-a-while. He saw the tiny burns from the cattle prod. He saw a scar the shape of a cigarette burn on the side of Lee's rib cage. And he saw the mottled bruises that had faded to yellow all over him. As though he'd been a blank canvas to Vornis and the rest, and they couldn't bear to leave a square inch of his skin unblemished. Up close, his multitude of bruises were yellow, brown, gray, and red. They were messy and random, but from a distance, they coalesced into a patina of light and shadow that defined the planes of his body. Like a postimpressionist painting. Like *The Boy in the Red Vest*.

There was a sort of sick artistry in it, Shaw thought.

Lee opened his eyes, and Shaw shot him a quick smile. *You're okay.* Lee's own lips quirked up gratefully, and then he squeezed his eyes shut again.

"Okay," the doc said. "Lie down on your stomach for me, please."

Everything was *okay* and *please* with Lee. It had to be.

Shaw watched as Lee shifted awkwardly onto his stomach. A shiver ran through his thin body. Too thin, Shaw thought; too thin and too broken.

"Good," said the doc. He patted Lee's shoulder gently. "Okay."

Lee was holding himself tensely. Shaw could see him trying to force himself to relax under the doc's hand, but he couldn't. The muscles moving under his skin were tight. His breathing was shallow. And his hands were fisted.

Lee hissed through his teeth as the doc's fingers touched a burn. "Shaw?"

Shaw moved forward. "It's okay, Lee."

Lee reached out his hand, and Shaw took it. Lee was trembling, but he gripped Shaw's hand tightly and closed his eyes again. He frowned, and clenched his jaw.

Shaw exchanged a look with the doc and wondered if he imagined something censorious in the older man's expression. Maybe the doc was just reading Shaw's guilt. *I could have saved him at any time. I just chose not to.* Shaw looked down at Lee's hand in his own.

If I'd known you, he thought. *I want to know you, but not the way you are now. You deserve better.*

Shaw wasn't a human being. Not when he was working. He was something different then. He was a machine, programmed to do a task. He reduced everything to a simple calculation: risk versus reward. And he'd seen some god-awful things in his work as well, things that the machine could witness, the machine could process, but the man couldn't. Shaw had learned to compartmentalize everything. He had learned that there was a time and a place to feel, and it was always later, always at home, either in the debriefing or in the nearest bar with Callie. And it wasn't the fact that Lee had got under his defenses that bothered Shaw the most. It was the fact that nothing else ever had. What the hell did that make him?

A rhetorical question. Shaw knew the answer.

"You lie down with dogs, you get up with fleas," his mother used to say.

Shaw looked away from Lee and fixed his gaze on the eye chart on the wall.

His parents knew he worked for ASIO, but Shaw

told them he was an analyst in the Sydney office. Something with computers, they assumed, and Shaw had never corrected them. They didn't know about the work he really did in the field, the people he associated with — befriended and then betrayed because he was such a clever monster — and Shaw discovered that he shed it all like a second skin the moment he was home again. It was surprisingly easy to do. That had worried Shaw at first. He'd wondered if it made him a sociopath, but then he'd learned not to look that gift horse in the mouth. He only knew it was a very thin line that separated him from men like Vornis, and it had become increasingly blurred. But he was good at his job. That was what he clung to when he couldn't see for all the gray areas: he was good at his job. That was all that mattered.

Somehow, Lee had changed that. Shaw had thrown away his assignment. He'd made a moral decision, and it bothered him. It bothered him that he'd made it at all — the machine knew Lee's life wasn't worth the intel Guterman could have provided — and it bothered him that he'd made it so late. He should have found a boat and got Lee off the island the first time it had occurred to him, the first time he'd allowed the human being to override the machine's programming. All he'd done, in the end, was prolong Lee's suffering.

I'm so fucking sorry, Lee. He squeezed Lee's hand. *I am so fucking sorry.*

Lee flinched under the doc's examination and turned his face away.

CHAPTER SIXTEEN

Two steps back. Shaw could sense the impending crisis.

"What do I say?" Lee asked in a small voice when Shaw set the laptop in front of him. He bit his lip.

Shaw raised his hand before he even realized. Raised it to touch Lee's face, to soothe away Lee's frown, to run his thumb along Lee's lip until his teeth released it. And then what? Well, that was the fucking problem, wasn't it? Neither of them knew where to stop. Shaw moved back. He sat down and leaned his elbows on the table. He smiled slightly. "I dunno, mate. Just tell them you're okay."

This wasn't Shaw's idea. This was the DEA's idea. And Shaw thought that it was bullshit. Two days. Why couldn't they give him two days and let him do this inside a psychologist's office? What difference would two days make to the people who had thought Lee was dead?

Shaw was not qualified for this.

Lee squinted at the screen. He sucked in a breath. "Yeah," he said. "Yeah."

Shaw had read Lee's file that morning, or at least what the DEA had passed on to Callie. Lee Anderson, twenty-four years old, DEA, Denver office. He had been born in Andover, Minnesota. Shaw had been right about his accent.

"What were you doing in Colombia, Lee?" Shaw asked him. He couldn't imagine a Minnesota boy ending up in Colombia via Colorado. Which was a conceit, probably, because Shaw had been born in Ayr, a small town on the north Queensland coast with a population of about eight thousand. But Lee was still so young. Not as young as Shaw had first thought, but still young. He must have been ambitious at one point. He must have been assertive. Shaw couldn't imagine that.

What a difference two months made. Would the people back home even recognize him?

Lee's gaze flicked up from the screen. He looked grateful for the distraction. "*Um,* surveillance."

"I know that." Shaw smiled. "I meant you, specifically."

"Oh." Lee flushed. "I wanted to get more field work. I was on a temporary transfer to the Miami office. It was a joint operation . . ." He bit his lip. "Shit, I don't know if I'm allowed to tell you any of this."

Shaw shrugged. "Nah, I guess not. I was just curious about you. I wondered why you joined the DEA."

"I wanted to be a cop, but . . ." Lee said. A shadow crossed his face and he looked away. "Doesn't matter."

"I wanted to be an astronaut," Shaw told him and waited until Lee looked up again. "But it turns out we don't have those."

Lee rewarded him with a hesitant smile. "So you became James Bond instead?"

"Something like that," Shaw agreed.

Somewhere under there was Lee Anderson, and Shaw was slowly drawing him to the surface. Shaw wanted to see him as a human being, just once, before it was all over. He wanted to know about his life. He wanted to know what sort of person he'd been before Vornis had broken him.

"Write your e-mail," he said gently. "They've already been told you're alive, Lee. They just want to hear it from you."

Lee hunched over. "I don't know what to say."

"It doesn't matter," Lee said. He reached across the table and caught Lee's hand. "Dear Mum and Dad, I'm okay. I'll see you soon. Love, Lee."

"Mum," Lee said and snorted with amusement. "*Mum!*"

Shaw felt his breath catch in his throat. Was that the first time he'd heard anything like a laugh from Lee? Jesus, he wanted to hear it again! He raised his eyebrows. "Are you taking the piss out of my accent?"

"*Mum,*" Lee muttered and then laughed.

Shaw laughed as well. "Okay, *Mom.*"

He saw the moment Lee sank into himself again. The light faded from his eyes, and he pulled his hand away. He hunched his shoulders and stared at the screen of the laptop. "Yeah. Do you think I should say that? Do you think I should say I'm okay?"

Shaw forced an encouraging smile. "I think that's enough for an e-mail. I think anything else you need to tell them should be done face-to-face."

"I guess," Lee said. He closed his eyes for a brief moment. "I didn't think I'd see them again. I was sort of glad."

Shaw didn't say anything. He wondered if Lee was waiting for him to condemn him, to call him selfish or deluded, but Shaw didn't believe in black and white. Shaw existed in shades of gray. Other men painted themselves into idealistic corners, but never Shaw.

"I don't want them to know what happened to me," Lee said at last, his voice strained.

"I know," Shaw said. "You tell them what you think they need to know when you see them, and keep what you need a secret. You look out for yourself first, Lee."

Fuck. That was harsh. For all he knew, Mom and Dad Anderson were the kindest, most loving, most understanding parents on the planet. For all he knew, they both had advanced degrees in psychology. And what was Shaw's stellar advice? Avoidance. That was the best thing about avoidance, though. You got to avoid shit.

You sure you should be giving advice on mental-health coping mechanisms, king of the night terrors?

And there was that look again: full of trust and hope. Shaw hated that look.

"I'm going to tell you something," Shaw said, "and I want you to really try and listen, okay?"

"Okay," Lee murmured.

"When I get home," Shaw said, "to my flat, I mean, not just Sydney, the first thing I'll do is get undressed and get in the shower. And then I'll take the dog for a walk to the dry cleaners. And when I get those clothes back, I won't wear them. I'll put them in a box at the back of my cupboard. Those are my work clothes. Suits, boxers, T-shirts, it doesn't matter. I won't wear them except for work. I won't even look at them. You understand?"

Lee narrowed his eyes. "You mean I should put everything that happened to me in a box in the back of a cupboard?"

"If you have to," Shaw said. "Not forever, not always. Just until you need to take it out again."

Lee wrinkled his nose. "I thought you were James Bond, not Dr. Phil."

"You and me, Lee," Shaw said. "We're out of Dr.

Phil's pay grade."

Lee's lips quirked.

"Everything that happened," Shaw said, "it will always be there. But you have to learn how to put it away. I'm not the same guy I was on that island. That was work, and shit, Lee, I hope you know that. I hope you know that me, the real me, wouldn't have let it go that far."

His heart was thumping. Shit. What was that? He hadn't meant to unburden himself like that. Lee didn't need to have the passenger seat on Shaw's personal guilt trip along with everything else.

"You saved me," Lee said. He blinked in confusion.

Shaw knew his regret showed on his face. "Lee, I could have saved you the night I met you."

Lee shrank back. His mouth worked for a moment, but nothing came. The look on his face, Shaw thought— stricken, trapped—must have been the one Vornis saw in Colombia. The one when Lee came face-to-face with a monster.

Shaw gazed back. *I want you, Lee, but you deserve better. You have to know that. You have to know what I am.*

Someone has to.

"I understand," Lee said at last. "You think I don't, but I do. I know why you waited. I know it was important."

Shaw frowned slightly. "No, you don't understand. I'm not your savior, and I'm sure as hell not your redemption. You need to remember that I let Vornis take you back all those times without a single objection."

"What difference does that make?" Lee scowled, jutting out his chin. "A few more sessions after so many. What difference is it?"

Aggression, Shaw thought; that's interesting.

Shaw folded his arms across his chest. "It doesn't make a difference to you, Lee, not in the long run, but it makes a difference to *us*. You trust me because your head isn't in the right place yet. But when it is, you'll see exactly what went down on that island. At the moment, you don't understand what I mean."

You'll see exactly how I failed you.

"Don't tell me what I'll see," Lee said. He was breathing heavily. "Don't tell me what I'll feel. You are the only one who looked me in the eye in that place. You are the only one who saw *me*. And you saved me."

"I did," Shaw said. "But not soon enough."

Not soon enough to deserve you.

"I don't—" Lee managed, and couldn't finish the thought: *I don't understand.*

Shaw smiled slightly. He'd proven himself right, and there was a sort of a grim satisfaction in that. God knows it was the only satisfaction he warranted out of this whole sorry incident.

Lee chewed on his lower lip, and hell, that was distracting.

"There's something else," he said, keeping his tone gentle.

Lee's brilliant green eyes flicked up and down but not before Shaw saw the tears.

Shaw's stomach churned. "You'll be okay," he said. "You will be. You'll go home, and you'll see your parents, and you'll see a shrink, and you'll be okay. You've done your time, Lee. You get to relax now. You get to have your life back. Any life you want."

Oh, Jesus. He had a sudden vision of Lee, old and fat and happy. And it made him want to laugh. It made him want to be the other old, fat, happy guy in that mental picture. He wanted them to take turns yelling at kids to get off their lawn.

"Maybe . . . maybe it's you that doesn't understand," Lee said, blinking away his tears. "I know you think I'm just a weak kid. I mean, I am, I know that, but you made me stronger. You didn't hurt me. I believed you when you said you'd help me. I didn't expect you to save me. I thought you'd just make a call, like you said, and that was more than I could have hoped for. You think I didn't know what you were risking by telling me you'd help me? I might not have known what you were, but I knew Vornis would kill you as well."

Shaw had no answer for that.

Lee trailed his fingers across the keys of the laptop. "You think he didn't ask me about you? You know what he couldn't get over? The number of times you showered. Know what I told him?"

Shaw shook his head.

"I told him you liked to force my head back and see how long it took before I started to choke under the water." Lee shivered. "He got a kick out of that."

Shaw swallowed with difficulty.

Lee looked up at him. "So don't tell me that I don't understand what was going on. I was your fucking accomplice every time I was with Vornis." He frowned, and his eyes flashed. "And don't ever tell me that you didn't save me, because that is bullshit!"

"Okay," Shaw said. Lee's sudden fierceness surprised him. He reached out and took Lee's hand again. "Okay, Lee."

Lee pulled his hand back quickly, like he'd been stung. He breathed heavily for a moment. His teeth were clenched, and there was a tic in his jaw. "Don't do that."

"Okay," Shaw said again. He fought to keep his face impassive.

Lee swallowed. "I just mean, when you touch me, I want more."

Holy shit. From any other guy in any other circumstances, Shaw would have been flashing a cocky grin: *I know it!* But this wasn't right. This whole conversation had been a mistake. It wasn't Lee's job to soothe Shaw's conscience, and it wasn't fair of Shaw to put this shit on him now. He should have just shut his mouth until Sydney and walked away. Because that was all that could happen. "Write your e-mail."

Lee nodded, relaxing his jaw. "Okay."

Shaw looked away.

He'd chosen this job. And he'd been good at it, until Lee. And he'd always known that with this job there were things he couldn't have. Normal things. And it hadn't bothered him, not really. Until Lee.

* * * * *

"Huh," was all Zev said when he came by Shaw's cabin later that night and found Lee asleep in Shaw's bunk. "Come for a cigarette with me, Shaw."

Shaw rose from the chair he'd been dozing in and stretched. He didn't really care what Zev thought. Lee needed the reassurance of Shaw's company, as simple as that. If he slept better in Shaw's cabin, what of it? It was no business of anyone's.

Except it would be, in Sydney.

Shaw sighed and followed Zev outside. Zev's escort was waiting in the hallway. He looked young and spotty enough to still be a teenager.

"Get lost, kid," Zev said. "Shoo!"

Shaw nodded at the kid. "I'll make sure he doesn't steal the silverware."

"Yes, sir." The kid vanished.

Zev rolled his eyes. "What if you tell the captain I am a perfectly nice spy and not at all planning on building a machine to control the weather?"

"His boat, his rules," Shaw told him.

They headed up on deck.

Shaw sniffed the salt air. He loved the Pacific. It had always felt like home. The stars were brilliant. They felt close enough that Shaw imagined he could reach up and snag them with his fingertips.

"Are you gonna ask me why Lee's sleeping in my bunk?" Shaw leaned on the rail.

Zev shrugged as he lit a cigarette. "Seems like that's none of my business now." He exhaled pale smoke that was lost in the night air. "You know what I don't like about this work?"

Jesus, where to start? Shaw could think of a hundred things.

"I get homesick," Zev said. "And then, when I get home, I get restless."

Shaw nodded. He knew that contradictory feeling well.

"My wife is a schoolteacher," Zev said. "I don't think I've ever told you that."

"I didn't even know you were married," Shaw said.

"I would show you a picture, if I could carry one," Zev said. "She's my other half, I tell people, but it's not true."

Shaw raised his eyebrows.

"I wish she was," Zev said. "But my other half is whoever they tell me it is. Do you understand?"

"Yeah," Shaw said, wishing he didn't.

"I can't tell my wife about my work," Zev said. "And I think that if I did, I would not like the way she would look at me. And then I think I should have married someone else in my line of work, and then I wonder if I would be able to look at her without always wondering. So I tell myself I am very happy with my schoolteacher wife, and she tells herself she doesn't need to know what I do."

Shaw felt regret close in on him. Was that what he had to look forward to? A life of shared solitude, if he was lucky?

"You should get out while you can," Zev said.

His frankness surprised Shaw. He felt his stomach clench. "Maybe."

This was Zev's idea of a pep talk, he supposed. It was probably kinder than the one he'd get from his boss. Frank's would probably go something like, *Don't let the door hit you on the arse on the way out.* It surprised him, coming from Zev. Zev was a consummate professional, or at least that was the impression he gave. Shaw supposed he should have stopped being surprised by the impressions people gave years ago.

He didn't know Zev that well. They'd met a few times before, but crossed paths undercover only once before the island. Pakistan, Shaw remembered. Shaw had been posing as a journalist, and he'd hated it. That was a line he didn't like to cross, but it had been short notice and only a week. Still, he hated knowing that every time a journalist was accused of being a spy, it was because of men like him.

Zev had been posing as a businessman, and they'd met at a restaurant in Islamabad. Zev had shaken Shaw's hand enthusiastically and introduced him to the men he was dining with. Coffee and cigars and aliases, Shaw remembered. It had all been very congenial, and then they'd gone their separate ways. Shaw still had no idea what Zev had been doing there, and it was probably mutual.

And once, Shaw had seen Zev torture a man.

Shaw had hardly known Zev before he'd put his trust in him in Vornis's dungeon. It occurred to him for the first time that he'd taken a leap of faith after all, as desperate as the one Lee had taken.

Shaw looked down into the black water.

"What happened back there," Zev said, "was a bloodbath. When I'm not smoking, my hands are shaking."

Shaw looked at his face in the darkness, wondering if it was true. He was never sure with Zev.

"Lucky for you," Zev said calmly, "there's a boy in your cabin who saw the whole thing and still wants to be in your bunk."

"He won't," Shaw said with certainty. "Not once he's back home."

Zev only shrugged and watched the smoke from his cigarette curl away into the darkness.

* * * * *

It was what it was, Shaw thought later. It was two days of artificial happiness. They were adrift on the Pacific, just as he'd always imagined, and it felt right. Lee felt right. He was coming out of his shell. He was smiling. He was relaxing. Shaw wished it could last forever, but he knew better than that.

On the final day, Shaw watched the approaching coastline with a strange mixture of relief and regret. It was good to be home, even if he'd be walking into what Callie had called a shit storm. And he knew he wouldn't see Lee again. That felt like the biggest waste of all. He was only just starting to know Lee.

He was a baseball fan. That was no surprise, probably, but the night before, they'd sat in front of the TV with some of the crew and watched a few hours of cricket.

"I have no fucking idea what's going on here," Lee had announced at last, watching the animated duck stalk along the bottom of the screen as the batsman was dismissed. "This doesn't make any sense."

"At least when we have a world series, we're not the only country in it," Shaw had told him.

"The World Series was named after a newspaper," Lee had informed him. "At least we don't play for ashes!"

Lee gave as good as he got, and Shaw liked that. If he'd met him under different circumstances, he would have wanted to get to know him just for that. It didn't have to be about beauty and brokenness and protection. It could have been about laughter and desire. Shaw wished they'd met as equals. He wished they could have fucked as equals. It felt like Lee was finding his way again, taking back control, but it was too late for Shaw. Every hour that passed was one less hour they had.

"He's doing well, I think," the doc had told Shaw. "I mean, he'll need psychiatric help, but he's doing okay for now."

"Did he tell you what happened?" Shaw asked curiously.

The doctor shook his head. "No, but he didn't have to. It's written all over him."

Lee liked television. They were close enough to pick up the broadcasts from the Australian commercial channels, and Shaw had found Lee sitting in the rec room at three o'clock in the morning watching an old rerun of *Spyforce*.

"Is this what you do?" he asked Shaw with a smile.

"Yeah." Shaw laughed. "I just got back from blowing up the Burma railroad."

"Hey, turns out we didn't need to help out at all in the war," Lee told him. "You guys had it covered."

"Oh, we needed the help, I'll admit," Shaw told him. "And you were only three years late."

Shaw gave as good as he got as well, and he liked the way it made Lee's eyes light up. Letting him go would hurt.

Zev, who spent his time on deck smoking and doing crosswords, looked at Shaw curiously when he saw him with Lee. It was the same look he'd given Shaw several times back on the island: *What are you planning?*

Shaw hadn't had a plan back on the island, and he sure as hell didn't have one now.

The final day on the HMAS *Stuart* was a flurry of activity for the crew. They scrubbed and swabbed and worked furiously. By the time they entered the harbor, the crew was lined up on the deck in brilliant white dress uniforms. Other boats sounded their horns in greeting, welcoming them home.

White, Shaw had always thought, was such an impractical color for a uniform of any sort. But they looked good as they entered the harbor.

Sydney Harbour was the most beautiful harbor in the world. Shaw had never seen anything to rival it. It was the world's largest natural harbor. It glittered. Shaw felt an ache when he saw the familiar arch of the Harbour Bridge rising up in front of them and the Opera House gleaming like a shell on Bennelong Point. That was Sydney's real triumph: postcard views from every angle.

Shaw looked at the sun gleaming off the bridge. He was home, he was alive, but he ached.

"It's beautiful," Lee said, leaning on the rail beside him.

"Yeah." Shaw felt it again: regret. There would be no more quiet moments like these between them. He wondered if Lee had realized it. Every minute that brought them closer to the port pushed them further apart.

Shaw wanted to reach out for Lee. Couldn't. He fixed his gaze on the sunlight gleaming on the water and let it blind him. He thought hard about not touching Lee. He shifted, and their shoulders bumped together, and that was it. That was probably the last time they would touch.

Don't. Don't.

The sun burned the back of his neck as he stared at the water.

There were families waiting on the dock. Wives and husbands and children. And, Shaw saw, a fiery little redhead with an excited yellow Lab on a lead. Shaw smiled at that, even as he felt a tug of sadness. There was his life, waiting for him, and there was no room in it for Lee.

Lee shifted closer to him, nervous at all the people. "What happens now?"

"You'll be okay," Shaw said.

They didn't have any luggage. They didn't have anything except their borrowed clothes. They let the crew go first, down to the waiting smiles and tears and hugs.

Zev lit a cigarette on the gangway. "Where's our next ride?"

Shaw could see it. Behind all the happy families there was a cluster of dark sedans and men in suits and sunglasses. None of them were smiling.

Lee tried to take his hand when they reached the dock, and Shaw shook his head.

He could hear Lee breathing heavily. He was terrified.

"Agent Shaw?" A cheap suit pushed an ID in his face. "John Meyers. United States Embassy."

Shaw shook his hand.

"Mr. Anderson," Meyers said. "Welcome to Sydney."

Lee swallowed and nodded.

Meyers opened the car door. "Come with me, please."

Lee looked at Shaw anxiously, and Shaw forced a smile. "Good luck, mate."

"I want to stay with you," Lee whispered. "Please."

Shaw felt his chest constrict. *Oh Jesus, Lee, don't. Not now.*

"Please, Shaw," Lee said. His green eyes were wide. His breath caught in his throat. "Please, can't I stay with you?"

Shaw felt the disapproving gazes of the embassy officials turned on him. Disapproving and maybe disgusted. Should have seen how pitiful he was a week ago, Shaw wanted to tell them, but Lee didn't deserve that.

"You'll be okay," Shaw told him firmly. He hated himself when Lee looked at him, *trusted* him, and nodded. Shaw kept his smile until Meyers had bundled Lee into the car and let it fade again as they drove away toward the main gates.

He wondered where they were taking him. Some hotel in the city, probably. He hoped they'd let him sleep, at least, and not attack him with questions immediately. Nine weeks ago, Lee had been with the DEA in Colombia. Now he wasn't the same person anymore, and Shaw hoped they'd go easy on him.

Shaw frowned. Why was he even worrying about Lee anymore? He had his own problems. It was supposed to have been infiltration, not a bloodbath. However he looked at it, Shaw knew he'd fucked up. The intel alone he could have got from Guterman and the others was easily worth the cost of Lee's life. The worst part was, he didn't regret saving Lee. He just didn't know how he was going to justify it to his bosses.

The night before, after *Spyforce*, Lee had found an old rerun of *I Love Lucy. Lucy, you've got some 'splainin to do!*

Shaw knew that feeling.

"That kid's got Stockholm Syndrome," Zev announced, dropping his cigarette butt on the ground and standing on it. He looked at Shaw curiously. "Unless he doesn't."

"Shut up, Zev," Shaw told him. What the hell was wrong with him? Why didn't he want to let Lee go? He couldn't keep him, couldn't fix him, so why did he even want to try?

Zev clapped him on the back. "You're an odd one, my friend."

"How's that?" Shaw asked as they pushed their way back through the small crowd toward Callie and Molly.

"You blew your operation to save that American," Zev said. "You stood up to a room full of killers for that kid, outran armed security patrols, and escaped an island for him, but just now you didn't tell Meyers to go and fuck himself."

"Well, I wasn't sure you'd back me this time."

Zev clapped him on the back again. "It didn't stop you before."

Before, Shaw thought, was a different world with different rules: a world full of gods and monsters, life and death, judges and executioners. None of that worked here. It didn't even feel real. Here, Shaw was a middle-grade public servant with a mortgage and a daily commute. He put the other side of him away when he was home. Callie hadn't come to meet the man Shaw had been on the island.

Callie's face lit up with a brilliant smile as Shaw approached. She tugged Molly forward to meet him. She flung her arms around Shaw's neck and squeezed. Her hair tickled his face. "Welcome home."

A wave of relief caught him.

"Thanks, Cal." Shaw held her for a moment.

"You okay?" she murmured in his ear.

"Yeah." Shaw released her and knelt down. He opened his arms, and they were suddenly full of dog; wriggling, squirming, tail thrashing, tongue everywhere, the whole package ready to burst with excitement. "Hey, Molly!"

This was good. This was right. He was home, his girls had come to meet him, and Lee would be okay. Shaw would shake this off, same as always.

He didn't have to turn around and see if the dark sedan was still in sight. He didn't have to think about Lee. He was home, he was covered in dog hair and slobber, and in that sea of happy reunions beside the dock, he had no right to want more.

CHAPTER SEVENTEEN

Three months later

What's the first thing you remember?

It was difficult to sleep without the sound of the ocean. The endless sigh, back and forth; white noise that drowned everything else, that swept it all away. The ocean and the moonlight and the unfamiliar stars. Strange that he'd slept so well there.

The sheets itched. They smelled of laundry powder.

There were no insects here, buzzing in the night. No breath of wind. No salt on his lips.

You shouldn't miss the place where they ruined you.

It was the quiet moments Lee missed. Those moments when his body was racked with pain, those moments of fear and horror, all of them had left him open to the stillness afterwards. To the ocean and the night and to Shaw. He'd never slept as deeply anywhere as on that last week on the island, and that was fucked-up.

He couldn't sleep now. He hadn't been able to, not since getting back. Not at night. Now he lay awake and counted the hours until dawn, trying to relearn the rhythms of his childhood home.

His dad usually watched television until eleven. The third step creaked when he walked upstairs to bed. That third step had creaked forever. Lee remembered how he'd had to dodge it when he was sneaking out of the house as a teenager. Straight out into the night, breathless with exhilaration, because nothing scared him back then. Now he was a hostage to every nightmare in the world.

Except for those quite moments on the island. He'd had nothing to lose there, nothing left to fear. Nothing except a glimmering thread of hope, the sound of the ocean, and Shaw sleeping beside him. Now, every step he climbed toward recovery, he was afraid he had further to fall. He wouldn't survive that again. He couldn't.

And it was irrational. He knew that. It wasn't going to happen to him again, but *something* would. What if his dad had a heart attack? He hadn't been watching his cholesterol lately. What if his mom was in a car wreck? She never paid enough attention when she was driving. Tornados, disease, crime, and plain dumb luck: Lee was afraid of it all these days. Everything was so fucking fragile, and he felt it most acutely at night.

His scars hurt. The skin felt too tight across his back where his welts had healed. There was some muscle damage as well, and he had a list of exercises he was supposed to do and an appointment with a physical therapist every two weeks. Between that and the regular appointments with the psychiatrist and the psychologist, Lee felt he might as well be living in Minneapolis, he spent so much time driving there. Well, his dad drove. He always found some excuse to go into the city on the same day as Lee's appointments. He'd even closed up the hardware store one morning, which was stupid. Lee didn't need a chaperone.

His dad had asked him to come back and work in the store, like he had when he was a kid. Lee had refused. He wasn't ready to face people yet. Not people who were his dad's long-standing customers and who'd gone to Lee's memorial service. Shit, no. He felt enough like a ghost already.

The day after he'd arrived home, he'd found a card shoved in the drawer of the bureau in the dining room. His parents must have missed it when they'd thrown the others away. *In deepest sympathy.* He'd felt a sick thrill when he'd opened it and hadn't known whether to feel invincible or like an interloper. They'd mourned him. Not for long, but it didn't matter. Coming back, he didn't know if he was the answer to his parents' prayers or their worst nightmare—a broken thing that had crawled out of a grave.

They kept finding excuses to touch him, as though they were assuring themselves he was really there. If he was, he didn't feel it. He wanted to be better; he wanted to be healed. He was sick of feeling like a stranger in the house he'd grown up in.

What's the first thing you remember?

The question was instinctive in him now, and he hated it. He should have been able to shed it now he'd left the island, now he no longer needed it, but it always came back to him at night.

Stop it. You're home; you're safe.

The psychiatrist had prescribed sleeping pills and antianxiety meds, and Lee still couldn't sleep at night. He slept during the day instead, on the couch in front of the television, but not at night. Never at night. At night, he was watchful.

Lee looked at the patterns of shadow and moonlight on the ceiling. They were fading. It would be morning soon. The sunlight would creep in the window, and gradually the room would brighten, and at seven o'clock, he would hear Mr. Keller rattling past in his old truck, and then the day would begin.

He snaked his arm out from under the covers and squinted to read his watch. Five-thirty. An hour and a half to go, and then he could stop pretending he was sleeping and get out of bed.

"He's sleeping so much," his mom had said on the phone to someone the day before.

Not true, Mom. He got a couple of hours in during the day, and that was it. At night, he lay awake and tortured himself with his memories, but his parents didn't know that.

"Come on, why are you torturing yourself?" Shaw had asked him on the ship. Frigate. Whatever.

"Got no one else to do it for me now."

That was fucked-up as well. Everything was fucked-up. His life and his parents' lives. When was the last time his dad had kept the store open late like he used to? And his mom had quit her job. Just quit, like the past twenty-five years didn't matter. She'd always talked of retiring. She'd mentioned it again at Christmas, but she'd talked about it like it was at some indeterminate, distant point in the future, because she loved teaching those kids. She'd done it so long that she was teaching her kids' kids. She loved it. She always had, and now it was gone.

No more finger-painted pictures on the refrigerator: *I love you, Mrs. Anderson.*

No more lopsided cookies or cupcakes with the frosting sliding off. *"I made this for you, Mrs. Anderson."*

No more shy trick-or-treaters on Halloween, peeking out from behind their masks. *"It's me, Mrs. Anderson!"*

And Lee had taken all of that away from her.

Lee had tried to ask them about money. The shop wasn't doing great anyway, not with the chain store just a couple of miles away, and now his mom wasn't earning.

His dad had waved the question away. *"We're doing fine, Lee. You concentrate on* you, *okay?"*

Lee was sick of concentrating on himself. He'd lived in his head for eight fucking weeks on the island. He didn't want to do it anymore. Sometimes he wished he could just go to sleep and never wake up.

That, Doctor Fisher said, was passive suicidal ideation.

"Do you want to hurt yourself?" she had asked him at one of their earlier sessions.

No. Not exactly. He couldn't do that to his parents, not after everything. But would he care if he accidentally walked in front of a truck? He didn't know. He wanted it to be over, that was all, over for good. He was sick of these long nights that stretched out forever. He was sick of not sleeping. He was sick of always feeling like shit.

He closed his eyes as he heard his bedroom door squeak open. One of his parents checking on him. A moment later, it closed again.

Apparently, nobody was sleeping at night these days. He rolled over, the scars on his back tightening and itching, and shoved the pillow over his head.

Everybody just wanted to help, and it was so fucking cloying.

God, he felt like he was five years old again. Every time he turned around, one of his parents was there. It was like they didn't trust him to be alone for five minutes. They'd been like this ever since Doctor Fisher had given him the booklet on Acute Stress Disorder and PTSD to take home and his dad had found it. Lee wished he'd thrown it out instead, because now his parents treated him like they were afraid he was going to break or snap. And it wasn't fair on any of them. Moving back home had been a mistake. He should have stayed in Denver, although it was stupid to think he could have slipped straight back into his old life like nothing had happened. Lee knew there were things he needed to work out first. He needed time. And he probably needed space as well. Coming back to Andover, to the house he'd grown up in, had been a mistake.

His relationship with his parents had never been worse. It threatened to smother him. His mom hadn't retired, Lee realized. She'd just traded teaching for full-time suicide watch.

He closed his eyes and lay there, and nothing happened. He was tired, but nothing happened. He couldn't sleep.

What's the first thing you remember?

Maybe he should pick up one of those white-noise machines and see if that helped. That seemed like an eminently practical thing to do, and something Doctor Fisher would approve of. Doctor Fisher was always encouraging him to find coping strategies, to identify his triggers, and to celebrate the small steps forward without dwelling on those times he'd jumped two steps back without realizing.

Or ten steps, like the time his mom had screamed when she'd caught him getting out of the shower and seen his scars. And at the time, all Lee could think was: *Well, now you know why I'm wearing long-sleeved shirts these days, Mom.* Afterward, though, he'd retreated to his bedroom and sat in the closet for hours. And he hadn't done that since he was seven and throwing a stupid tantrum. Weird.

He realized only much later that it wasn't about his bedroom closet at all. It was about the closet in Vornis's house where he'd slept on that filthy mattress. It was about the tiny prison that was his sanctuary before Shaw. And after, apparently. At least it had given him and Doctor Fisher something to talk about.

That night, his dad had taken him aside. *"The scars, Lee. What did the doctor say about those? Should you be doing anything for them? The ones you can't reach, I mean."*

His dad meant applying cream to soften them, Lee had supposed.

"We've talked about dermabrasion and maybe surgery. I can't have anyone touch them, Dad, not now, okay?" He hadn't been able to look at his dad when he answered. *He knows I was whipped. He knows I was burned. They both know, and they can probably guess the rest.*

The scars itched at night when they rubbed against his sheets. They pulled when he moved, and he couldn't imagine they would ever be better. He couldn't imagine *he* would ever be better.

"It's a process, Lee," Doctor Fisher always said.

Well, he was sick of the fucking process.

Lee thumped the pillow and squinted at his watch again. It wasn't even six yet. There was still an hour to go until Mr. Keller's truck roared past and the day could begin. Physical therapy in the morning, and Doctor Fisher in the afternoon. Another full day of staring his memories in the face, of dissecting them in front of strangers.

His throat ached with tears. Fuck, he was so sick of this. At least on the island, he'd always been able to sleep after they tortured him. Seemed like a fair trade-off now.

What's the first thing you remember?

The sound of the ocean.

Shaw.

This.

* * * * *

He was tired. His whole body ached with it. If he

closed his eyes, he thought he'd just drift off, and that would be okay. That would be nice. Except he was in the middle of a session with Doctor Fisher.

"I should be happy, right?" Lee asked, passing a hand in front of his stinging eyes. "My blood tests came back clean, and that's a fucking miracle."

"It's good news," Doctor Fisher said. She leaned back in her chair. "You say 'should' a lot, Lee. I wonder if you've noticed that."

"Do I?" He glanced at the windows. Looked like a nice day outside.

"I *should* be happy. I *should* be better. I *should* be able to get on with my life," Doctor Fisher said. "These things don't have a timeline. It's a process."

Lee shrugged.

"Did you go out last night?" Doctor Fisher asked him.

Lee nodded, wondering if she could smell the alcohol still on him, or if it was something they'd talked about last week. Something they thought he might be ready to try. "Yeah, to a club."

"And how did that go?"

"Badly," Lee admitted. He'd hated the thump of the bass and the press of strangers' bodies. The strobe lights had made him nauseated, and he'd drunk too much. That was a habit he needed to break before it became an issue, he knew, but he hadn't found a reason to stop yet. "I keep thinking that if I can get laid and get it over with, it'll be okay."

"Is that what you thought on the ship?"

Frigate, Lee thought automatically. *The crew gets shitty if you call it the wrong thing.* He studied the pattern of the carpet for a moment. "I guess."

"Sex isn't a hurdle you need to jump, Lee," Doctor Fisher said.

"Well, I didn't," Lee said. "I had a few drinks with some guy, but I chickened out."

The look on the guy's face had made him anxious. He'd looked at Lee like he was just a hot body, which had been the whole point of the fucking exercise, but he'd freaked out about it. He'd muttered his apologies and got the hell out of there. The guy had been too predatory. A few months ago that would have been a turn-on. Now it made him want to be sick. He'd almost had a panic attack right there in the club. He'd had all the symptoms: sweaty palms, elevated heart rate, and the constricting pressure in his chest that was the weight of his own fear.

Panic attack. It sounded almost mild. The reality was completely different.

He'd had one full-blown attack before, a few weeks ago now when he'd heard Mr. Keller's truck rattling up the street and the association had taken him straight back to the island, to the session where he'd hallucinated home. *It's not real! You're still in that room!* He hadn't been able to breathe. He'd thought he was having a heart attack. He'd been sure he was dying. It had been terrifying. His mom had called the paramedics.

Lee looked toward the window again. His dad was waiting outside for him, just like last week and the week before that. This time, he'd made up some bullshit story about needing to come into the city to drop his printer off to be repaired, as though there was nowhere in Andover that did that.

Rob. That was the guy's name from the club. Rob, like steal or take. Like force. And he probably wasn't a bad guy, but Lee had been too afraid to risk it. Anyway, what would Rob have said when he took his clothes off? He would have asked what happened, anyone would ask, and all those scars would have turned him off. And if they hadn't, if he'd been the type of guy who wasn't turned off by scars, then it would have been even worse. Lee wondered if that was his only option now: some sadistic freak who was turned on by marks of torture. Vornis had ruined sex and relationships for him forever. He'd managed to destroy Lee's life without killing him. He was probably smiling in hell.

Maybe it would have been better if he'd died on the island. Passive suicidal ideation. Lee recognized it now.

"I'm not sleeping," Lee said. It all came out in a rush when he let it. "I hate the way my parents treat me. I feel like a kid. I feel like I'm climbing the walls. I need some space, I need to get away sometimes, and I don't even have my fucking car."

His car was still in Denver. His whole life was still in Denver, and he wasn't sure he wanted it back. Could he really walk into the DEA office there like nothing had happened? Or, worse, acknowledge to all his colleagues that something had? It's not like it would be in the staff newsletter, but Lee knew how it would go. Everyone would find out sooner or later, if they didn't already know.

Lee liked Doctor Fisher. He hated his sessions, but he liked her.

He raised his eyes and looked at her. She was wearing the same even, nonjudgmental look she always did. The light gleamed on her square glasses as Lee looked at her. He looked at the carpet again. "I think I want to quit my job."

"Now may not be the time to make those sort of big decisions, Lee," Doctor Fisher told him, "but it's certainly something you can think about. What would you do if you didn't go back to the DEA?"

And that was the problem right there. He shrugged.

He couldn't stay in Andover forever, and he didn't want to go back to Denver. Was it because the island had broken him that he didn't want his old life back? Or had it given him something completely unexpected — clarity? Maybe it wasn't an admission of failure that he couldn't just pick up the pieces of his life like nothing had happened. Maybe another man would have made a different decision: *I won't let those bastards beat me.* But did it have to be about victory and defeat? Maybe it was time he thought about what he really wanted in life instead, and it wasn't his job. Because life was too short for regrets. Shit, if he'd learned anything, wasn't that it? He couldn't tell.

He looked at the window again, the carpet again, and then back to Doctor Fisher. Admission time. "I miss Shaw."

"That's not surprising," Doctor Fisher told him. "We've talked a little about that before. We've also talked about how post-traumatic stress disorder actually changes the chemical balance in your brain. It physically changes the way that you think. This is why it's important that you don't make any big decisions now."

Like she was worried he was going to jump straight on a plane and head for Australia. Jesus, his head might have been fucked-up, but Lee still wasn't that stupid. Shaw deserved better. Shaw deserved someone who was as strong as he was, as brave, not some emotional cripple with scars all over his body.

"Did you masturbate this week?" Doctor Fisher asked him.

That was another thing. A few months ago, the thought of having to answer a question like that would have made him squirm. Not now, though. This was sex for him now: something horrible, something frightening, and at best something clinical.

"Twice," he said.

"Do you remember what you thought of?" Doctor Fisher asked.

"You," Lee said, his mouth quirking. "Sorry, that sounds sick, right? I mean, I thought about how you'd ask me about it, then I got on with it."

She smiled at that.

Lee glanced at the window. "I thought about Shaw. About fucking Shaw. Like we did the second time, when it was good."

Although, not exactly good. If it had been good, Shaw would have wanted to do it again before Sydney. They'd both come, but it hadn't been enough. And Lee couldn't blame Shaw for that. Shit, who wanted someone who cried when they came? Who wanted someone that broken? Lee wouldn't have, and that was what he was reduced to now. Someone so screwed up, so desperate and needy, that it was more trouble than it was worth to fuck him. He hated himself for that.

For that and for so much else.

"Did you enjoy it?"

Lee closed his eyes briefly. "Sort of, I guess. But my brain got in the way, and I started to think about Vornis."

"You must like that, boy; you're getting hard."

Fear, Doctor Fisher had told him, sometimes provoked the same biological reaction. And sometimes, Lee knew, when people were assholes, they made you like a thing just so they could throw it back in your face. Just so you were an accomplice in your own torture. So it was never just Shaw when he jerked off in the shower. Now it was a race against time: *Think of Shaw. Think of him and come before Vornis gets here. Hurry!*

There was no part of him that Vornis hadn't ruined, no corner of his mind that it was safe to hide in.

"It's my head," he told the carpet. "It's been

fucked-up since Colombia."

"It's your survival mechanism," Doctor Fisher told him. "It's part of your lizard brain. Logic and rational thought don't come into it. Your brain got you through eight weeks of hell, Lee, where you were reduced to one thing only: the need to survive. All of those coping mechanisms you developed, all of those chemical changes, they served their purpose, because here you are talking to me."

"I hate my lizard brain," Lee muttered.

"It's more powerful than we give it credit for," Doctor Fisher said.

"Except it wasn't my brain that got me off the island," Lee said. "It was Shaw."

"You stayed alive," Doctor Fisher said. "Don't underestimate that."

"And it wasn't my lizard brain that said to trust him," Lee said. He picked at a thread in the hem of his shirt and frowned. "I don't know what that was. It wasn't instinct; it was very much a conscious choice. It was because of the way his face changed when he looked out at the ocean. It was because he had bad dreams. He didn't seem like a monster. I mean, he talked like one, but he never acted like one. Not to me."

"It's not uncommon to develop feelings for the person who saves your life."

Lee shrugged. "Except I developed these feelings before he saved my life."

"You developed a strong emotional attachment to the one man who didn't torture you," Doctor Fisher said in her quiet, steady voice. No judgment, no censure, just concern. "And that was the smart thing to do. That was what you needed to do, on the island. But you're safe now. Do you think that it could in any way be an even relationship?"

Maybe that's what I was thinking on the ship. Fucked that up as well.

"I don't know," Lee said. He rubbed his temples. "I mean, you say don't make any big decisions. You say my brain isn't working properly, and I know that, but what if it was real? If I can't trust my logic, how about this: do you throw away a six-year assignment to save the life of a guy you don't even know?"

"Maybe," Doctor Fisher said. "If you're a moral person."

"I don't think morality comes into it," Lee said. "Not for people in that work." He sighed. "I just want to know, I guess. I want to know if the one person who looked me in the eye when I was at my worst could still do it now."

Doctor Fisher didn't say anything.

Lee sighed. "How will I know when I'm better?"

"It's a process, Lee," Doctor Fisher said quietly. "It's going to take time, and it's going to take work. Do you feel better compared to last week?"

He shrugged.

"Well, you went out to a club," Doctor Fisher said. "That's something you wouldn't have done a month ago."

"It didn't exactly go well."

"Do you remember what we said about celebrating the small victories?" Doctor Fisher asked him. "This is important. You took a big step. You should be proud of that."

Lee leaned back in his chair. "I don't think I want to go to clubs anymore. I don't think I want to go back to my job. I don't think I want to try and be the person I was before the island, because it will always be a lie. I was an arrogant asshole, you know. I thought I owned the fucking world."

"You're young." Doctor Fisher smiled. "You're smart. You're good-looking. I think most people would agree that you owned the world. We all did when we were twenty-four."

"I was wrong," Lee said. He rubbed the whorl of scar tissue near his throat and thought of Vornis. "I don't even recognize that guy anymore. Shit, last night I didn't even want to get into the taxi because I saw the way the driver frowned at me when he saw me coming out of a gay club. The guy I was would have been dry humping some random stranger in the back seat, and to hell with what the asshole driver thought."

Doctor Fisher's smile grew. "I'd like to meet that guy one day, Lee."

"I'm fairly certain he's gone." Lee sighed. "It's easy to be brave when you've got nothing to be scared about."

"Don't sell yourself short," Doctor Fisher said. "Not now, and not then."

Lee sighed again. "Yeah, I know. It's my brain, right? I'm just sick of feeling like I'm not getting anywhere with this."

"You are," Doctor Fisher said. "You're taking bigger steps than you realize."

Lee looked at his watch and thought of his dad waiting in the parking lot, and the long, awkward drive home.

Doctor Fisher looked at her watch as well. "Okay, then. Homework for this week."

Lee smiled at that.

"You're going to write down all the steps you take, however small you think they are, and next week we'll discuss them all."

"One foot in front of the other," Lee murmured.

One sand dollar and then another.

CHAPTER EIGHTEEN

"Thank you, Mr. Shaw," said the woman. "You're excused."

Shaw gathered up his notes and walked outside. He sat in the foyer and looked out at the miserable weather. Another cold, gray, gloomy Canberra day. He'd liked the city once, when he'd been young and naive enough to be impressed by the dense population of power brokers, politicians, and public servants. Canberra was the heart of the nation, or at least it told itself that. The rest of the nation seemed to get along just fine without it.

And there was a reason Shaw worked out of the Sydney office. Canberra had to be the most boring city in the world, once the initial glow wore off. Trying to find somewhere open for dinner after nine p.m.? Good luck with that. No, fly-in, fly-out was how Shaw liked it now.

And now here he was again, staying in a dull, three-star hotel with Callie, missing Molly, until the end of the inquiry. And an inquiry headed by politicians, of all people. It had taken the first week just to get them *au fait* with the acronyms ASIO used. Shaw still wasn't convinced some of them knew what ASIO stood for. It had been hard not to let his contempt show. Politicians didn't care about national security. They only pulled that card out when it came to refugees arriving on boats. They didn't know the real thing when it bit them, and they were completely out of their depth here.

It felt like a Star Chamber deal. Shaw recognized one or two of the faces sitting in judgment of him, and he was fairly certain they didn't like him. And the rest? No fucking clue. Faceless bureaucrats. They were the real authority here, and that shouldn't have rankled so much. What was Shaw himself but a faceless bureaucrat?

Shaw sighed. It was raining again. Why was winter in Canberra always so miserable? It rained, and the only time it stopped raining was when it actually snowed. Jesus, it was enough to make him wish he was still on that Fijian island.

"Why the long face?" a voice asked him.

Shaw looked up and smiled. "Zev! Are you a part of this circus as well?"

"Trained seal," Zev said, slapping his hands together and yelping.

It attracted the attention of others in the lobby.

"What are you going to say?" Shaw asked.

"I'm going to be silent and mysterious," Zev said. "But I thought, with your permission, that I'd remind them that your country has very strong ties with the U.S., and that maybe it wasn't such a bad idea to rescue one of their DEA agents. The Americans will like that."

Shaw nodded. "The Americans will like that."

"I already blamed you at my inquiry," Zev said with a quick grin. "The least I can do is spin a new tale in there."

"I'd appreciate that," Shaw said.

A woman flittered out into the foyer. "Mr. Hirsch? Mr. Ari Hirsch?"

"Showtime," Zev said, and headed inside.

Zev was inside for less than an hour. Shaw doubted that was long enough to rehabilitate his reputation, but

Zev gave him a wink as he sailed outside to the car that was waiting for him.

Shaw flicked through his notes again. There was nothing new in there. Either the government would support his decision to scupper an entire six-year operation to save Lee, or they wouldn't. And worrying about it wouldn't change the outcome.

Callie sighed as she sank into the seat next to him. Her face was pinched with cold. She'd been outside to use her phone.

"How's Molly?" Shaw asked. He didn't really trust Callie's latest boyfriend to dog-sit. *Latest* boyfriend. That made her sound like there was a queue of them lined up around the block or something , which was unfair.

"She's fine." Callie brushed her curls back behind her ears. She'd been going for a severe bob the last time she'd had her hair cut but failed to take the curls into account. "Steve wants to know if we can keep her all the time."

"Over my dead body," Shaw murmured.

Callie raised her eyebrows. "Well, that was always the plan."

Shaw snorted and found a newspaper to read. He heard the automatic doors roll open but didn't bother look up.

"Shaw?"

Shaw recognized the voice before he recognized Lee. His dark hair had grown into the soft curls he had imagined it would. He wasn't pale anymore. He had a healthy glow and no bags under his eyes. He'd filled out a bit. He looked good. And God, he'd *missed* him. It all flooded back in an instant.

"Jesus, Lee!" He stood, stuck out his hand, and

caught an eyeful of the sour faces of Lee's escorts. A man and a woman, but they were cut from the exact same mold. They both wore sunglasses and dark suits with American flag pins on the lapels.

Lee shook his hand. "Good to see you, Shaw."

"You too. You look good." Fuck, was he gushing? That sounded a lot like gushing.

Lee smiled hesitantly and wiped his hand on his jacket. He was nervous, Shaw realized. It wasn't his job on the line, but they were going to make him relive it all inside that room.

"Yeah," Lee said. His brows drew together in a frown, and Shaw resisted the urge to reach out and smooth it away. "I didn't recognize you in a suit."

Shaw shrugged. "No. You either. Good luck in there, hey?"

"Thanks."

Lee allowed his escorts to draw him off to the side. He sat in a seat, staring at the carpet and jiggling his leg until his name was called.

Shaw watched him go. He heard the doors to the chamber open and close and wondered what Lee would say about him.

"Cute," Callie murmured.

Shaw made a face. He read the newspaper again, never more conscious than now of the clock ticking slowly on the wall. What the hell were they asking him in there? What Shaw had done? He didn't care about that. What Vornis had done? It wasn't fair.

He looked around the foyer for the boss and found him fighting with the coffee machine. Shaw approached him.

"Frank, I've already testified," he said. "Can I go in and listen?"

"Sure." Frank swore as he spilled coffee down his

tie.

Shaw headed up the corridor and opened the door quietly. He slipped into the public gallery. It was closed, of course, but there were several heads of various agencies there, suits and uniforms, taking notes for their departments. Probably all headed: *How not to fuck up like ASIO.*

Lee was speaking in a quiet, assured voice when Shaw sat down.

The chairwoman waited for him to finish before she hit him with the million dollar question: "Agent Adam Shaw has already made mention of what he called the *peepshow.* What do you understand by that?"

Lee moistened his lips nervously and leaned forward toward the microphone. "*Um,* the first time I didn't really know what was going on. I was still drugged. But I realized there were cameras, so I played along. We did that a few times."

"Did you feel that Agent Shaw was taking advantage of your condition and your circumstances, Mr. Anderson?" the woman pressed.

"No, ma'am," Lee said in a steady voice. "If he hadn't pretended, Vornis would have done it for real. I was grateful."

"Did Agent Shaw every touch you inappropriately?" the woman asked.

Did making him come count? Shaw wondered. What about letting Lee suck him off in the shower? None of those things had made it into his report. If Lee spilled his guts now, he was up to his neck in shit.

Except what was *inappropriate* anyway? It was Vornis's island, for Christ's sake, not a Sunday-school picnic. And you had to do things among people like that, because if they didn't trust you, then you were dead.

That's what had rankled from the beginning of the inquiry. None of those men and women on the panel seemed to get that.

"No, ma'am," Lee said. "Not once."

Shaw kept his face impassive. Nothing to see here, move along.

He should have known. Lee hadn't given him up to Vornis, and he wouldn't give him up to the inquiry either. He still trusted Shaw, apparently, when Shaw hadn't trusted himself in a long time.

"Did you tell Agent Shaw you were with the DEA?" the chairwoman asked.

"As soon as I remembered, yes, ma'am."

The chairwoman shuffled her papers. "Do you recall the night of the eleventh of March?"

"I don't know what date it was," Lee said. "Do you mean the night I got rescued?"

"Yes." The chairwoman looked at him over her glasses. "Did Agent Shaw tell you he was going to rescue you?"

Lee hesitated, and Shaw knew he was trying to figure out the motivation behind the question. He stuck to the truth. "No, ma'am. He'd said previously he would call the DEA when he was off the island. The night in question, he told me to shut up and take it." He paused, suddenly hearing how bad it sounded. "But that was before Vornis said he was going to kill me."

"And did you believe that threat?" the chairwoman asked.

Shaw almost snorted. She had no clue the sort of people he had been dealing with. None of them did.

"Yes, ma'am," Lee said, and there was a quaver in his voice. "He, *um*, he always carried through on his threats."

"And after Vornis threatened to kill you," the

chairwoman said, "did Agent Shaw tell you he would rescue you?"

"No, ma'am," Lee said. "There wasn't time for that. But I knew he would." His voice was strong again.

Shaw's chest constricted, and his heart skipped a beat, and he wondered if it was true. He'd known? Lee had *known*? Christ, he hadn't known himself until he'd seen the cattle prod on the wall.

"Did Agent Shaw tell you who he really was?" the chairwoman said through pursed lips.

"No," said Lee firmly.

"And did he reveal to you that Ari Hirsch was an ally?" the chairwoman asked.

Lee looked lost. He glanced around the room but couldn't see Shaw sitting behind him. "I don't know that name."

Of course he didn't. It was one of Zev's many aliases. Unless, Shaw reflected, it was actually his real name, and Zev Rosenberg was the alias. It didn't matter in the grand scheme of things, but it was the sort of inconsequential little detail inquiries liked to tie themselves in knots with.

"The, *ah*, man who initially identified as Ali Ibn Usayd," the chairwoman told him, turning back through her notes.

"No," Lee said. "I didn't know that until we were on the shi-*um*, frigate."

Frigate. Anzac class. The crew gets shitty when you call it the wrong thing.

Shaw raised his hand to cover his smile. He wondered if he imagined the smile in Lee's voice as well.

"Did he tell you then?" the chairwoman asked.

Lee sounded a shade sarcastic. "Yes, ma'am. He

sort of had to say something, you know, after a navy frigate picked us up."

Shaw hid another smile. He liked snarky Lee.

The chairwoman frowned slightly at him over her glasses. "Thank you for your time, Mr. Anderson. We appreciate how difficult this must have been for you."

"Can I say something?" Lee asked and didn't wait for her to answer. "Agent Shaw saved my life. My government didn't even know I was still alive. He saved me. He didn't have to, but he did. He's a good guy." A flush rose on the back of his neck. "That's all. Thank you."

He rose, turned, and saw Shaw sitting there. His eyes widened, and then he pushed his way back outside.

Shaw waited for a minute and followed. Lee's escorts were still waiting in the foyer, but there was no sign of Lee. Shaw looked up the hallway and saw the sign for the toilets. He headed toward them.

As soon as he pushed the door open, he could hear the sounds of retching.

"Lee?" He pushed open the doors to the stalls and found Lee on his knees in the third one. "Lee, are you okay?"

Lee pulled himself up, wiping his mouth. He flipped the toilet seat down and sat on it heavily. "Yeah. It's good to see you, really." He started to cry.

Shaw's heart raced. The same protective instinct he'd always felt with Lee came rushing right back like no time at all had passed. He knelt in front of Lee and put his arms around him. Lee leaned forward and rested his head on his shoulder, and it felt right.

"They shouldn't have called you up," he said. "That's just fucking cruel."

"I wanted to help," Lee mumbled into his collar. "You shouldn't lose your job because of me."

Shaw shrugged. "Don't worry about that. I made a

call. It was the right one, but it did fuck up an entire intelligence operation."

"Yeah," Lee said. "And now we're locked in a bathroom stall together. That's gonna look bad."

Shaw laughed. "Yeah, won't it?"

Lee sniffed.

Shaw patted him on the back and released him. "How've you been, anyway?"

Lee shrugged. "Okay, actually, until this. I went home, but since it's all classified, I can't talk to anyone but my shrink about it. My parents don't know what the fuck happened." He frowned and looked away. "My mom saw my back once when I got out of the shower, and just started screaming."

Shaw reached up and touched his hair. He stroked the curls gently.

Lee shuddered. "I think I'm gonna have to move out."

"I'm sorry," Shaw said, reaching for his hand. "But, you know, there's classified and then there's classified."

"How do you mean?" Lee asked him, chewing his lower lip.

Fuck, that was distracting. Shaw pulled his thoughts back with difficulty. "I mean make something up. Tell them a drug lord tortured you. You don't have to tell them everything. They probably just want to help."

Lee shrugged dismissively, so Shaw didn't press the point.

Lee looked at him worriedly. "Did I do okay in there?"

"Yeah," said Shaw. "Don't worry about it. You did great. If they want me gone, I'm gone. If they decide I'm worth the trouble, they'll find a way to spin it so I come out smelling like roses. It's just politics."

"And what if they want you gone?" Lee asked him with a frown. "It's my fault."

"No," Shaw said. He shook his head. "None of this was ever your fault. And I will never regret getting you off that island."

I only regret I didn't do it sooner.

"But what will you do if you lose your job?" Lee asked.

"I've put some thought into that," Shaw told him with a smile. "I'll head back up to Ayr, buy myself a tinny, and spend my days wetting a line with Molly." He almost laughed at the look on Lee's face. "Molly's my dog."

"I didn't understand half of what you just said," Lee said, wrinkling his nose. "But I'm glad Molly's a dog."

They both tensed as they heard the squeal of the door. "Mr. Anderson?"

Lee rolled his eyes. "Gimme a minute, okay?"

The door squealed shut again.

"They're like fucking guards," Lee said. He leaned forward and brushed his lips gently against Shaw's. "I gotta go. I'll miss you."

Shaw rose, his thighs aching. "I'll miss you too, Lee. Take care of yourself, okay?"

Lee straightened his tie. "Yeah," he said. "You too."

Shaw waited until he was gone before he let himself out of the stall.

* * * * *

"So," Callie said that night as she looked for the remote control, "this is you now? Drunk and miserable?"

Shaw knocked the top off another bottle of beer. "I'm not drunk. Yet."

They were sharing a room. It wasn't an issue for either of them, but Shaw knew it would have been different if he had been straight. In some respects, the service had come a long way, he supposed. Twenty years ago, he wouldn't have been sent into the field. Thirty years ago, he wouldn't have been able to get a job with ASIO. Forty years ago, he wouldn't have been able to get any government job at all.

Callie found the remote at last and turned off the television. She flopped onto the bed on her stomach and flipped open her laptop. "The Americans are very interested in the outcome of the inquiry, you know," she said.

Shaw shrugged.

Callie checked her e-mail. "I'm telling you this because I don't think they'll be happy if the inquiry hangs you out to dry."

"And we must keep the Americans happy," Shaw muttered.

"You should be glad when it works in your favor," Callie told him sternly.

Shaw shook his head. "You know, Cal, I don't even care much at the moment."

Callie picked at a piece of fluff on her pajama top. "I think you do, and that's the problem. I've got your e-mail right here. *At what point am I a fucking monster?*"

Shaw looked at her sideways. "Christ, Callie, you know that's all about context. I felt like shit that night."

It was always about context with Shaw. Context or interpretation or perspective. There was nothing he couldn't get a philosophical crowbar underneath, and maybe that was part of the problem. Maybe he'd lived so long in that world that he wasn't fit to live in normal society. And he'd always trusted that Callie would warn him when he was too close to the edge, but maybe she'd lost all perspective as well. Shit, maybe they all had.

Shaw sighed. Or maybe Callie was right, and he was just drunk and miserable.

"And you think I didn't?" Callie asked, raising her brows. "What did I send back? *It's not your job to give a fuck.* Meanwhile, I was ready to have a breakdown in the middle of the bloody office! Frank threatened to have me pulled off your support team. All I could see was that photo you'd sent. This young, cute guy, and you were going to watch him be tortured. I went and cried in the toilets because I had to be the one to tell you not to give a fuck."

"Jesus." Shaw sighed. "I'm sorry."

"Don't be. It's my job to pick up the slack for you," Callie reminded him. "God, I wish you'd seen Frank's face when we got the call from the *Stuart.*"

"I'm glad I didn't," Shaw said.

"Oh, he called you everything under the sun," Callie said. "For *hours.* And then he asked if you'd got the American out. None of us *wanted* him to die. It's just none of us wanted to throw in a six-year op either. And the next morning, Frank was on the phone telling everyone he supported the decisions his agents made in the field."

"It's probably not enough to save me," Shaw reminded her.

Callie shrugged. "But we all know you're not a monster. And that's the important thing, right?"

Shaw finished his beer. "Yeah, I suppose it is."

Callie fetched a beer from the bar fridge. "You know, that picture you sent didn't do him justice."

Shaw smiled slightly.

"He's cute," Callie said. "And when he doesn't look twelve anymore, he'll be hot."

Shaw snorted. "He's twenty-four."

"He's a twink," Callie said, throwing Shaw a sly smile. "And apparently that's your type."

"I don't have a type," Shaw said.

"Bullshit," Callie said. "I can tell you're head over heels for that kid."

Maybe, Shaw thought, but I don't have a type.

"You can't call him a kid," he said at last. "You're like two years older than him."

"And hugely jealous that he looks so young," Callie said. She flicked her bottle cap in Shaw's direction. "You can bet he doesn't even use any moisturizer!"

"Yeah, he's cute," Shaw said and looked out the window for a moment.

It was a three-star view of a car park.

"And more than that," Callie said. "You miss him."

Shaw turned his face to look at her sharply.

Callie raised her tinted eyebrows. "Don't even try to bullshit me. I know you too well. You had a thing. Or, if you didn't, you wanted to."

Shaw knew better than to answer that. He shrugged.

"You could go to his hotel," Callie said.

"I don't even know where he's staying," Shaw said.

"We're ASIO, for fuck's sake," Callie said. "If anyone can find out, it's us, right?"

Shaw laughed. "I suppose so. But we're not going to stalk him. Look, maybe some stuff happened that didn't make my report, but it doesn't matter. He needs to put it all behind him and get on with his life. He doesn't want me. How could he? Not after I saw the things they did to him."

Callie inspected a thread on the hem of her pajama shirt. She raised her eyebrows. "Did you ask him?"

"What?" Shaw asked.

"Did you ask him?" Callie repeated.

"It's too late now," Shaw said, wiping a droplet of moisture off the neck of the bottle. Jesus, how could he have asked something like that? Lee had enough to deal with without Shaw laying that emotional blackmail on him: *I saved you, stay with me!* It would have been too cruel.

"If you're sure," Callie said and flashed him a grin. "Because, you know, if this was a movie, I'd be the mad bitch who drove the wrong way in traffic so you could catch him at the airport and declare your love."

Shaw snorted with amusement at that mental picture. He didn't doubt for a second it was true. "Cal, whatever happens you'll always be my mad bitch."

She raised her bottle in a toast. "Damn straight."

Shaw laughed despite himself.

He wondered if he should tell her how often he dreamed of Lee, and how, surprisingly, it wasn't sexual. Okay, so sometimes it was. Sometimes his subconscious took him back to that day when Lee had gone down onto his knees in the shower, and he'd looked fucking gorgeous with his eyes closed, his mouth around Shaw's cock, and the water running over his skin. But most of the time, he dreamed they were still adrift on the Pacific, before they'd been rescued.

Stay with me, Lee.

Zev wasn't with them in the dream. It was just the two of them, their fingers entwined. Just the two of them and the Pacific and the stars.

Stay with me, Lee.

And they drifted together in the Milky Way.

CHAPTER NINETEEN

"Are you okay, honey?" His mother slipped an arm around him.

Lee leaned on the patio railing and showed her a smile he wasn't sure he meant. "I'm okay, Mom."

He stood as far as he could away from the steps. Away from the light that pooled out of the back door. He felt more comfortable watching from where he couldn't be seen.

The backyard was strung with party lights. Smoke came off the barbeque and brought the scent of grilled steak all the way back to the house. Lee could hear talking and laughter, and someone's kids squealing as they chased one another around the yard.

At the back of the yard, behind the tool shed, there was a wilderness. Kids were always drawn right to the narrow patch of untamed grass and creepers that hung between the back fence and the shed. It was a pirate's jungle. It was an unexplored planet. It was a magical land. Lee had played there every day when he was a kid, until he hit adolescence. He had a sudden urge to see it now, but he didn't want to thread his way through the party just to be disappointed because it wasn't what he remembered.

Lee rested his beer bottle on the top of the railing

for a moment. It had gone warm, and he'd hardly drunk any of it. He'd been carrying it like a prop. *Can't shake hands; I'm holding this beer. Can't stop and talk; it's a party — look, I've got a beer and everything. Here I am with a beer like a normal guy.*

His mother released him. "Maybe you'll want to come down and say hello to some people later."

"Yeah, sure." It surprised him how natural that sounded when he was already planning to sneak away upstairs and hide in his bedroom.

He'd overheard his mother on the phone earlier in the day. "Yes, he'll be here, he got back last night. Just don't bring it up, please."

His parents had collected him at the airport. Between his escorts and his parents, he hadn't had a moment to himself since Canberra. It had felt more like a hostage exchange than a homecoming. He'd given his mom the fuzzy koala toy he'd bought at the airport — the closest he'd made it to the real thing — and she'd burst into tears. Lee still wasn't sure why. Relief or pity. He'd looked like shit, he guessed. He was so tired after everything — the inquiry, seeing Shaw, the flight back — that he'd ached all over. He could have fallen asleep on his feet in the terminal. He had fallen asleep on the ride home and woken up at one point to see the lights on the highway flashing past.

"He's just tired," his dad had been saying. "He'll talk when he wants to talk."

"I want my son back," his mom had said.

Lee didn't know where to find him.

"Okay, honey," his mom said now and headed back inside to get the salads.

There were fewer than twenty people in the yard, but it might as well have been a crowd of thousands. These were the people Lee had known since he was a kid, the same people who came around every few weeks. The same people, he kept reminding himself, who had worn black at his memorial service. He didn't feel ready to face them yet, and he wondered if he ever would.

Lee took a sip of his warm beer. It tasted sour. He left the bottle on the patio and slipped back inside. He headed upstairs, avoiding that squeaky third step, before his mother came back out of the kitchen.

He closed his door and crossed the room to push his window open. The cool breeze smelled of steak and barbeque smoke, even on the other side of the house. Lee's stomach growled, and he tried to remember if he'd eaten lunch earlier. There was a chart taped in the kitchen he could check—his nutritionist was a dictator—but that would mean sneaking downstairs. He'd rather just wait in his room until the barbeque was cooked.

He hated small talk these days. *Hi,* he said when people noticed him. *Good,* when they asked how he was doing. It sometimes felt like those were the only two words he used in a day. His customer-service skills sucked, so his dad had him working in the stock room at the hardware store. And that suited him fine. It got him out of the house, which everyone from his parents to Doctor Fisher agreed was a good thing, and it got him busy, which he needed. Stocktaking, ordering, and doing the books; he even enjoyed it. He just couldn't work out on the floor.

Lee lay on his bed and took a deep breath. Small steps, one foot in front of the other just like always. And maybe he was getting somewhere after all.

He heard a car and then the crunch of tires on the shoulder of the road as it pulled in. Doors slammed, and people laughed. A moment later, the doorbell rang. More guests.

Lee closed his eyes and wondered if tonight would be the night he actually started talking to people again. Maybe. Maybe not.

The third step squeaked, and he heard footsteps in the hall. There was a knock at his door.

"Hey, babe."

Lee's eyes flashed open, and he smiled before he even thought not to. He sat up quickly. "Chas!"

"You look okay," Chastity told him, "for a corpse."

There was nothing subtle about Chastity. There never had been. She regarded him frankly with her eyebrows raised, as though she was daring him to react badly. That was Chastity through and through.

Lee felt his smile grow. "I feel okay, for a corpse."

"Your mom sent me to come and get you," Chastity told him. "But I say I go downstairs and get us some burgers, and then I sneak back up here, and we eat 'em. What do you think?"

"I think you're just what I need right now," Lee told her. He sighed. "You won't ask, will you, Chas? About what happened?"

"No, Anderson," she said. She tossed her hair back and gave him the same haughty look he remembered from high school. The grade-A-bitch look. "I'm just here for the burgers."

Lee felt relief wash over him.

"Do you want ketchup?"

"What sort of dumb question is that?" Lee asked.

She laughed. "Ketchup it is! I'll be right back."

Lee kicked off his shoes while he waited.

Later, sitting on the floor with their beers and burgers, he saw how fragile their masks were. They talked about school, college, and how the last time either of them had seen Shaun, he was pumping gas, but they didn't talk about the thing that was right there between them: Lee's death and resurrection into a man who would never be the same one Chastity had mourned.

She caught his wrist once when he reached for his beer bottle and then bit back whatever she had been going to say. Lee's answering smile had wavered.

"Remember how we used to go up to the lake?" he asked to change the subject.

He'd gone there that morning with his dad. Round Lake had gleamed in the sunlight. Lee walked along the bank, one foot in front of the other. He kept his eyes down as he walked, looking at the stones, at the grass, at the mud, and half looking for sand dollars he knew wouldn't be there. His lips quirked.

One foot in front of the other.
One sand dollar and then another.

The lake was popular in the summer, with fishermen during the day and with high school kids at night. It had been early in the morning when they'd arrived, and a few beer cans had littered the lake's edge from the night before. Beer cans, Lee thought, instead of sand dollars.

When he was a kid, he'd thought that Round Lake was as big as an ocean.

"Have you ever seen the Pacific?"

His dad looked at him sideways. His forehead was creased in a worried frown. "The Pacific? No."

"It's beautiful," Lee told him. He thought of the shards of sunlight that had bounced off the ocean's glittering surface, blinding him. The roar of the Pacific had comforted him. He thought of the whispering waves that had chased up the beach and slipped back to reveal gleaming sand dollars. And he thought of Shaw and the way his face had softened when he had stared out at the horizon. The Pacific had revealed Shaw as well.

Lee wondered now if the *wish-wash* of waves on a white beach would still comfort him and lull him gently into sleep.

"God, yeah." Chastity's blue eyes shone. "We had great times at the lake. Remember all those times I tried to tease you by pretending I'd forgotten my suit so I had to go skinny-dipping? Goddammit, I should have known you were gay long before college. You never even looked, and meanwhile, Shaun used to follow me around with his tongue hanging out."

Lee leaned back against his closet door. "Yeah, also, Shaun would have punched the shit out of me if he'd caught me looking."

Chastity screwed up her nose. "What did I ever see in him?"

"He was the quarterback. You were the cheerleader. It was mandatory."

She snorted. "God, I was so stupid."

Lee picked at the label on his beer bottle. "Yeah, well, we all were."

"I *missed* you," Chastity said suddenly. She leaned forward, and her blonde hair curtained her face as she picked at a spot on the carpet. When she looked up again, her eyes were wide. "I don't mean the last few months, Lee. I mean since we graduated. I miss snuggling up and watching bad sci-fi movies at night. I miss going to brunch every Sunday. I miss getting together and bitching about men!"

Lee took her hand. His throat ached. "I know. I missed you too."

She flung herself at him, and they ended up entangled on the floor together. The smell of her perfume made his chest tighten. He hugged her tightly. "It's good to see you."

"You too, babe," she mumbled into his chest and then rolled off him.

They lay close together and stared up at the bedroom ceiling.

"Are you gonna stay in Andover?" she asked him after a while.

"I don't know yet." He turned his head to look at her.

Chastity shuffled closer. "Well, there's always room on my couch if you ever find yourself in Chicago."

"I know," he murmured, but he couldn't picture it. The problem was that he couldn't picture much beyond these four familiar walls, the stockroom of his dad's hardware store, and Doctor Fisher's office. Three fucking places in the world where he didn't feel afraid. And, apparently, that bathroom stall in Canberra where he'd cried all over Shaw, just like he always did.

Three places and one person. Maybe that meant something.

He'd always trusted Shaw. Maybe it was time to trust himself.

"*I'll miss you too, Lee,*" Shaw had said in Canberra, and it had sounded like the truth.

"Do you want me to go and get us more beer?" Chastity asked him.

Lee squeezed her hand. His heart raced, but he ignored it. He had to see if he could do this. "You wait here. I'll go."

* * * * *

After the barbeque, Lee sat in the darkness of the

steps and listened to his parents in the kitchen. Their conversation drifted up to him, punctuated by the clatter and splash of dishes being washed.

"Well, there's no harm in going," his dad said. "Just to see what they want."

"I know what they want," his mom returned, "and I'm retired. I've got enough to keep me busy around the house. I don't need to go back to teaching."

"Karen," his dad said, and Lee could hear the tender smile in his voice, "you're going stir-crazy around the house."

Lee leaned his head against the banister and watched the play of light and shadow on the walls. This is not a sanctuary, he'd thought of the closet on the island; this is a prison. It was important to know the difference still. For him and for his parents. They all deserved better.

His mom changed the subject, like she always did when she didn't want to admit his dad was right. "Linda is pregnant again. That's good news, isn't it?"

Whatever his dad said was drowned out by the noise of the sink draining.

"Chastity's looking well," his mom said. "I think it was good for Lee to see her again. I wonder if she'll be staying in town for a while. I should call her to see if she'll take Lee out for lunch tomorrow."

"Lee's old enough to make his own lunch dates," his dad said.

"If we didn't push him, he'd stay in his bedroom every day," his mom replied.

Lee closed his eyes. True, probably. He relied on his parents to push him because he had forgotten how to push himself. And that was unfair on them. He just wished he wasn't so afraid. Maybe he would always be afraid. Maybe getting better didn't mean entirely losing that fear. Maybe it just meant living his life again despite it. And maybe, in time, it would go away. What was the harm in believing that?

Lee smiled to himself. There was hope again. Stupid, breathless hope. He wondered why he still distrusted it so much. It had saved him on the island.

He rose to his feet and moved downstairs. The third step from the bottom creaked.

His parents were drying the dishes with their backs to him.

"Hey," he said, and they turned around.

"Can't you sleep, Lee?" his dad asked him.

"I'm not tired," he said, looking at his dad's face and wondering when he'd gotten so old. He hadn't looked this gray, this weary, at Christmas. His mom too. Jesus, Vornis cast a long shadow.

He reached for the cookie jar on the bench and opened it. His mom made the best macaroons.

"I think you should take your job back, Mom," he said.

Her mouth tightened, and her eyes flashed with worry.

"I'm not going to stay in Andover," he told her. "Not forever. And you miss those kids, right?"

She raised a hand to her mouth.

Lee fought not to back away, not to run up the stairs and hide in his closet. He was so scared of confrontation these days. So scared to look anyone in the eye, even his own mother. His heart pounded. He swallowed. "I don't want you to feel like you have to choose between your life and me, Mom. You'll just end up resenting me."

She reached out and caught his hands. "I would *never...*"

"It's okay." A shower of cookie crumbs fell to the floor. Lee withdrew his hands and wiped them on his jeans. "When you retire, it should be for you, not me; that's all I meant."

Tears shone in her eyes. "I want to be here for you."

"You are," he said. "You always are. Both of you."

His dad put a hand on his shoulder and squeezed lightly.

Lee closed his eyes briefly. The touch felt so good. When he opened his eyes, his parents were both still watching him, both of them wary, hopeful, and afraid. Just like always. And shit, they deserved more than that. They deserved not to have to hold their breath every time they talked to their son. They deserved not to be so scared of hurting him that they were afraid to be themselves.

Lee was sick of fear.

Lee brushed his fingers against the button of his shirt. He looked at the crumbs on the kitchen floor and then back at his parents' faces. "I think, *um*, I think maybe I can tell you guys what happened now, if you want to hear it."

His dad nodded slightly. His face was set, but his eyes were wide with concern.

His mom bit her lip.

Lee pulled his top button free and then began to work on the one below it. His fingers trembled. His heart was racing again. He could hear the blood pounding in his ears, and it sounded a little bit like the ocean.

Every scar on his body told a story, and maybe it was time to share them with the people who loved him. He thought of what Shaw had said in Canberra: *"You don't have to tell them everything."* But Lee thought that maybe he did. He hated the space that had grown between his parents and himself. He hated feeling ashamed and angry and afraid. They needed to know why he was like this. They deserved the truth.

"It is what it is, Lee," Shaw had told him on the island. No judgment. There didn't have to be judgment, just acknowledgment.

His fingers hovered over his last button. He looked down at the crumbs on the floor, unable to look at their faces just yet. Not yet, and maybe not while he was talking, but afterwards. He would be able to look at them afterwards. He was strong enough to ride this out. He wasn't going to break now.

Not now and maybe not ever again.

"Just, um, just don't freak out, okay?"

Lee shrugged off his shirt.

CHAPTER TWENTY

Two months later

    His parents had a weekend place at Alva Beach just up from the caravan park. It wasn't much more than an old beach shack, but it was all Shaw needed. He had been spending time here since he was a kid. Walking through the place was like revisiting his childhood. The back cupboard was full of board games with missing pieces, old issues of *National Geographic* that went back generations, chipped saucers, and candle stubs. The place never changed. The laminate on the kitchen bench was the same hideous orange-brown it had always been, and that piece of tin on the roof still rattled in a high wind. Shaw slept on the enclosed back veranda instead of the bedroom, the same as he always had. He even liked to hear the possums screaming in the trees at night, however much the noise grated. It took him back to all those long summers of his childhood; the hot, humid days and the nights that were just as humid, and sneaking out to go swimming in the moonlight.

    Molly loved it. She'd gone feral. She'd worked out how to squeeze through the sagging wire fence. Every lunchtime since Shaw found her at the caravan park, looking sweet and hungry for the tourists at the barbeques. Shaw headed into town at the end of the week to the hardware shop to get supplies to fix the fence.

Ayr hadn't changed a lot either. Shaw liked that about small towns. It made them good to come back to, even if he'd been bursting to leave at the end of high school. He liked how people still stopped on the street to catch up.

Shaw still had friends in Ayr. They tended to be like him, the ones who had got out before coming back. Paul, a mate since kindergarten, was now the principal of the primary school. Mike was a doctor. And Kate, who'd dropped out of high school to start a punk band, had moved back from Melbourne after her divorce to raise her kids. She was running her parents' cane farm. Shaw knew he could rely on all of them to meet up at Alva Beach every Friday night, bottles of cheap wine in hand, to relive their teenage years. It took about half a glass each before they had all regressed into giggles and rude jokes, and saying *shh! shh! shh!* like they were afraid they were going to get busted every time a car drove past.

It wouldn't be so bad here.

Shaw picked up a roll of fencing wire and then headed down the street to get some groceries. Such ordinary, everyday things, and a part of him still couldn't get his head around it. Five months ago, he'd tortured Pieter Guterman with a cattle prod and watched as Zev cut his throat, all their throats. Now he was buying dog food and toilet paper and wondering what to make himself for dinner. He'd seen some horrible things, done some horrible things, and he was standing in a supermarket aisle trying to decide between light milk and skim milk. Or, fuck it, full cream.

He'd been able to shake things off so easily once. Before the island.

Shaw spent the afternoon fixing the fence. Molly

thought it was a game. She kept bouncing away with his tools, and Shaw ran her down every time.

"*Molly*," he coaxed when she was heading for the beach for the third time. "Come on, girl. Come on, Molly."

A pair of sunburned backpackers crossed the road behind them, laughing.

When Shaw finally got the pliers off her and turned back to the house, there was someone standing by the fence. Shaw thought he recognized that height, that stance, but he was looking into the sun now and couldn't be sure. Couldn't stop his heart racing either.

Shaw was a mess. He was covered in sweat, sand, and dog hair. His shirt was the tattiest one he could find, and his shorts were possibly his dad's. He'd found them in the back cupboard that morning. They had to be at least twenty-five years old if they fitted Shaw. His dad liked his beer too much these days.

He walked back toward the house, Molly at his side.

It was him. It couldn't be anyone else. It was impossible, but it was him.

"Hey," Shaw said and really didn't know where to go from there.

"Hey," said Lee.

"How did you find me?" Shaw asked, setting the pliers down on the gatepost.

"You said you'd be here," Lee said.

"I said I'd be in Ayr," Shaw said. "This is a little, *ah*, specific."

"ASIO's in the phonebook, you know," Lee said.

And not exactly in the habit of giving out addresses, Shaw thought. He waited.

"It took a while," Lee said, "but I got through to your friend Callie. She told me where you were."

"Callie?" Shaw frowned. Why the hell would she do that? Of course. He thought back to the hotel room in Canberra. She was being his mad bitch. Shaw didn't know if he wanted to kill her for it or send her chocolates.

Lee looked hesitant. "Um, do you mind that I'm here?"

Shaw raised his eyebrows. "I'm surprised, that's all. I didn't think you'd want to see me."

Lee shook his head. "Why would you think that?"

Shaw stuck his hands in the pockets of his borrowed shorts. "Don't I remind you of everything that happened?"

"You saved me," Lee said, and his voice was as certain as the day he'd spoken at the inquiry. "You saved my life. You're one of the good guys."

His eyes shone, and Shaw wanted to kiss him then and there. But he was filthy, and he stank, and maybe it was still a bad idea, but Lee was here. Lee had come here. They both still wanted this.

Chocolates. He'd send chocolates.

"Come in," Shaw said, and Lee picked up his bag and followed him inside.

* * * * *

Shaw watched as Lee looked at the family photos on the wall. His eyes slid over them as though he was afraid to study them too closely. Shaw had no problems with that. He'd spent half his adolescence wearing braces and outgrowing his own limbs.

"This is, um, this is a nice one," Lee said.

Two kids in shorts and singlets held fishing rods way too big for them and squinted into the sunlight.

"That's me and Emma, my sister," Shaw said.

Lee frowned slightly. "You said you didn't have a sister."

Shaw didn't know whether or not to laugh. He shrugged instead. "I lied, Lee. It's what they pay me to do."

"Okay," Lee said.

"Well," Shaw said, heading for the fridge for beers, "it's what they *paid* me to do."

"Did you really lose your job?" Lee asked.

Shaw handed him a beer and gestured at the laminate table. "Have a seat. No, I'm still gainfully employed. I'm just on leave." He twisted the top off his beer. "And I don't think they'll be putting me back in the field anytime soon."

"I'm sorry," Lee said, sitting.

"I'm not," Shaw said, and it was the truth. "It was starting to fuck with my head."

Lee looked like he wasn't sure how to respond. He looked down instead, to find Molly's head on his knee. He rubbed her head, and her tail thumped against the floor.

Shaw drank his beer faster than he should have. He was sure that Lee was fussing over Molly to avoid looking at him.

It's a long way to come to avoid eye contact. You could have done that from Minnesota, mate.

"I need a shower," Shaw said, rising from the table. "You can put your stuff in the bedroom if you want." He saw Lee's anxious face. "I'm sleeping out the back."

And he wondered, when he collected his fresh clothes from the sleepout, what that was about. He wondered what Lee hoped to gain by coming here and what his expectations were. Was sex even in the picture? Shaw wouldn't push it, but what else could Lee have thought? Shit, maybe this wasn't about Shaw at all. Maybe this was about closure.

Shaw closed the bathroom door and turned on the shower. It didn't matter, he supposed. At worst, they could watch TV and talk. He didn't want anything from Lee that Lee wasn't ready to give.

Shaw relaxed under the hot water, closed his eyes, and wondered how he felt about having Lee here, in this house that belonged to his childhood. His life was designed so that the two worlds never met. He liked it that way. This was his safe place. This was his sanctuary. But suddenly he didn't hate the idea of sharing it with someone who needed it.

The shower door squeaked open, and Shaw opened his eyes.

Lee was fucking gorgeous. He'd put on weight since the island, filled out a bit, and it suited him. His bruises had vanished. His scars had faded. He didn't look fragile anymore, but he still looked afraid. His green eyes were wide.

"Do you mind?" he asked in a low voice.

"No," Shaw said, reaching out to draw him closer.

The shower had always been their confessional. Shaw wondered if Lee would always need the feel of the spray on his skin to make the words come.

"I missed you," Lee murmured as Shaw's lips found his throat. He let his head fall back. "I want you."

Shaw's chest constricted. Hope rose up, and he tried to force it down again.

"Want you too," he said, his voice straining. He turned Lee around, following the tracks of the scars on his back with his fingertips. Lee braced his hands against the tiles of the shower wall and pushed back against him, and Shaw resisted. "No, not like this."

"How?" Lee asked, his breath hitching as Shaw's hands slipped down to his buttocks.

Shaw nuzzled his neck. "On the bed."

"Okay."

Shaw twisted the taps off and reached for a couple of towels. He wrapped one around his waist as he stepped out of the shower and held the other one out for Lee. Lee stepped forward into it, and Shaw wiped it gently over his skin. Lee's cock was hard, engorged with blood, and Shaw wanted nothing more than to sink onto his knees and take it into his mouth. But not on the bathroom tiles. He satisfied himself with a quick stroke of that rigid flesh, loving the way that Lee trembled and gasped under his touch. He was so responsive.

Shaw took him by the hand and led him to the bedroom.

"Shaw," Lee asked cautiously as he looked around. He tucked his towel around his hips. "Is this your *parents'* bedroom?"

Shaw took in the room with fresh eyes. The sagging double bed, the patchwork quilt, the World's Best Dad coffee mug on the bedside cabinet—filled with shells collected by Shaw and Emma twenty-odd years ago.

Lee's gaze fell on the coffee mug, to the dusty sand dollar on the top of the pile of shells. His eyes widened for a moment—Shaw heard his sharp intake of breath and wondered at it—and then his gaze travelled up the wall.

Crap. Straight to the awkward family portrait hanging over the bed. Very eighties. His dad had a mullet. Baldness was the best thing that had happened to Shaw's dad.

"*Um*, yeah," Shaw said. His face cracked with a grin. "Too weird?"

"I don't know," Lee said. He wrinkled his nose, and Shaw wondered if he knew how fucking cute that was. "Are they gonna walk in on us?"

"This is their weekend place," Shaw said. "They let me stay here when I'm in town. They're not going to walk in on us."

Although, now the thought was in his head, it was difficult to shake. And it would be typical of his dad to drop in to see if he wanted to go fishing, or his mum to pop by with something she'd made for his dinner because she still thought he couldn't be trusted to eat right.

Yeah, too weird.

"Sleepout," Shaw decided, and drew Lee through the house onto the back veranda.

"What's a sleepout?" Lee asked curiously.

Half of the back veranda had been partitioned off when his parents had bought the house. Shaw, as the oldest, had claimed it as his own while Emma had to sleep on a trundle bed in the small lounge room. The roof of the veranda extended far enough to protect the sleepout from the weather. The veranda rails had been enclosed with wood, and the space from the top of the rails to the roof was done in mosquito netting. Or had been, when Shaw was a kid. His dad had since replaced the flimsy netting with the proper security stuff.

The sleepout looked the same. The screens let in the light and the breeze. Shaw could lie in bed at night and hear the ocean. The only difference was that Shaw couldn't peel back this netting back and escape. Not that he had any intention of escaping now. This was exactly where he wanted to be.

Lee raised his eyebrows as he looked at the single bed. "Transformer sheets?"

"Have you got a problem with the Transformers?" Shaw asked him.

Lee raised his eyebrows. His brilliant green eyes sparkled. "No, not at all. In five minutes here, I've learned more about you than the whole time on the island."

His voice was even when he spoke, but Shaw saw the flash of worry in his eyes. He wondered if it would always be there. He wondered if the sound of the rolling ocean took Lee straight back there.

Lee flushed suddenly. "It's okay to mention it. I just...I just didn't know if you would be okay with it."

Shaw curled his fingers through Lee's. "Have you been seeing someone about it?"

"A good doctor," Lee said, squeezing Shaw's hand gratefully.

"I bet he thinks this is a bad idea," Shaw said before he could stop himself.

"Actually, *she* thinks I'm ready," Lee said. He showed Shaw a shy smile. "We talked about you a lot."

"Huh," Shaw said.

"We agreed that you were a nice guy not to take advantage of me on the island," Lee said. He shrugged. "And we disagreed on who took advantage of who on the *Stuart*."

Shaw frowned. "You did?"

"You're kidding, right?" Lee asked him, dropping his hand. "God, I threw myself at you!"

Shaw's breath caught in his throat. "That's not exactly how I remember it."

Lee shrugged and looked away. "Anyway, here I am again. Throwing myself at you."

Shaw's heart thumped. Lee was scared. It wasn't the same as it had been on the island. This time, he wasn't scared of pain. He was scared of rejection. Jesus, as if he had to worry about that. Not now and not ever.

"Lee," Shaw said in a low voice.

Lee raised his gaze.

"Whatever you want," Shaw told him.

Lee swallowed. "What?"

"Whatever you want," Shaw repeated. "Whatever you came here for. Just tell me, and it's yours."

Lee shivered suddenly, crossing his arms across his chest. "That's a dumb fucking thing to say."

Shaw shook his head. "I mean it. You know what I am, Lee, and you still came all the way here." He remembered what Zev had said on board the *Stuart*: *There's a boy in your cabin who saw the whole thing and still wants to be in your bunk.* "So, whatever you want."

Lee looked at him anxiously. "What if I want to stay awhile? If we're good together, I mean."

"You can stay as long as you want," Shaw told him, swallowing. He tried for a cocky grin. "And we'll be fucking *awesome*."

Shit, no pressure!

Lee's lips quirked, and then he stepped forward and kissed Shaw.

Everything fell into place.

This time, they were equals, and it felt good. Shaw didn't have to direct Lee, to reassure him, or to distract him. This time, Lee was right there with him and nowhere else. This time, there was no island, no Vornis, and no fear.

"How do you want it?" Shaw asked him, running his hands down Lee's back.

"I want to see your face," Lee said, his breath hot and fast against Shaw's ear. He squirmed as Shaw's fingers slipped under the towel and grazed teasingly against the cleft of his ass. "Oh God."

Shaw liked the way he said that. The sharp exhalation of breath was impatient with anticipation and thick with desire. He wanted to hear it again and again. For the rest of his life, if he could, but there was no point spooking Lee with that just yet. Shaw knew how to run a covert operation. But it would happen. He'd make it happen. He smiled as Lee's lips found his throat.

Hell yeah. He'd make it happen.

"I meant top or bottom, Lee," he said.

"Oh," Lee breathed. He drew back. His green eyes were wide. "You'd do that for me?"

"Whatever you want," Shaw reminded him. He leaned forward and brushed his lips against Lee's. "And it's not a big ask, you know? I like to bottom as much as anyone."

Lee raised his eyebrows. "Really? You seem like a natural top."

"I'm versatile," Shaw told him. "Try me."

For a moment, Lee's gaze faltered, and then he wrinkled his nose. "Maybe we could try that next time? I want to, but this time I want you inside me."

"Okay," Shaw said. "I mean, hell yes!"

Lee laughed, and Shaw thought it was the most beautiful sound he'd ever heard in his life. He caught Lee's face between his palms and looked at him wonderingly for a moment—the real Lee, at last; the impish green eyes, the messy dark hair that wanted to curl, and those gorgeous lips curved in a smile—then pulled him close for another kiss.

Lee moaned, drawing Shaw's lower lip between his teeth and worrying it gently. Shaw moaned as well, his cock hardening. He rocked his hips gently against Lee's and felt Lee's cock pressing against him. They were both at the same place. That was good.

Stop worrying and fuck him.

Shaw didn't have to take charge. He didn't have to push Lee gently toward the bed. He didn't have to maneuver, to manipulate. Lee did it all. Lee's hands were on Shaw's hips, and he was pulling him to the bed. By the hips, by the lower lip his teeth refused to relinquish, and by the force of the heat that rose between them.

The springs on the old bed squealed in protest as they fell onto it in a tangle of limbs and towels.

"Shit!" Shaw leaned out of the bed and reached underneath it. Somewhere, between the collections of comic books and model planes and shoeboxes full of Legos, *somewhere* was his cabin bag. He'd shoved it there when he'd arrived and thought he wouldn't need it for a while. He hooked his fingers around the strap and pulled it out. He hunted through it quickly, twisting his head to look back at Lee.

Lee slid his hands behind his head. "No rush."

Gorgeous and a smartass. Perfect.

Shaw laughed at that, his fingers closing on the foil packet of a condom. He had to dig a little deeper for the lube. By the time he pulled himself upright again, he was breathless. "Found it!"

Lee's eyes shone with lust. "You gonna get me ready?"

"Yeah, baby," Shaw said and wondered where the hell that endearment came from. He'd never called anyone baby before, but it felt right. "I am."

Lee bit his lip.

Shaw twisted the top off the lube and squeezed it into his palm. He slicked up his fingers and knelt between Lee's legs. Lee's cock was hard, pressing up against his abdomen. It was dark with blood, and the tip glistened with a pearl of precum. It twitched as Shaw looked at it, and Lee moaned again.

Lee bent his knees and drew his legs up, and then

let them fall open. The muscles in his thighs were taut. Shaw slid his hands along them, and Lee sighed.

Shaw leaned forward and cupped Lee's balls in his palm. Lee's body jerked as though Shaw had put electricity through it. He shifted his arms back down to his sides and gripped the sheets tightly. "Feels good."

Shaw squeezed gently. There was such a fine line between pleasure and pain, and he couldn't walk it with Lee. Not now, but maybe one day. And he'd wait. He'd wait until Lee was ready. Because anything that Lee gave him willingly was more than enough. It was more than he deserved.

Lee's fingers turned white, and he groaned. "More. I need more."

Shaw slipped his fingers down to Lee's tight entrance, teasing it with his fingertips. He circled it, pushing gently, and watched Lee's face. Watched his brilliant green eyes, and the way he bit his lip. Shaw pushed a fingertip inside of him, and Lee arched his back. He drew a shuddering breath.

"More," he murmured and widened his thighs.

Shaw took it slowly. Not just for Lee. For himself as well, because he wanted to see every flicker of sensation translated into Lee's eyes, his face, and his trembling body. He wanted it to last forever.

He pressed a finger inside Lee, and Lee breathed heavily and moved restlessly. He fixed his gaze on Shaw's face. "Please."

Shaw withdrew his finger for a moment and then pressed two fingers inside Lee's tight passage. He felt Lee tense and then breathe through the mild sting. Shaw sighed as Lee's body slowly opened and accepted him. So hot. So tight. He felt the moment Lee allowed his muscles to relax, and that was when he crooked his fingers against Lee's prostate.

"Holy fuck!" Lee almost jumped off the bed. He sank back against the mattress, wide-eyed. "Do that again!"

Like he even had to ask. Shaw's cock was rock hard now, throbbing desperately. He'd almost lost it when Lee had reacted like that. He'd almost come like a teenager, without even being touched. Jesus, weren't those the days? Shaw crooked his fingers again and had to take a deep breath to prevent himself from coming as Lee shuddered on the bed and clenched around his fingers.

Lee gripped the sheets tightly. "I need you inside me now!"

"No argument here," Shaw said breathlessly. He withdrew his fingers and tore the condom open. He rolled it over his aching cock, and slathered it with lube. He shifted forward, positioning the head of his cock against Lee's puckered entrance. He leaned over Lee, bracing his weight on one arm. He gripped his cock tightly, pushing slowly forward into Lee.

Lee arched his back. "Oh God."

Shaw stopped. "Too much?"

"No," Lee said. His hands found Shaw's shoulders. "More!"

"Jesus." Shaw gasped, feeling Lee's tight muscles squeeze his cock.

Lee began to rock back and forth slowly, drawing Shaw deeper and deeper inside. His wide eyes searched Shaw's face, and he smiled as he felt Shaw's balls come to rest against his ass. "Oh yeah. That's it."

Shaw drew a shaky breath. Hell yes, that was it. It was everything. Lee was giving him everything. Shaw's chest swelled with hope. He lowered himself and kissed Lee.

Lee's mouth was hot and hungry. He dug his fingers into Shaw's shoulders. He hooked his legs around Shaw and began to rock his hips. His mouth left a wet, hot trail from Shaw's lips to his ear. "Fuck me. Fuck me, please."

Shaw tilted his pelvis, changing the angle of his penetration, and Lee gasped. Shaw drew back and began to thrust. Jesus, Lee was so tight. Every stroke was fucking heaven, and the way that Lee was rising up to meet his thrusts and moaning in his ear and digging his fingers into Shaw's shoulders so hard it would leave bruises...Shaw had to squeeze his eyes shut. The sensations were enough. If he had to look at Lee's face as well, he wouldn't be able to stop from coming too soon.

Shaw's universe contracted. Just him, just Lee, just the feel of them moving together, and just the ragged sound of their gasps. And it was just right. It felt like coming home.

The wind picked up outside, and a shower of seed pods rattled on the tin roof.

He was home.

Lee came first, his cock rubbing between their straining bodies. He cried out and froze, and then his body spasmed. Shaw felt the hot spray of his cum burst between them, and he came as well. His balls contracted, and he thrust quickly into Lee as he came, riding out the crest as long as he could before falling forward into Lee's embrace.

Lee curled his hand around the back of Shaw's neck. "Oh God."

Shaw pressed his lips against Lee's jaw. He tasted of sweat. "Awesome?"

Lee turned his head, his mouth searching for Shaw's. They kissed, and Lee's smile broke it. "Fucking awesome." His laugh was breathless. "Arrogant asshole."

Shaw smiled as well, rolling off Lee carefully and

then drawing him into a gentle embrace. "Welcome to Alva Beach, Lee."

Because Lee was home as well.

* * * * *

"Hello?" a voice called. Shaw heard the screen door squeak open. "You home?"

"Shit," Shaw said, scrambling for his clothes. It was Paul. "It's Friday, isn't it?" He raised his voice. "Give me a minute, mate!"

He pulled the doors of the old wardrobe open, wincing as he stood on a long-discarded piece of Lego.

Lee sat up, reaching for his towel.

"I forgot it's Friday." Shaw pulled on a shirt and a pair of jeans and tossed some clothing Lee's way. "My mates are coming over for drinks." He caught Lee's worried look. "You'll like 'em."

Lee stood and began to dress. "Are you sure?"

"Yeah." Shaw crossed the floor and pulled him close for a moment. He smelled of sweat and cum, and Shaw kissed him softly. "They'll like you too."

Lee pulled back. "What are you going to tell them?"

The ghosts of the island flashed through his brilliant green eyes.

Shaw hooked his fingers through the belt loops of Lee's jeans. He kept his voice low. "I'm going to tell them we met through work. I'm going to tell them you're my boyfriend, and you're moving in with me."

"Am I?" Lee asked him, fumbling with the buttons on the shirt. He worried his lower lip with his teeth. "Is that really happening?"

"If you want," Shaw said. He held Lee's gaze. "Do you trust me?"

The moment of truth. Shaw didn't think he could breathe.

"Always," Lee said seriously.

And shit, it was true. It had been true since the moment they'd met. Shaw hadn't deserved it then—he'd *hated* it—but now he wanted Lee's trust more than anything. And he'd make himself worthy of it. He'd treasure it; forever, if Lee let him.

"I don't deserve you," he murmured.

Lee frowned slightly. "You're a better person than you think, you know."

Shaw couldn't remember the last time someone had believed in him like that. He swallowed with difficulty around the sudden lump in his throat. "Jesus, I *really* don't deserve you, Lee. You're amazing."

Lee flushed and wrinkled his nose. "Shut up."

It was another moment Shaw wanted to last forever, but he could hear Paul stomping around in the lounge. A moment later, Paul yelled out again: "I got some chips. Did you want anything else?"

"No, we should be good," Shaw called back. He kissed Lee again. "You okay?"

"I'm okay," Lee said. He drew a deep breath. His eyes shone.

"Jesus Christ!" Paul called out from the lounge. "What the bloody hell are you doing back there, Matty? My beer's getting hot, and your dog is molesting me!"

"Mate, you know where the fridge is!" Shaw frowned at the look of confusion that crossed over Lee's face. *Shit.* "Yeah, about that . . . "

"Your name's not Adam Shaw, is it?" Lee asked him quietly.

"It's Matthew," Shaw said. "Matthew Sinclair."

He waited, his heart thumping, for Lee's response.

Lee looked at him for a moment, his green eyes wary, and then he relaxed and smiled.

"Fucking spies," he said and stuck out his hand. "It's nice to meet you, Matthew Sinclair."

They walked outside together.

ALSO BY LISA HENRY

He Is Worthy
Tribute
Dark Space
Darker Space (Dark Space #2)
Sweetwater
One Perfect Night
Stealing Innocents, writing as Cari Waites

By Lisa Henry & Heidi Belleau

King of Dublin
Bliss (Bliss #1)
Tin Man (Bliss #1.5)
The Harder They Fall

By Lisa Henry & J.A. Rock

The Good Boy (The Boy #1)
The Naughty Boy (The Boy #1.5)
The Boy Who Belonged (The Boy #2)
Mark Cooper versus America (Prescott College #1)
Brandon Mills versus the V-Card (Prescott College #2)
When All the World Sleeps
Another Man's Treasure
The Two Gentlemen of Altona (Playing the Fool #1)
Merchant of Death (Playing the Fool #2)
Tempest (Playing the Fool #3)

By Lisa Henry and M. Caspian

Fallout

LISA HENRY

ABOUT THE AUTHOR

Lisa Henry likes to tell stories, mostly with hot guys and happily ever afters.

Lisa lives in tropical North Queensland, Australia. She doesn't know why, because she hates the heat, but she suspects she's too lazy to move. She spends half her time slaving away as a government minion, and the other half plotting her escape.

She attended university at sixteen, not because she was a child prodigy or anything, but because of a mix-up between international school systems early in life. She studied History and English, neither of them very thoroughly.

She shares her house with too many cats, a dog, a green tree frog that swims in the toilet, and as many possums as can break in every night. This is not how she imagined life as a grown-up.

Website: www.lisahenryonline.com
Blog: http://lisahenryonline.blogspot.com.au
Twitter: https://twitter.com/LisaHenryOnline
Facebook:https://www.facebook.com/lisa.henry.1441